M000074255

Readers' Favorite®
Book Reviews and Award Contest

2019 INTERNATIONAL BOOK AWARDS
In recognition of excellence in writing

Gold Medal Winner
Fiction - Mystery - General

Don't Dare to Dream

Dan Friedman

Congratulations on your award!

The Readers' Favorite Team

PRAISE FOR DON'T DARE TO DREAM

"One of the best crime novels I've read in ages, full of breathtaking twists and turns."

—WILLIAM BERNHARDT, NYT BEST-
SELLING AUTHOR

"When reading a good psychological thriller, I hold to a couple of mantras: "Trust no one," and "Believe nothing." Great advice for anyone planning to dive into Dan Friedman's immensely entertaining debut *Don't Dare to Dream*, a story in which almost nothing is as it seems.

Friedman has created a masterful braiding of truth and lies that's guaranteed to leave readers amazed and satisfied. A fine first outing for this talented author, and I predict new fans will be clamoring for more."

—WILLIAM KENT KRUEGER, NYT BEST-
SELLING & EDGAR AWARD WINNING
AUTHOR

"A brilliantly plotted and enthralling thriller, Don't Dare to Dream by Dan Friedman is a huge literary achievement for a debut novel, with sophisticated characters, a strong premise, and fascinating twists.

Dan Friedman doesn't just keep the reader riveted to the pages as they follow this emotionally-charged story but keeps them guessing as well from page to page... an emotionally rich story imbued with psychological depth.

A great read told in a smooth, irresistible voice. It kept me awake through the night."

—READERS' FAVORITE BOOK REVIEW

"An impressive thriller. When even the FBI can't solve the entirety of the problem, the narrative is sure to please. Reader is hooked by the back cover summary, and ready for the story to unspool... Resonant and exciting. There is a lot to like about this story. Well done,"

JUDGE, 27TH ANNUAL WRITER'S DIGEST
SELF-PUBLISHED BOOK AWARDS

"With *Don't Dare to Dream* Dan Friedman hits the sweet spot between the paranoia of Hitchcock and Highsmith and the subtle fear bred by the uniquely American cult of self-help and motivational thinking.

Twisted and thrilling, you'll hate these characters one chapter and cheer for them the next.

Highly recommended."

—BRYON QUERTERMOUS, BOOK EDITOR
AND AUTHOR

"It's a great page-turner and would make a perfect vacation read."

—KEN DARROW, EDITOR

"Read this! Kept me wondering what was going to happen all the way through.

Recommended!"

—AMAZON REVIEWER

"Fast paced thriller. I read this book in 2 sittings, taking a break for sleep and work.

I love the way the author creates and builds the characters, makes you feel like you are sitting right next to them and are a part of their lives.

Highly recommend."

—GOODREADS REVIEWER

"A good story, well told. Good characters and an enlightening view of the tech world. Hard to believe this is a debut book."

"I thoroughly enjoyed this book. I haven't devoured a novel like I did this one in years.

It's refreshing to have a hero who's a pudgy, out-of-shape techie so out of touch with humanity that a complete stranger can become his best friend in minutes. He's a real human being, tossed into circumstances out of his control and dependent on others to make it out alive.

I thoroughly recommend it."

"It was an enjoyable and thoroughly entertaining book. Fast paced and obviously well researched.

If you like police drama and technology, you will very much enjoy this book with its unexpected twists and turns. I hope to read much more from this author."

"Excellently written, full of twists and turns in the plot and in the way the reader relates to the characters, the book is breathtaking and thrilling.

It is highly recommended!"

"A great book-Read it in one day and loved it!-Definitely a can't put down type of book-I would like more from this author."

"Captivating. Very much enjoyed this book.
    I recommend."

"...it's one of the best thrillers I have read.... The characters are well described and easy to relate with. Multiple twists made it hard for me to stop reading (plus I was too nervous to walk around the house at night).

    Don't miss it!"

DON'T DARE TO DREAM

DAN FRIEDMAN

For my parents
Thank you for everything,
I love you.

PART 1
DARE TO DREAM

ONE

David held his breath as he watched the pickup truck storm toward a woman and her little girl, about to step into the crossroad.

The woman steered the red Target cart out of the store using her elbows, eyes glued to her phone. The girl, wearing a pink dress and a matching hair bow, strolled behind her.

The pickup truck driver eyeballed his phone.

David had only wanted to get snacks for dinner, but what happened next felt like a scene in slow motion; he saw the driver blow through the stop sign, and with a force only God could explain, he ran, grabbed the girl, and tried to finish crossing the road.

He had not run in over ten years.

The pickup truck screeched to a halt a few inches from them.

David exhaled slowly and tried to smile at the girl, but she was crying for her mother.

The next thing he knew, someone was helping him sit on one of the red concrete balls in front of the store while a man offered him water. People gathered around him, staring. Someone pulled his arm and asked if he was okay. A woman squatted in front of him, her hand over her mouth.

He thought he heard someone somewhere say the word *hero*.

Every inch of his body ached. His heart raced as he gasped for air. The little girl stared at him from her crying mother's arms. She hugged her mother and inspected the crowd around David. When the crowd dispersed, the mother bent over him, hugged him tight for a few seconds, and kissed his cheek.

Some of her tears wet his face.

"Thank you, sir. Thank you so much."

He tried to smile.

Almost dying was worth the hug and the kiss.

Too bad she was probably married.

———

Rick MacMillan sat in his new Chevrolet Camaro in front of Target and couldn't believe what he had just seen.

TWO

David drove up to the black gate at the entrance to his apartment complex and pushed the remote a few times until it opened. The stupid thing worked randomly, and when it did, it took ages for the gate to open.

The management had installed the gates following a few burglaries, and the paint on it was already peeling. They wanted the tenants to feel secure but never offered actual statistics. The gate was like putting a Band-Aid on a broken skull—anyone could wait for a tenant to open the gate and drive in after them.

David tried to feel good about saving the little girl's life, but his body ached from the short run. He'd pulled every muscle in both legs. He wondered if he'd really moved that quickly. Maybe it just felt that way.

A sidewalk separated the car from his apartment, which kept him from parking even closer. He lifted a foot to climb it, but his legs couldn't hold his weight and he tumbled backward, missing his car by an inch. He crashed to the ground, his head hitting last, and he felt as though he'd made a dent in the pavement.

He tried, but failed, to push himself up. After a few tries, he decided to wait for someone to help him.

But what if no one came? Maybe I should call 911.

That would be embarrassing.

He thought of the old commercial: *I've fallen and I can't get up.* He was too young for that.

He fumbled for his iPhone, but it took him a few minutes to roll his wide body over and get it out. As he tried to overcome his blurred vision, a man kneeled down next to him and grabbed his arm. "Are you okay, buddy? What happened?"

Where the hell did he come from?

David had met Rick last week, when the tall, handsome neighbor from upstairs came knocking on his door. Rick was at least a head taller than David and wore a tight T-shirt, which emphasized his muscular physique. His body seemed as if it could burst out of his shirt.

Rick said he'd scratched David's car while moving his furniture in and insisted on reimbursing him, despite David's protests that the car was old and that he didn't intend to repaint it.

Rick was standing in his way of getting his daily dose of junk food, so David had to wave him off.

Now, as he lay in the parking lot looking blankly up at Rick, he thought having a friendly neighbor wasn't so bad after all.

"I'm fine. Thanks," David whispered.

Rick's eyebrows rose. "Let me at least help you up."

Rick dropped a gym bag from his shoulder and tugged at David, his big muscles flexing under his shirt, but he was too heavy even for Rick. It took a joint effort to get David to his knees and then for him to sit on the curb.

Rick looked at him. "Do you need an ambulance?"

David shook his head. He hated doctors.

Rick retrieved his bag, pulled out a bottle of water, and handed it to David.

After David took a few sips, Rick helped him up and walked him into his apartment, gripping his arm until David settled in his recliner.

Rick examined the apartment. "Would you like me to call someone?"

David stared up at him from his recliner, then shook his head and gazed at the ceiling.

"Is there anything I can get you?"

David shook his head.

"Would you like me to stay for a few minutes?" Rick asked, but David had already dozed off.

———

Rick watched David sleeping in the recliner.

He sighed. *This man needs to change his life. It's a wonder he's still alive.*

He went to the kitchen and saw a sink full of dirty dishes. He inspected the unopened mail on the counter—medical bills, bank statements, junk mail.

He moved to the bedroom and saw an unmade queen-size bed without a frame. He doubted the fatso's bed saw any action. A single brown plastic nightstand stood next to the bed with an old night lamp and a phone charger on it. A small desk with a printer covered with dust filled the corner of the room, dirty clothes scattered on the chair next to it. He opened the nightstand drawer, but a noise from the living room startled him. He closed the drawer, sprang to the bathroom, and flushed the toilet. When he returned to the living room, David was still sleeping.

Rick sat for a few minutes, then returned to the night-stand drawer. He feared a sex toy jumping out at him, but instead saw an old iPhone, earphones, and batteries.

He returned to the living room and stared at David. Rick shook his head and slipped his hands into his front pockets.

———

David opened his eyes and saw a man in his bedroom.

What the hell is he doing there? Is this a dream?

He dozed off again. When he awoke, a man lay on his couch a few feet from him, reading from a phone. David wanted to speak, but his tongue was too heavy. He gazed at the man.

"You're up?" Rick dropped his feet to the floor and sat up.

David said nothing, so Rick continued: "It's me. Rick. Your neighbor. You fell outside, and I helped you into your apartment. How are you feeling, buddy?"

"You're still here?" David asked.

"I hope it's okay. I didn't think I could leave you like this." Rick rose, bent over to look at him, imitating a doctor, then sat back down. "Are you feeling better?"

David stared at him.

"You want me to take you to a hospital or call an ambulance? I'm kinda worried."

David shook his head. After a moment, he said, "Why are you still here?"

"I didn't go to med school, but I looked it up online"—Rick held his phone up—"and saw you might've gotten a concussion. I didn't want to leave you alone like this. I almost called an ambulance a few minutes ago. Are you sure you're okay?"

David nodded.

"Do you want me to go?"

David nodded again. "I'm sorry. I want to be alone."

Rick rose and straightened his shirt. "Sure. I have a meeting I have to go to anyway. I'll leave you my card. Don't hesitate to call me if you need anything."

"Thank you," he whispered.

As Rick turned the doorknob to leave, David asked, "Did you go into my bedroom?"

THREE

David looked at the card. The neighbor's full name was Rick MacMillan, and his title read "Life Coach."

I should have known. A scammer.

That's how he got his shiny new Camaro. He had noticed it when they walked together to their cars and Rick had nagged about reimbursing him for the scratch.

He wanted to stand but didn't have the strength. He felt like tearing the business card to pieces but couldn't.

He read an online article once with tips on how to improve your life. They suggested some bullshit New Age stuff and recommended getting a life coach. He felt so bad back then he almost considered it, but he came to his senses soon enough.

Rick's the only person in the world who helped me.

David turned on the TV, then turned it off. Maybe he should have gone to the hospital. Someone would have taken care of him. He'd get meals, probably bad ones, but better than nothing.

Would you like me to call someone? Rick had asked as if he didn't know there was no one.

He wanted to tell Rick he'd saved a little girl's life. He wasn't a complete loser. Someone called him a hero.

But what good is it now? No one would remember.

He looked for comfort food but had none. He'd gone to Target to get more food, but saving the girl stopped him from getting the snacks he liked.

He recalled having something in his trunk—some chips he'd bought and forgotten.

He ambled weakly to his car. It was almost dark, and he had to lean against his car so he wouldn't fall again. When he tried to open the door to his apartment with the bag of chips in one hand, he heard high heels going down the wooden stairs.

Music.

He looked up and saw a tall, blonde young woman floating down the stairs. A white blazer covered her top, and a black miniskirt covered little of her long, skinny legs, on top of four-inch heels. She checked her phone, which he considered a dangerous combination.

If she fell, I could catch her.

Two rescues in one day.

He stared at her, mouth open slightly. She didn't notice him until she reached the bottom of the stairs.

When her eyes met his, she smiled.

He'd never seen such a perfect white smile.

Unlike the smiles of a lot of the women he had seen in Target or Walmart, hers seemed genuine. She was younger than the women he usually went for.

"Hello." Her smile grew. "How are you doing?"

The heartburn he had suffered since morning disappeared.

He'd been wasting time at Target when his amazing apartment complex had *this*.

Oh my God.

"Hi," he whispered.

Okay. The moment of truth. *I must talk to her.*

Or maybe not. If she lived there, he could talk to her on any other day. But what if she didn't? What if she was only visiting her parents? Then he may not see her for a couple of months. It would explain why he'd never seen her before.

He couldn't risk it.

He had to talk to her.

He'd thought about the perfect opening line a million times. He had not started a conversation with a potential wife for many years. Should he talk about the weather? Should he compliment her on her looks?

His mouth dried up.

Maybe he should introduce himself. Maybe ask if she'd just moved in.

I hope she didn't notice I stopped breathing.

She advanced as if walking on a runway. She stopped a foot away from him, still smiling, and extended her gentle hand. "You must be David," she said. "It's nice to meet you."

She knows my name.

She was taller than him, but not as tall as Rick. He shook her soft hand, and she almost had to force it out of his grip.

"How did you know my—"

Heavy footsteps going down the stairs interrupted him.

He looked up and saw Rick.

I should have known.

Rick wore a black suit with a white button-down shirt and no tie. Rick put his arm around the beautiful woman's waist. "I see you met my wife, Angela."

They looked like *Barbie and Ken*.

David's heartburn returned.

FOUR

David sat in his recliner with the bag of chips. The TV was boring, and he felt like puking.

He glared at his dirty apartment, his body, his life.

"You'll never make anything of yourself again," he said.

Since losing his job, he'd found it hard to get back on the horse. He couldn't find a woman either. Meeting the new neighbors made him feel worse. He'd never look like Rick. He'd never find a woman like Angela.

His iPhone dinged. A reminder he had set a few years ago stabbed him in the chest. He'd forgotten to cancel it.

Or maybe he didn't want to forget it.

The next day would be Mia's birthday.

He had not seen or talked to her in almost two years. As far as he knew she still lived in Tulsa, on the other side of town. Thankfully, he didn't have to run into her at the grocery store.

He needed more information, and Facebook was the best way to spy on people. She had unfriended him as soon as they separated. She wanted nothing to do with him.

When he found her profile, he could see some of her pictures. She probably blocked most of them.

In the third picture, she wore a wedding dress.

She got married.

It felt as if someone dropped a truck on his head.

He tried to breathe but had a hard time filling his lungs. The text under the picture read, "I married the love of my life!"

Another stab in the chest.

Did she do it on purpose? Did she make sure I could see her happy with another man?

David had tears in his eyes. Slowly they became longer, heavier. Then he sobbed. He held his belly, then his face. The tears came down through his fingers.

He looked at the picture's date; it was over a year old.

He had no idea.

Did she meet him right after she dumped me?

Did she meet him before she dumped me?

He had no job, no woman, no life. He wiped his eyes and rose from his recliner.

Too bad I didn't get a gun. It's easy to get one these days.

He walked slowly to the bathroom and opened the medicine cabinet, which only contained pills for headache. *I have a headache, right?* The box suggested he shouldn't take more than six pills a day.

But she got married.

He grabbed the pill bottle and went to the kitchen. He took a glass, filled it with water, and snapped off the bottle's protective cap.

Will it work?

He took a pill.

Don't do it! an inner voice tried to shout.

He took another one.

He saw many more pills inside the bottle. He shook two more into his hand and swallowed them.

He was refilling his cup with water when his iPhone ring startled him.

Who could it be? It's been a while since someone called.

Should I get it?

Could it be Rick? Does he have my number?

Could it be Mia? Maybe she got divorced and wants me back?

He put the pill bottle and water cup on the counter and went for his phone. He recognized the number. It was the complex management office. Did he not pay the rent?

Who cares.

They'd be happy to get rid of me.

He went back to the bottle with the blue pills, peered inside, and saw the abyss.

She got married.

He stopped counting the pills. He kept swallowing them until the bottle was empty.

Was it enough?

Did I make a mistake?

No one'll know. No one'll care.

Who would want to live in this apartment after I die?

When he started feeling dizzy, he walked toward his recliner. On the way there, his world became blurry, and he fell to the floor.

FIVE

Rick stopped next to David's door.

"David?" he said after a few knocks.

When nobody replied, Rick went up the stairs.

Angela greeted him with a long kiss. They drank coffee, and he told her about his meeting. She told him about her day studying at the university, and then they moved into the bedroom where he took off everything but her underwear. They kissed for a while, then he stripped her while she closed her eyes. He kissed her body from top to bottom and undressed himself. They made love for the second time that day.

When he hugged her in bed, he told her about what had happened with David.

"That doesn't sound good. I think you should check on him. I think he's in terrible shape. Mentally and physically."

"You're right. I'll go tomorrow."

"Are you sure?"

"Yeah. I'm too tired. Had a long day. And I need a shower."

She blinked at him.

DON'T DARE TO DREAM

"He wasn't cooperative anyway. I'm thinking of giving up on him. He's hopeless."

"Rick!" Angela sat up in bed. "Forget about your plans for now. The man needs help." She removed the blanket and uncovered her naked body. "Maybe I should go there right now. Like this. What do you say?" She smiled.

"Wouldn't *he* like that?" Rick laughed.

"I'm going." Her feet touched the carpet.

"Okay, okay. I'll go." He took off the blanket and sat on his side of the bed. "I'll do anything to stop you from cheating on me with the handsome neighbor downstairs."

They burst out laughing, but Angela tried to stop herself. "Don't be cruel."

"Can I take a shower first?"

Angela considered it. "Make it fast. When you come back, maybe I'll let you watch *me* shower."

He sprang to the bathroom.

———

Rick knocked on David's door for a few minutes. He turned to go back to his apartment when he heard coughing. He knocked a few more times, then tried to open the door.

Unlocked.

Doesn't he lock his door?

Rick opened it slowly and glanced inside. He made sure no one saw him from outside and entered the apartment. David was not in the recliner.

"David?" he said. "Um...the door...was open. I'm sorry, I wanted to make sure you're okay." He closed the door behind him. "David?"

Rick meandered through the apartment. He walked slowly into David's bedroom and considered investigating it

17

again. He turned the light on in the bathroom, closed the medicine cabinet, and checked behind the shower curtain. He walked back out to the living room.

"Dav—"

Rick saw David on the floor. He kneeled and could barely turn him. He checked for a pulse and called 911.

SIX

FBI Special Agent Bob Alexis entered the investigation room with a huge file in his hands. There were only three pages about the suspect, but the file seemed thick. It was full of blank pages from Bob's printer. It was a trick many investigators used, to make the suspect think they had a lot of information about them.

The suspect was sitting with his head on the table.

Is he asleep?

Bob slammed the file on the table which startled the suspect and made him raise his head up to Bob.

"You know we want him?" Bob remained standing. "Not *you*. Right?"

The suspect said nothing.

"If you give us the information we need, we'll let you go. You can trust me."

No reply.

"If you don't help us, we'll put you in jail for what *he* did. Is it worth it?"

The suspect licked his lips.

"He's a bad man. He'll hurt more people if we don't put him away."

Nothing.

Bob clenched his teeth. "If you don't help us, I'll make sure you'll go away for a long time."

Bob picked up the file, turned away, and slammed the door on his way out.

———

David opened his eyes to a bright light blinding him. He blinked, squinted, and tried to block it with his hand.

Am I dead?

Where the hell am I?

He lay in a single bed, covered with a white blanket. Next to him he saw a big nightstand. The walls were off-white and a small, faded painting was hanging in front of his bed. A man sat to his right on a big blue-cushioned armchair. The familiar man slept.

David waited for a while, then cleared his throat. When that didn't wake the man, he whispered, "Rick?"

Rick awoke, startled, only after David finally yelled his name. He stood on his feet as fast as a man sitting on hot coals.

"How are you doing, buddy?" Rick asked as he hunched over him.

David stared at him. "I'm thirsty."

Rick returned to the room with a glass of water and a straw in his hand. He held David up and helped him drink.

"Do you remember what happened?" he asked.

"I took some pills." He stared at the painting.

Rick nodded.

"How did I end up here?" David asked after drinking more water.

"I knocked on your door a few times," Rick said. "When you didn't answer, I got worried, so I opened the door—which was unlocked. I saw you lying on the floor. I thought you were dead at first. I called an ambulance. They took you to the hospital and pumped your stomach."

David nodded.

Should I thank him? If he hadn't found me, all this shit would have been over.

A doctor in a white coat entered the room, introduced himself to David, and said, "I have good news and bad news. The good news is that your liver is okay. The bad news is that you have to drink charcoal to absorb the pills that did not get sucked out during the stomach pump."

It tasted worse than diet cola.

A few hours later, another doctor came in and introduced himself as a psychiatrist. He asked what had happened and if David tried to kill himself.

I thought these guys were supposed to be smart.

The psychiatrist did not seem concerned. Was he used to it?

David wished Rick would leave. Rick was a complete stranger but also his best friend. He didn't have the courage to ask him to leave. *Did it matter, anyway?*

David told the psychiatrist what happened. Rick listened carefully and filled in the parts where he came in and saved him.

The psychiatrist prescribed antidepressants and asked Rick, "Can you be with him for the next few days?"

"I'm...his neighbor." Rick fidgeted. "But yeah. Sure. Me and my wife can check on him."

"That's good." The psychiatrist turned to David. "Is

there anyone else who can come more often or even stay with you?"

David shook his head.

"Okay. I also need you to go to therapy. At least once a week. Can you do that?"

After almost a minute, David nodded.

————

The hospital discharged David a few days later. He convinced the doctors he didn't need to be committed into a mental hospital. They didn't insist.

He promised he'd never do it again.

He didn't think they cared.

Rick drove him to his apartment and helped him in.

"I can stay the night, if you want." Rick pointed at the couch.

"Won't Angel...Won't Angela mind?"

"Nah, she knows I'm not into guys."

David stared at Rick. *I don't need him here all the time.*

"It's okay," he said after a while. "You don't have to worry about it. I'd rather be alone. I won't do it again."

Rick nodded.

"Thank you. For everything."

Rick nodded again.

David tried to wipe the tears from his eyes without Rick seeing it.

Rick walked over to the recliner, leaned over David, and hugged him. Instinctively, David put his right arm on Rick's back.

Two hugs in a week. *I must be doing something right.*

He almost smiled.

Both times it happened after he'd almost killed himself.

"I have a meeting soon, but I'll be back to check on you later today. Okay?"

———

I need you also to go to therapy. At least once a week, the shrink at the hospital had told David.

Yeah, right, like I'm gonna pay someone hundreds of dollars to listen to me whine. What a waste of money. *Who needs that? It doesn't help.*

But having someone listen to him could be a nice change.

Nah, it's too expensive.

A few hours later, a loud knock on the door awoke him.

"I brought dinner." Rick raised a big plastic bag over his head.

Is he crazy? David thought, but he just nodded.

Rick took the food out and invited him to the table. When David rose from his recliner, he almost stumbled. Rick rushed and helped him walk the ten feet.

Rick had set the table for two.

Healthy stuff. Grilled chicken, brown rice, and a salad.

Yuck.

"You mind if I stay and have dinner with you? I brought enough for two."

Can I say no?

David nodded. He played with his food and his fork like a child. He forced himself to eat. He didn't raise his eyes or speak.

Rick didn't change that.

SEVEN

The following evening, Rick brought a plastic bag again. David smiled a little at him when he opened the door.

"I'm glad to see you're smiling," Rick said.

David flattened his lips immediately. Rick entered, set the table for two, and poured himself a glass of water.

"Water?" Rick asked.

"Nah, I only drink the good stuff."

"Beer?"

"That too, sometimes. But I meant the black stuff in the fridge."

David drank cola, and they ate the good-for-you-but-bad-for-your-taste-buds dinner again.

Rick broke the silence. "Tell me your story."

David stared at him.

"No problem," Rick said after a while. "Maybe some other time?" He cleared the table and stuck the dishes in the dishwasher. "I love those dishwashers. Big, fast, and they get the job done. We have the same one upstairs."

"That's the only good thing about this place. Maybe also the ice maker in the fridge."

"I like this place. It's comfortable, clean, close to what we need. And it's also quiet." Rick finished loading the dishwasher and turned it on. "There are also some nice neighbors."

David nodded.

"I have to go now. But you have a great evening, okay?" Rick walked to the door.

"I'm not as lame as you may think."

Rick stopped and turned. "I never said you were."

"I know what you think. I know what *people* think." David interlocked his fingers on the table.

Rick came back to the table and sat across from him.

"I used to work in high tech, you know?" David said. "I didn't used to be like this. I worked for seven different companies. I used to be a programmer, then I did business development and sales. I was good at it, but I guess I could never live up to my manager's—or my partner's—expectations. I always had horrible managers. One screamed at me all the time. Damn near abusive. I stayed there for more than a year. One of them was a liar. Another one stole my great ideas and told *his* bosses they were his. I even opened a few start-ups of my own."

Rick held his chin with his hand, eyes squinted a little, and nodded slowly.

"I lived in Silicon Valley, New York, and even Tel Aviv," David continued. "Most of the high-tech capitals of the world."

He sipped from his cup, only to discover it was empty. He put it back down on the table. Rick filled it with cola and returned it.

"The last one"—David stared at the ceiling, then at Rick —"was the worst one. After that I gave up."

After a few minutes of silence, Rick asked, "What happened?"

"I'm not sure I'm ready to talk about it." He rubbed his eyes. "Maybe some other time?"

Rick nodded. "Whenever you're ready."

After a while, Rick rose. "Tomorrow I'll be out of town for a seminar. If it's okay with you, my wife can stop by to check up on you. Would it be okay?"

David's mouth opened a little. He almost smiled.

"Sure," he said finally.

Rick smiled and left.

———

Why is he being so helpful? Does he have an ulterior motive? Does he think I'll leave him a lot of money when I die?

David opened his iPhone and launched Facebook. In the past, he had tried to use it to meet women, with little luck. Not a bad tool, he thought more than once, but the women with the status *Single* were too young for him. After a while he moved to women with a *Divorced* status, but those women were not for him either. Some of them had children. Some of them did not look good. Most of them did not write back.

Maybe I was the problem?

He considered trying it again. It gave him access to women all over the world, not only those from the local grocery store. David heard stories of couples who met online. Were they true stories or just fantasies? Facebook should be easier than Target. No need to leave the house. He also found it easier to write than to talk to women.

Maybe someday.

He would never return to dating apps, that was for sure.

In his profile picture, Rick MacMillan looked a bit younger, almost like a kid. Rick wore a suit, similar to the one he'd worn the other night, and stood with a microphone in his hand. The picture was taken from a low angle, which made him look even taller. It seemed as if Rick was talking on a stage, maybe in front of a crowd.

Did he speak at conferences?

David found only four profile pictures of Rick on his page. He could not find day-to-day pictures. Rick always dressed well and smiled. He'd posted a few clichés on his timeline but nothing else. After reviewing all of them, David noticed they were all timed to Sunday mornings. Those clichés had stopped appearing about two months ago. Rick did not have his hometown or current town specified.

David considered friending him.

Rick's relationship status was *Married*, but, strangely enough, it did not specify to whom.

I'd show off a woman like that.

David ran a search for Angela MacMillan. Unfortunately, she had even fewer pictures. David found only two profile pictures, both with Rick. Rick wasn't tagged in those pictures, which excluded them from Rick's timeline. Besides those pictures, Angela had nothing on her wall. Either she was inactive or she blocked prying eyes like his.

It would be nice to be friends with her.

After closing the Facebook app, David considered getting good-tasting food from the store. He had not left his apartment since returning from the hospital.

Instead, he fell asleep with his iPhone in his hand.

———

27

Angela came to David's apartment the following day and knocked gently on his door. She wore the same miniskirt she had worn the first time he saw her. But this time she had no jacket on, only a bra.

He did not want to wake up from the dream.

He let her in, closed the door, and turned to her. She undressed herself and exposed her perfect body.

Won't Rick mind? he asked.

Rick's out of town. She lay on the couch.

It had been a long time since he'd seen a naked woman. He had never seen such an amazing body in real life.

EIGHT

David awoke in the morning in his recliner with a huge grin on his face. Too bad it was only a dream.

At least I can still look Rick in the eyes.

He took a shower, then gathered his clothes from his bedroom floor, did a few loads of laundry, and stored the clean clothes in his closet. He tucked his bed, cleaned the bathroom and the kitchen, and took out the old, unused vacuum cleaner and cleaned the carpet, which covered most of the apartment.

All the hard work made him tired. He napped in the recliner, but when he awoke, his whole body ached. Rick would have been proud of his workout. He showered again, shaved, and even combed his hair.

He sat in his recliner and checked the time on his phone. He turned on the TV, then moved to the couch. He turned the TV off and walked around the apartment. Every step from outside made him jump and peer through the peephole.

When Angela finally knocked softly on the door, he straightened the wrinkles on his shirt, checked his hair in his reflection in the window, and opened the door. Angela did not wear the amazing miniskirt from the dream but instead was in a simple T-shirt, jeans, and sneakers. She held the same kind of white bag of food that Rick usually brought.

She had the biggest and prettiest smile in the world.

"Come in," he said. "Please." He opened the door wide and showed her in with his arm, almost bowing.

He took the bag from her hand, thanked her, and set the table. She sat across from him, still dressed.

"I see you and Rick like the same tasteless food."

She smiled. "He got me into this eating healthy stuff. It grows on you."

"I'll let you know if it ever does, but I doubt it." The healthy food tasted better that evening. He wondered if he'd gotten used to the food or if the company improved it.

Angela kept her mouth closed when she chewed, covered it when she laughed, and wiped it every few bites, using a napkin she brought with the food.

He asked the number one question when getting to know someone, and the one he dreaded most: "What do you do for a living?"

He hated that question. He did nothing with his life and talking about it only made it worse.

"I'm getting my master's in psychology," she said, "I started a few weeks ago. I got a scholarship. That's the main reason we moved to Tulsa."

"Wait. *Psychology?*"

She nodded.

He hated psychologists almost as much as he hated life coaches. Or whatever. On second thought, maybe she could treat him. It would be much nicer to talk to her than to the old psychiatrist from the hospital. He imagined her sitting on his couch and—

"I still do some modeling just to make a few bucks here and there."

Modeling?

"Modeling?"

"Yes, I used to be a model but hated it. I still hate it, but I do it from time to time to make money. Just until I get my degree and start my *real* job."

"Why...do you hate it?"

"I'm a feminist, and I feel that it's degrading. I don't like it when *men*—excuse me—look at my body and drool."

He swallowed hard. He hoped she didn't notice. *I didn't think models cared. I thought they liked it. But then again, I never stopped to think about it.*

Nor had he ever met one.

She must never learn about my dream.

"I grew up poor, so in order to pay for college and rent, I needed to do something," she said. "I was approached on the street by model scouts all the time. I had enough sense to reject most of them, even at a young age, but at a certain point, I gave it a shot. My mom came with me when I was underage. I did it for a few years after high school and before college. I never had to take my clothes off, so I kept doing it for the money. I made good money for the first time in my life. I could even help my mother."

Talking to her seemed much easier than talking to her husband. She didn't ask David what he did for a living. She didn't ask any significant questions. He wondered if she didn't care or was just tactful.

Or maybe Rick told her? David heard couples tell each other stuff.

He wanted to ask her what she thought of her husband's sleazy profession but figured it might be rude.

A few minutes after they finished eating, Angela said,

"I'm sorry, but I have to leave. I have an early class tomorrow, and I must go to bed early. I wanted to see how you were doing. Thank you for the conversation."

His heart sank. He wished she would stay longer.

He walked her to the door.

"I'm glad to see you're getting better."

He nodded. He wanted to tell her what had happened. He wished she'd asked. Maybe he should say something. He needed more time to build courage. Maybe if he had another hour. Or two.

But she left.

———

He watched her climb the stairs, almost running, and heard her open and close the door upstairs. He stood there for a few minutes, holding his door open. When it became chilly, he closed it and went back to his recliner.

Modeling?

He Googled her name plus "model" for images. He found a few images, which proved she'd told the truth. She lay on a white leather couch, which seemed much more expensive than his. She rested her head on her hands and looked at the camera. She wore a light pink dress, not too tight, which showed her legs but almost no cleavage. He'd never seen her wear that much makeup.

He found many more poses of the same photo shoot. He found a few more pictures of her in a few different wedding dresses, some in tight jeans and some in a bathrobe.

No bikini shots. No naked shots.

Did it make him happy or sad?

He stared at them for a while.

A loud bang from above startled him. With the paper-thin walls, he commonly heard noises from his neighbors.

Was someone trying to hurt her?

As he considered going up to check, he heard a loud laugh. *Her* laugh. Was she laughing at him? Was she talking to Rick on the phone, both laughing at him?

He turned on the TV and watched a reality show. After a while he thought he heard bedspring squeaking sounds coming from upstairs. Was she cheating on Rick? Impossible. She was not the type. He peeked outside the window to make sure Rick's car was gone. Maybe she was jumping on the bed? Were they still laughing at him, or had she gotten good news?

Cybersex?

He turned up the volume on the TV.

———

Angela returned to her apartment, climbing the stairs two at a time. She did not look back at David or hear him close the door before she entered her apartment.

"How did it go?" Rick asked after she kissed him.

"I'm not comfortable with what we did."

"I parked the car far away. Don't worry."

"I meant I hate lying."

"I know. But sometimes we do what we gotta do."

"You were right. It worked." She smiled.

"I knew it." Rick raised his arms in the air.

"There's something weird about him. For a while I was afraid he'd hit on me."

"Nah. He's harmless."

"I don't mean he'd try to rape me, just that—"

"He'd want to fuck you?" Rick asked. "*All* men do."

"You know I hate that word."

"I know. But that's what, um, men—*other* men—use."

He moved toward her, but she pushed him away.

"I feel bad for him."

"I know. Me too. But I know a way you can make it up to me."

"*You* need to make it up to me." She kissed him again, this time slower. He took off her shirt, then her bra. She helped him with her pants, and after Rick undressed, they kissed passionately on the couch.

She couldn't explain why, but she didn't feel comfortable doing it there, and they moved to their squeaky bed.

———

Michael finished his shift at The Little Italian Restaurant and walked home to his small apartment in Oklahoma City. He entered the apartment, kicked his shoes off, and laid on the couch with his feet on the coffee table in front of the TV.

Not many tips tonight, he texted Cindy. He'd met her at the restaurant, and they'd been dating for the past few weeks. She was cute, and she stuck around longer than most of his previous girlfriends.

I'm sure it'll pick up, don't worry, she texted back. *I can't come over tonight. Too tired. Tomorrow?*

He texted her a thumbs-up and a kiss. He wanted to see her but was too tired anyway.

He got up to get a beer when two huge men came out of his bedroom.

"What the hell—"

Mark, the smaller of the giants, hit Michael in the face and threw him halfway across the apartment.

"What do you want?" Michael screamed. "Leave me alone!"

Trever laughed and gestured to Mark. Mark raised Michael to his feet only to punch him in the gut.

Michael screamed.

"You have three weeks," Trever said.

NINE

David ambled into Target after he parked his ten-year-old Honda Civic closest to the handicapped spots. It wasn't the cheapest place to get food, but it was closest to his apartment, and the women who came there were prettier, for some reason.

He didn't have to run this time, so he grabbed the first red cart he could find and walked inside. The smell of sweet popcorn filled his nose.

A skinny blonde woman in her late thirties walked toward him; she wore shorts showing off her long, tanned legs, and a tank top. He tried not to stare.

She smiled at him. She must not have seen him staring. He forced a smile back. *Should I talk to her? Nah, she's probably married.*

He bought a big bottle of Coke, a six-pack of beer, and two of the biggest bags of Doritos he could find.

When he returned to his apartment complex, he saw the black Camaro parked in his favorite spot. *Did Rick do that on purpose?* He parked next to it, in the third-best parking spot. He almost scratched Rick's car when he opened the door.

I owe him, don't I?

He almost smiled but then watched himself in the rearview mirror and shook his head. *What the hell happened to me? I used to be nice.*

He held his door tight, away from Rick's car, as he exited.

He got ice for the Coke, sat in his beloved recliner with the Doritos, and flipped through the channels.

I should switch to diet cola, he thought. *I tried it once. Tasted like shit.*

———

David opened the door the following morning after a loud knock woke him. "Man, it's the middle of the night." David yawned. "What are you doing here so early?"

"I thought I'd surprise you." Rick wore blue shorts, a black shiny T-shirt, and running shoes and held a bottle of water in his hand. "Let's go for a run."

David burst out laughing. "Yeah, *right!*" He gestured for Rick to enter.

"At least I made you laugh." Rick slapped his shoulder as he entered.

"Wait. Weren't you supposed to be at a conference?"

"A *seminar*. Yes. But I got back early this morning. Too boring to stay another day."

Rick inspected the apartment, eyebrows raising. "How was your date with my wife last night?" He smiled and sat on the couch.

"*What?*"

"Just kidding. How was dinner?"

"Oh, that. Fine. She's nice." He grinned. "Much nicer than the other guy who brings food every day."

"I keep getting that. But I guess that's why I married her."

"Question is," David said, "why did *she* marry *you*?"

"You need to ask her that."

"I will, on our *next* date." He poured a glass of water for Rick and a glass of Coke for himself. Rick gazed at David's glass.

After they drank, Rick said, "Go put on your best workout gear, and let's go for a walk."

"You don't give up, do you?" he asked. "*Food*, even the bad food you bring me, is fine. But working out? Hell, no."

"You know," Rick said, "I started walking a few years ago. I walked every morning, pushing for an hour a day. I now walk for five minutes to warm up, run for forty-five, and then cool down with five more minutes of walking. I call it my hour of power and—"

"That's only fifty-five minutes."

Rick laughed. "You're right. I call it my hour of power because it sounds good. I do this every day. I learned it from a master—"

"Good for *you*. But not for me. Thank you, though."

"Come on. Just a walk. It's not hard, and the benefits are amazing."

"Did you get a look at me? I *can't*."

Rick stared at him. "You know, someone once said that if you say you can or if you say you can't, you're right."

David seemed to consider. "You *are* right. I said I can't, and *I'm right*."

Rick looked at him and tried not to laugh.

"You think only *you* can be a smart-ass?" David asked.

Rick shook his head. "I meant you need to say that *you can* do something so that you *could* do it."

"I know. Who said that, anyway?"

"Henry Ford."

David nodded. "Wasn't he the guy who also said his customers could have their cars in any color they wanted as long as it was black?"

"He was right about that too."

"Wasn't he an anti-Semite?"

"I don't know about that."

"I'll look it up. I didn't know he did coaching in his spare time." David brought out coffee. "To be honest, I thought it was another one of *your* clichés. No offense, but I'm not into that."

"What do you mean *another* one of my clichés? I haven't shared my cli—my *good* ideas with you."

Oops.

"I saw what you wrote on Facebook." No point lying.

"You looked me up?"

David nodded.

"Why didn't you friend me?"

"Didn't think you'd want me to."

"Sure I would."

"Besides, I have enough of your clichés in my apartment. I don't need them all over my Facebook wall."

"I give up. I'll go alone. You have a great day."

"I'll show him *my* hour of power," David said after Rick left. He poured a glass of Coke, opened the cupcakes he'd gotten recently, and sat in his recliner in front of the TV.

———

The following week, Rick came back every morning and asked David if he would join him for a walk.

"And here comes my morning stand-up comedy," David said every time.

One morning, after almost two weeks, David opened the door wearing blue jeans, a T-shirt, and an old pair of tennis shoes.

"Okay," he said, "let's do this. But only *once* so you'll stop nagging me every day." He pointed at the door. "And damn you for making me do this."

Rick's jaw dropped. "Really?"

"Let's go before I change my mind."

Rick stared at him from top to bottom and finally said, "We need to get you better workout gear."

"No need. This is a onetime thing."

He almost pushed Rick outside and locked his door. "Where do we go?"

Rick pointed toward the back of the building.

They ambled passed the Dumpster next to the building. He never walked there—he put his garbage bags over the hood of his car, drove as close as possible, got out, and tossed the trash. His breathing became heavy as they passed another building. He sat down on the curb.

"You okay?" Rick stopped and looked down at him.

"Look at me?" David said. "What do you think?"

"I see a dying old man."

David's eyes opened wide, but Rick smiled.

"You want to take me to the hospital again?"

"I think we had enough of that," Rick said. "You know you shouldn't throw your life away. It's much better for your body and mind to be healthy. A healthy mind needs a healthy body."

"Enough with your clichés, please."

"They call them *clichés* for a reason."

"Yeah, they are boring, stupid, and overused."

Rick crossed his arms over his chest.

"Do you want to leave me here and go home?"

"The thought crossed my mind."

David nodded. "Don't you know by now I don't care much about my body?"

"You *should* care. It will improve your life. A lot."

"I'm past that point. I'm only trying to survive."

Rick sat next to him on the curb, examining him.

David's breathing became shallow after a while.

"Look around you," Rick said. "What do you see?"

"What?"

"What do you see?"

David stared at him. "I see a white, skinny, *slightly* built, annoying young man who, even when he sits down next to me, I still need to look up to see his face."

"What do you mean *slightly* built? I'm very muscular."

After a while, Rick asked, "What else do you see?"

"Nothing."

"Come on. Humor me. What do you see around you?"

David explored the area. "I see dry grass, ugly cars, and dirt everywhere."

Rick nodded and looked around again. "Where do you see dirt?"

"That cup over there." He pointed across the parking lot.

"I didn't notice that," Rick said. "But I agree about the ugly cars. Most of them, anyway. You don't see anything else?"

"What am I supposed to see?"

"You can choose what you see. For example, I see tall, green, beautiful trees, well-maintained green grass—well, most of it is green. When we started walking—right next to your apartment—I saw some nice flowers and a huge yellow butterfly." Rick pointed at the building near them. He smiled as if he was riding a cloud in the sky. "And I also see two grown men working out and having a great conversation."

David stared at him. "Who said anything about a great conversation?"

"Well," Rick said, "one of them is complaining all the time, and the other is being polite."

David looked around him. "Where do you see all the beautiful stuff you talked about?"

"You can *choose* to see the good, like I tried to point out to you, or you can *choose* to see the bad. As *you* just did. And I'm assuming that's what you usually see. It's all up to you. If you choose to see the good, your life will be much better, and you'll be much more optimistic. If you choose to see the bad, your life will suck."

"Like it does right now."

Rick nodded. "I'll give you another example. How full is my bottle of water?"

David tilted his head.

"Humor me."

"It's half-empty, of course."

"You see?" Rick said. "*You* see it as half-empty. *I* see it as half-full."

"Isn't the cliché 'a glass half-empty'?"

"Yes." Rick sighed. "My point was how you choose to look at things."

David's eyes rolled down to the pavement, and he said nothing.

———

On the third day, they walked for ten minutes before David called it quits. They sat on the curb outside his apartment where he had fallen recently.

"I think the grass here is a little greener than I used to notice," he said.

Rick put his hand on David's shoulder and nodded. "What else do you see?"

"You know I was messin' with you, right?"

Rick punched him in the shoulder.

"Hey, don't hit an old man."

"You're not as old as you think. What are you? Fifty?"

His turn to punch Rick. "I'm hardly forty. Actually, a little over forty. But *not* fifty."

"Start acting like it."

They drank from the water bottles Rick brought.

"Are you ready for another exercise?"

"I think we're done working out for today. You're pushing your luck, big man."

"No, I meant a mental exercise."

"I'm not too sure about that. Your exercises are usually annoying."

Rick pointed at David with his index finger. "I want you to make a list of everything that's good in your life."

"That'll be a short list. *Nothing.*"

"Not that fast. I need you to make an effort. I'm sure if you sat alone and did some hard thinking, you could come up with a nice short list. I could help you get started, but I prefer you do it yourself."

After a while, Rick said, "Please? For me?"

David noticed a big red butterfly flying next to them.

"I'll think about it."

Trever hated going to people more than once, but Michael forced them.

It was time to let Mark, his partner, loose a little.

They broke into the young man's apartment again—the idiot didn't change locks or move—and made themselves comfortable in his living room, shoes on the coffee table.

When Michael opened the door, Mark jumped on him and forced him to the floor.

"Leave me alone!" Michael cried. "I told you I don't have it!"

Trever picked up the phone Michael had dropped and went through it. The only interesting thing he found was that someone by the name of Cindy had texted that she was coming over.

"I see your girlfriend's on her way." Trever grinned. "Don't worry. We'll take good care of her."

Michael's lips trembled as he leered up at Trever—who signaled Mark with his head and moved aside, not wanting to get his suit dirty.

Mark raised Michael's baseball bat slowly. The young man screamed as Mark hit him in the head with the bat.

Trever opened his little notebook and erased the young man's name.

TEN

An unfamiliar car was parked in David's favorite spot, so he parked next to it and smiled. He could use the extra walk. Parts of the grass turned gray, even though he noticed they'd tried to water it. The early morning cold killed it. He tried to see the green parts, but even Rick would agree that was too much.

A cold breeze made him shiver as he exited the car. He noticed the building's paint was chipped in a few places. They should fix that. It made the place look older. He should talk to them about it. He tried to focus on the few white flowers in front of the building, which made him smile.

He walked to his apartment carrying bags with fruit and vegetables. When he noticed a strange patch of paint on the wall next to his apartment, he stopped.

"What the hell?"

He had to step back to read the black graffiti.

YOU'LL PAY FOR IT.

He entered his apartment and put his groceries away.

What the hell did I do? He considered calling the police. *Will they take it seriously?*

His lips trembled. Who would want to make him pay? Mia? His ex-wife's new husband? His ex-business partner? It made no sense. Why *now*? It had been a long time since he encountered any of them.

He forgot the last time he'd felt scared. He could talk to Rick, ask for his help. A strong man like Rick could help if someone tried to attack him.

He did not want to see the graffiti again and decided the best action would be to call the complex manager and ask him to remove it. He would take pictures of it in case the police ever asked for evidence.

A few minutes later, he heard strange noises from outside his apartment. It sounded as if someone scratched something. He got out and saw Rick scrubbing the wall.

"What are you doing?"

"Oh, hey. This sucks, huh?" Rick's voice was lower than usual. "It annoyed me so much I decided to get rid of it. Will take me a few minutes."

"I was about to call the office, but I see you're doing a good job. You need help?"

"No, I'm good." He continued scraping the black letters off the wall.

"Any idea who did it?" David asked.

"Don't worry about it. It's nothing. Probably kids."

"No kids." A voice came from behind them. They turned and saw an older man standing in his doorway.

The neighbor from the apartment across from David's seldom got out. David had seen the old man only a few times since he moved in a couple of years ago. He considered knocking on the door to check on the neighbor but never felt up to it. He knew his name because it decorated the neighbor's door with big colorful letters.

"Hello, Barton. This is Rick, from upstairs."

The two men nodded at each other.

"Did you see who did this?"

"Hell, yeah," Barton said with a thick Southern accent. "Two big men." He emphasized each word. "They were being ugly. Knocked on your door. Loud. Woke me up. I peeked at them and saw them do this. I wanted to speak, but they seemed too dangerous. I even considered calling the cops, but they were gone fast." Barton stared at David. "What did you do?"

"*Me?* Nothing! I don't know what the hell's going on."

"Probably got the wrong address," Rick said. "Anyway, I'm done. It's as good as new." He tried to smile. "I gotta go now. Sorry, guys. Great meeting you, Barton."

Rick sprang up the stairs, leaving the two men to stare blankly at each other.

"There's something fishy going on here with y'all," Barton said. "I'd be careful if I was you."

"What do you mean?" David asked, but Barton shut the door behind him.

———

Angela entered their apartment and kissed Rick.

"Some kids painted graffiti next to David's apartment today." Rick crossed his arms. "It said, 'You'll pay for it.' So strange."

She stopped in the middle of taking her heels off. "Really?"

"Yeah. Strange."

"I didn't see anything."

"The maintenance guys came and cleaned it." Rick swallowed.

"So fast? David always says it takes them ages to fix things."

"I told them it was urgent."

She nodded. "You think someone's out to get him?"

"I doubt it. It's probably kids."

She took her other shoe off. "You don't think it could be *him*, do you?"

"No. No! I'm sure he doesn't know where you live. Don't worry about it, honey." He hugged her. "Even if it wasn't a prank, it was meant for David, not *you*."

She held him tight and nodded, her face against his pecs.

———

A few days later, Angela confronted Rick about cleaning the graffiti. "David told me you washed it off. Why did you lie to me?"

"I knew it was nothing and didn't want to worry you, honey."

He hugged her.

ELEVEN

After a few weeks, Rick and David did a twenty-minute walk. They sat on the two old stools next to David's kitchen counter and drank water and diet cola. David had bought the stools when he moved into the apartment but never used them.

"This sucks, man." David pointed to his diet drink.

"Yeah, but it has no calories." Rick raised his own drink. "This would be better for you." He pointed at his glass of water.

"I'll stick to the black stuff, if you don't mind."

"How's the list coming along?"

"I switched to Diet Coke. That's good, right?"

"That's one thing. What else?"

"I'm not sure I'm ready to share."

"You didn't do it, did you?"

"Actually, I did." David rose. "Your lack of confidence in me is insulting." He went to his bedroom and brought back a piece of paper.

"If I didn't have confidence in you, I wouldn't be here."

He let Rick get a glimpse of the note, then folded it and placed it in his pocket.

"Why don't you want to share it with me?"

"It's private."

"I can respect that." Rick sipped. "How do I know it's not your grocery list?"

They burst out laughing.

"Okay, buddy. No problem. Assuming it *is* a list, I need you to do one more thing for me."

"What might that be?"

"I need you to read it every morning, as soon as you get out of bed."

"It's starting to sound like you're coaching me."

Rick smiled.

"You know I hate coaches."

Rick nodded. "I almost forgot. I'll be right back." Rick left the apartment and returned after a few minutes with a Target bag in his hand.

"You bought me cupcakes?"

"You *wish*." Rick opened the bag and pulled out a black breathable T-shirt, like the ones he wore—only bigger—and put it on the kitchen table. Then he pulled out black shorts and a box with running shoes and put it on top of the clothes.

"You're showing me your new collection?"

"These are gifts. For *you*."

"What? Why?"

"Now that you're turning into my running—sorry, *walking*—buddy, I can't have you walking around in jeans. It's more for me than for you."

"I can't take this."

"Too late."

"I'll return it and give you the money back."

"I won't take it."

"I'll trade it for cupcakes."

"I want you to have it."

David pressed a hand against his chest, fingers splayed out, and sucked in a quick breath. He excused himself, went to the bathroom, and washed his face. He glared at himself in the mirror. *Why would he buy me such nice gifts? When was the last time anyone bought me a gift?*

He flushed the toilet and returned to the kitchen. He wanted to hug Rick but felt awkward. "Thanks, man."

"Don't worry about it. Angela helped me pick them out. If they're not the right size, we can go together and exchange them."

The thought of Angela picking out his clothes both flattered and embarrassed him.

David took out the note from his pocket, unfolded it, and sat on the stool. "It's not long," he said. "I have a car, a roof over my head, some money to buy food, *some* flowers outside my apartment."

Rick nodded. "That's good. Anything else?"

"The list does have two more items."

"Care to share?"

"It just says"—he swallowed—"Rick and Angela."

TWELVE

"Hey, buddy!" Rick said. "You look great in those clothes. Couldn't have picked better ones myself."

David tried not to laugh. "Yeah, well. You have good taste. What can I say?"

"Great. Let's take my car."

"I thought we were walking."

"You've earned something new. We're going to a better place."

"Heaven? *Finally!*"

"Not that far."

"The last time I tried it you stopped me halfway there, remember?"

Rick slapped his shoulder and got into the driver's side. "And I've regretted it ever since."

"Yeah, right." He entered Rick's car. "You did it 'cause you have a crush on me. It's okay. I don't mind. As long as you don't act on it."

"You know, I'm not sure God would have sent you to heaven."

"You're probably right." David buckled up. "Where are you taking me on our first date?"

"You'll see."

Rick started the car. The engine sounded like music to David's ears. He had heard it from his apartment but never from inside the car. He searched online and discovered it was the lower-end Camaro. The entry-level ones, not the sporty models. The more expensive Camaros had much louder engines. Still, not a cheap car. He wouldn't mind borrowing it from time to time.

David had expected the car's interior to be flashier, but it seemed almost like a regular car. The dashboard's speed and tachometer seemed like two big eyes staring at the driver. Testing him. A local pop station played music from the car stereo. Rick did not put his seat belt on until the alarm became unbearable.

"You drive like a grandma," David said when they crossed the bridge over the Arkansas River.

Rick revved the engine but did not drive any faster.

"You bought it to confuse the cops?" he asked.

"What do you mean?"

"Isn't it a cop car?"

"Cops drive Dodge Chargers. Actually, they have a special version of the car with better brakes, better cooling systems, and better stability."

"Wow, you sure know a lot about cop cars."

"I'm a guy. I know a lot about cars."

David looked out the window.

Rick turned his car without signaling into a parking lot in front of the river.

"Ah, the Arkansas River," David said. "I used to like it here. I used to come here to stare at the water."

"Yeah, it's nice. Me and Angela come to jog here every once in a while. I thought you might like it."

David nodded.

They got out of the car and looked around. "What do you see?" Rick asked.

"I see a river, even though it's drying up here and there." He pointed at the dry riverbeds. "Such a shame. I also see the trees starting to get yellow, which is nice. I see some trails for walking. I don't see many people, though."

"That sure is progress. You see both sides of things. I'll take that."

"I originally wanted to say the river's half-empty."

David smiled, but Rick's cell phone rang. He took it out, and his eyes widened when he saw the number. "I'm sorry, I gotta take this. Won't be long. Why don't you start stretching?"

Rick moved away. David stretched but could not help overhearing Rick's conversation. He couldn't hear actual words, but Rick yelled at first, then became quieter, and then it sounded as if he begged. It did not sound as if he was talking to Angela or to a client.

Rick returned after a while. They walked on the trail next to the river. After fifteen minutes, they turned around and walked back. When they neared the car, Rick pointed at a bench overlooking the river and used the backrest to stretch his thighs. David followed his stretching routine, and then they sat on the bench.

"You know I lost ten pounds because of you?" David slapped Rick on the shoulder. "Damn you."

"We should be running soon, you know?"

"No way in hell."

"That's what you told me a few weeks ago about walking." Rick inhaled. "I dare you to dream." He stood, raised his fists in the air, and faced the sky. "*I dare you to dream big!*"

———

David rose, walked toward the river, and gazed at it.

Rick texted someone, rose, and walked over to him. "Did you add this to your list?"

David nodded. "I even read the damn thing every morning. It doesn't do anything, but I'm a teacher's pet."

Rick smiled and raised a fist like a winner. "Look at yourself. When I first met you, you could hardly move. You hardly talked. Now you walk thirty minutes a day, you're much more vibrant, and—God help me—you talk *more* than my wife."

David giggled, still looking at the river. After a few minutes, he said, "I haven't seen Angela in a while. Is she okay?"

"Her mom lives alone in Chicago, so she goes to visit her for a few days every now and then."

"Oh. I didn't know that. Why didn't you go with her?"

"Sometimes I do. I don't like doing it often, though," Rick said. "Besides, I wouldn't want to miss out on our morning jogs. I mean—*walks*."

"You're crazy to prefer me over her."

"True. To be honest, I don't like her mom so much."

"How come?"

"To be more honest, she doesn't like me."

"I can relate." David giggled again, but Rick didn't. "Why doesn't she like you?"

"I'm not sure. I think she doesn't like what I do, and she probably doesn't think I'm good enough for her daughter. I don't have a college degree and all that. Her mother's a schoolteacher, and education is important to her." Rick gazed downward. "Angela is her only daughter, so she's overprotective."

"That's tough." David nodded. "Why *didn't* you go to college?"

"Didn't think I needed it. Didn't believe in it. I read a million books, went to seminars, learned a lot online. I'm kinda following Tony Robbins's route. You know him?"

David nodded.

"I want to be like him. I will be. He's amazing."

"I used to follow Steve Jobs. I thought I could be like him. A little like him. Unlike him, I completed two degrees, but besides that, I thought I could follow in his footsteps." David stared down at his feet. "I gave up on those dreams a long time ago."

"If you believe enough and work hard enough, you can accomplish anything you want." Rick's fists hit the air again.

"I used to believe that. But I'm not sure anymore."

"I hope I can take you to a Tony Robbins seminar one day. He'll help me change your mind." Rick checked his phone. "I'm sorry, but I have to go soon. I have a client in an hour, and I need to shower first."

"You mean a *real* client?"

Rick smiled and said nothing.

———

Someone knocked on David's door a few days later.

He stared at the door. Probably Rick. *Why is he coming here every day? Doesn't he have anything better to do with his life?*

After a few knocks, Rick left. *Thank God.*

But then David's phone rang.

"Why aren't you opening the door?" Rick cleared his throat. "Buddy?"

David opened the door and let him in.

"I'm sorry," he said. "I had a bad night."

Rick nodded. "I was worried about you. What happened?"

David went to the kitchen, plucked a banana Rick had made him buy, and almost tore it open. "Never mind."

David had taken three sleeping pills the previous night, but they didn't help. He stared at the ceiling and reflected on his life, not liking what had become of it. His heartburn —which had gotten less frequent in the past few weeks— gave him hell.

Staying up late thrusted him into obsessive thoughts. The major one was why he let a young man—almost a kid— tell him what to do with his life?

"Would you prefer I came back later?" Rick crossed his legs.

David shrugged and threw half of the banana in the garbage can. He noticed Rick held a set of books. "What's that?"

David moved back to the living room, and Rick put the books on the coffee table. "What do you see?"

"I see too many pages you think I should read."

"You want to know what I see?"

"Let me guess. You see flowers growing out of my table and smiling right at my face?"

"No." Rick ran his hands through his hair. "I see a huge bank of knowledge that'll help you get out of the depression you've been in for too long."

David rose from his recliner, face red, eyes opened wide.

"You don't tell me what I have or don't have! You understand me?" David yelled. "You're not my shrink. I did more than you ever did in your whole lifetime! Who do you think you are? You didn't even go to school. I have *two* degrees. Come back to me when you finish *one*."

He passed Rick, almost bumped him, and opened the door.

Rick's jaw dropped all the way to his pecs. "David, I'm sorry. I didn't mean that. I...I just wanted to help."

David looked outside the apartment. "I want you to leave."

"I'm sorry, buddy—"

"Stop calling me that! I hate it."

Rick nodded and left the apartment.

David slammed the door shut, cursed, and paced in his apartment. He kicked the coffee table, causing Rick's books to scatter all over the floor.

Who the fuck does he think he is? Just 'cause he looks good, is married to an amazing chick, and knows a few lines —he thinks he can diagnose me?

It's better to have him out of my life.

He grabbed the keys to his car and peered through the peephole, and after seeing no evidence of Rick, he left for his car. He decided to go all the way to Walmart, thinking they had different kind of women. He wanted more variety in his diet. He got two boxes of Twinkies, a box of cupcakes, and bigger-sized chips of a different brand. He returned to his apartment, ate all of it in front of the TV, and fell asleep.

When he awoke, he trudged to the bathroom. *Great to have my life back,* he thought as he urinated.

THIRTEEN

Someone knocked on the door that afternoon. *Too soft to be Rick. Maybe Angela? It would be nice to see her again.*

Or maybe not.

David stared at the door.

Is it too rude not to open it? On the fifth knock, he thought, *She did nothing wrong.*

When he opened the door, Angela smiled at him. Not her usual smile, but more of an *I'm sorry* kind of smile.

Too bad she married that idiot.

"Are you okay?" she asked.

He stared at her.

"Can I come in?"

He opened the door a little more, giving her enough space to enter. She sat on the couch. After a while, she said, "He never meant to hurt you. Please believe me. I know him. He doesn't want to hurt *anyone*. He likes you. And he likes to help people. That's what he does, and he does it well. He's a bit tough on people, but he gets results."

"Do you want a drink?"

"No, thank you."

She followed his gaze to the books her husband had left.

"You know," she said, "people pay him a lot of money for his help."

"Now you think I should thank him for it? What does he think I am? Charity?" He tried to keep his voice low.

Angela closed her eyes. "I'm sorry. That's not what I meant." She moved forward to the edge of the couch and leaned on her knees. "I meant he's good at what he does. And that he likes you and wants to help you." She leaned back in her seat. "He doesn't care about the money."

They were both silent for a while.

"Okay. I didn't mean to upset you even more. Rick and I have your best interest at heart. We both like you. I'm sorry."

She left.

He gazed at the closed door for almost an hour.

———

"It doesn't look like he's going to budge," Angela told Rick.

"He's so stubborn. I should have known," Rick said. "I didn't mean to offend him, but he *is* depressed. He tried to commit suicide, for crying out loud."

"Yes, but he's sensitive," she said. "Taking your help was a huge step for him. He didn't need you flashing it in his face."

"That's not what I did."

"*I* know. I meant from his point of view. He probably felt you were degrading him. You hurt his honor."

"*What* honor? That guy was a sorry-ass loser when I met him. I made him a human being again."

"You got him back on his feet and raised his confidence,

but from his point of view you shattered it when you confronted him."

Rick nodded. "I knew you were the smart one."

"You know I think highly about what you do," she said, "but in this case, I think he needs a psychologist alongside your coaching."

"I agree, but he won't do it. The psychiatrist at the hospital told him he should go to therapy, but I don't think he ever did. He probably would have rejected me if I'd offered him coaching like a regular client. I had to trick him into it, and it worked. The man lost ten pounds, smiles and talks and walks for almost thirty minutes a day! He could hardly move his ass when I met him."

"I know. I know. You're right."

"I don't know if he can afford a psychiatrist. I'm starting to think he spent all of his money." Rick shook his head.

"Didn't you say he won the lottery or something?"

"He sold his start-up. Internet says for ten million, but I don't know where the money went. I don't think he has much left."

Angela nodded.

"Maybe when you finish your studies you could give him some free therapy."

"It'll take me some time. Besides, it would be unacceptable and unprofessional since he's a friend."

Rick reflected on what she said. "You know, I have easier *paying* customers than him."

Angela thought for a moment. "You know what? I have an idea to help you take your mind off this."

"Sex?"

She laughed. "I guess that would work, but I meant going to a movie. I think there's a new comedy. What do you say?"

"And then sex?"

"I'll think about it. Let's go."

On the way to the car, Rick paused and stared at David's door.

"He'll come around," she said. "Give him a day or two to come to his senses. He'll probably call you tomorrow."

———

No one knocked on David's door for two weeks. No one came in; no one called him; no one told him what to do. No one brought him bad food. He got back to his lovely ritual of eating great food and watching TV. Life was good again.

Before he'd met Rick, David went to a nearby coffee shop every few weeks. He couldn't explain why, but it made him feel better. He didn't plan on meeting women there, but it was a highlight for him. Going out. Someone else making him a sandwich or soup.

David recognized some of the people from earlier visits. Some were in groups, some were in couples, and some were alone. Those who were not alone discussed their boring lives. At first, he made fun of them. Later he envied them.

At least they have friends.

Some of them, mainly the older ones, talked a lot about politics—how bad the president was, whom they should vote for, and how they would do things differently. Better.

David sat there, watched them, even eavesdropped. When he suspected they noticed him, he tried not to look. Why should he care? He did nothing wrong. The ones who came alone brought laptops and seemed to be working.

A few years ago, he was one of those people. He worked on his laptop, met other people, smiled.

David almost stumbled climbing the curb to his apartment. He leered at his belly, which had grown halfway back to where it had been a few weeks before. He dropped the grocery bags outside his apartment door and caught his breath. He stared at the door for a moment, then looked up the stairs. He climbed to the second floor, one step at a time. He walked to Rick's door and raised his hand to knock.

He held his hand in the air for almost a minute, then lowered it. He hoped someone would open the door. After a few minutes of staring at the door, he went back to his apartment.

He stared at the books Rick had brought him. Rick never asked for them back. He saw a book about a secret, two other books, and a few audio CDs from Anthony Robbins. *Who uses CDs these days?* He saw a book called *The 7 Habits of Highly Effective People.* He always thought he should have been one of them. He *had* been one of them. For a while.

A long time ago.

Another book smiled at him. Robert Herjavec, one of the nicer sharks from the *Tank*. He took the book and sat in his recliner. It had been a long time since he'd read a book. Watching TV took much less effort.

He ate all the food he'd bought and spent the day in his recliner, but he did not turn on the TV. He read the book.

For the next few days, the TV remained off. He didn't buy any more bad food and read all the books Rick had given him. He let himself skip a few boring chapters.

The books made him think about his life again. Think about Rick's lessons. *Do I want to be alone? It felt nice to have people come and go from my apartment.*

Having people in his life felt nice.

How stupid could I have been?

A few days later, David heard Rick walk down the

stairs. He peered outside and saw Rick looking at his door. He waited for him to knock, but he didn't.

A day later, David opened the door when he heard Rick's footsteps. Rick stopped as the door opened, wearing his running outfit. They looked at each other.

"You forgot to mention you stole that 'hour of power' from Tony Robbins," David said.

"You read the books I gave you?"

"I had to," David said. "They blocked my view of the TV."

Rick smiled.

"You need someone to help you with your hour of power?"

"Sure," Rick said. "Put on those sexy clothes I gotcha and join me. I'll stretch."

"You can do it inside." David opened the door wider. "But don't you get any ideas while I get dressed. Okay? I know you like me more than that average-looking wife of yours."

"I missed your stupid sense of humor, buddy." Rick walked in.

David smiled with his back to Rick.

It took David a few days to get back into shape.

"Let's start running," Rick said.

"No way in hell," David replied.

"Okay. Tell you what." Rick waved his hands in the air, the way he got when he gave a speech. "Tomorrow you go for a walk. *Alone*. You and your phone. Okay? You text me when you start. After about fifteen minutes, I'll text you a link to a song. It's a great song to start running to. You run the length of the song. Just about four minutes. When the song's over, you go back to walking. That's it. That's all you need to do. Okay?"

"I like the walking alone part."

The next day, he texted Rick: *I'm doing half of what you said. I'm walking alone but not running.*

Rick replied with a smiley face.

After fifteen minutes, Rick texted him a link to YouTube. *Kill my data plan, won't you?* But a good-looking blonde woman sang her "Fight Song." *Is she married?* David giggled.

He stopped and texted back: *I'm not listening to some kitsch song. You should know that by now. Some coach you are.*

As he walked again, he unlocked his iPhone. When no one saw him, he played the song. The pretty blonde sang about getting her life back.

He liked the song but would never admit it.

He picked up his pace and did something resembling a run. For almost a minute. He stopped and bent over, hands on his knees, and breathed heavily. When he caught his breath, he turned around and walked back home.

The trees turned green again.

Rick showed up after David showered. "How did the walk go?"

"Not bad. I had fun doing it alone, without all of your mantras."

"And how was running to the song I sent you?"

"It wasn't that bad. I wouldn't mind running with *her*."

They watched a comedy on TV. Watching a show with a friend felt good. David did not binge eat. He did not feel pathetic. He was not alone.

"I'm sorry," Rick said, looking at the TV. "I shouldn't have said what I said."

"It's okay. You *were* right." David looked at the TV as well. "I'm the one who should apologize to you. I'm not good at that. I was an asshole, especially about you not having a degree and all. It was a cheap shot. I'm sorry."

Rick nodded.

David hated to admit it, but he understood better what Rick did for a living. He started to believe in it, just a little. Maybe Rick was not a hack as he had initially thought?

"I'm only going to say this once, so pay attention." David rose from his recliner. "You are an amazing coach. I'm lucky to have you in my life."

———

A few days later, David walked alone while Rick left for a seminar. He ran for two minutes to a different song and felt both amazing and nauseous.

When he pulled the keys out of the back pocket of his shorts, he discovered his door was ajar.

FOURTEEN

"We can meet every couple of weeks. I'll fly here whenever you need me, and we can always talk on the phone." Rick shook the man's hand.

Another customer.

A paying customer.

The seminars he liked attending were great places to meet potential clients. Someone always needed coaching but couldn't afford one of the main speakers, and Rick was right there to help.

Hopefully, I'll be one of the speakers soon.

His phone vibrated in his pocket. He took it out and stared at it.

We didn't find anything, the text read.

———

David opened the door slowly to discover the apartment was a mess. Someone had turned everything upside down. He saw drawers opened and turned, things scattered all over the floor.

He considered entering, even though the burglar could still be inside. *What is my life worth, anyway?*

But when his chin trembled and his sweaty hand could not hold the door open, he decided to step outside and call the police. Two bulky police officers arrived, and after a short explanation, told him to wait outside. They entered the apartment, guns drawn. A few minutes later, they let him in.

The burglars had also emptied the drawers in the kitchen and in the bedroom. Everything that had been in them lay on the floor, next to the few books he had and the books from Rick. The only valuables in the apartment were the TV and an old laptop.

Both were there.

"They didn't steal anything valuable?" The police officers exchanged looks.

David shook his head. He told them about the graffiti a few weeks back, and when they asked for proof, he remembered he never had the chance to take a picture. Rick had cleaned it before he could do anything.

Rick.

I wish Rick was here.

Who is after me? Why is this happening? First the threats on the wall and now this. Who the hell could do this?

"It's probably *not* a crazy ex-girlfriend," one officer told the other as David returned from the bedroom. When they noticed him, they stopped laughing and glared at the floor.

After the police officers left, David shivered and wept for an hour.

———

A few days later, Angela knocked on David's door. He'd cleaned the apartment and put everything back in place.

"Rick and I wanted to invite you for dinner tonight. In a real restaurant. The three of us. What do you say?"

"Smart of him to send you. He knew I couldn't say no to *you*."

Angela smiled. It made him smile.

"It's great to see you smile again. Seven p.m.?"

He nodded.

He considered telling her about the break-in but was too embarrassed. *Would they laugh at me like the cops did?*

"Is that healthy food?" David asked at the nearby Mexican restaurant.

"It's okay to eat less healthy every now and then," Rick replied, "especially with friends. We just have to go easy on the chips."

David froze with a chip halfway into his mouth and put it on his plate instead. "Did I ever tell you about my failed start-up? My last attempt?"

Rick shook his head. "From what I understand, it happens a lot with start-ups, doesn't it?"

"It happened to me a few times. But the last one was special."

Angela looked at Rick and then at David. Rick gazed at him. David ate a few more chips, sighed, and then continued.

"I launched it with a partner who had the idea for the start-up. Back then, people came to me with start-up ideas all the time. I wrote a column for a big tech blog. I was famous in my circles. I would get two, maybe three ideas a week from literally everyone. I would discourage most of them—not trying to be mean, but, you know, most of them were crappy ideas or were done already."

"But can't you say that about practically everything?" Rick asked. "I don't think they have new ideas, do they?"

"You could say that." David sat upright, shoulders back, face serious. "But there's usually no point in going after a saturated or dominated market, sometimes by big players like Google or Apple, especially if you don't have anything unique to give the customers. You need a great new angle, something that solves a problem differently. Some people disagree with me on that."

The waiter interrupted them with their food. After they took a few bites, David continued, "Anyway, this guy had a great idea. The second he said he wanted me to partner with him, I said yes."

"What was it about?" Rick said.

"An app, more like a platform, for car sharing."

"There's...Uber, isn't there?" Rick said. "And Lyft?"

"Don't mention those names again," David said. "We tried to raise money with only a business plan I wrote, but the investors didn't like it. But *we* did, which is a good thing for a start-up. We knew about the competitors—they were starting out, but we believed we had a better product. We developed a working prototype, what we call an MVP—a *minimum viable product*, which I developed. We were able to get a couple of drivers—including ourselves—and even a few clients to start with. Then we tried to raise money again. After a few good meetings with potential investors, Uber was published to have raised two hundred and fifty-eight million dollars, which got them a lot of publicity, so no one wanted to invest in our company. Some accused us of copying them while not even trying to do a better job. Lyft raised much less, but it also hurt our chances of raising money."

"Didn't Uber raise a billion dollars?" Rick asked.

David nodded, ate some of his fajita, then continued. "Anyway, after we couldn't raise any money, my partner started blaming me for the failure, bad-mouthing me to investors and other entrepreneurs. I couldn't believe it when I first heard the rumors. Before that, I trusted him blindly. By the time I figured out what happened, it was too late. People stopped coming to me with new ideas. After a while I couldn't even get a corporate job."

His eyes became teary, but he wiped them. The couple looked at him with sympathy. He had not thought of his ex-partner for a long time. It led to other bad things. At a certain point after that, he gave up on life. Too hard to deal with work, people, money, not to mention the hard work and stamina needed to be an entrepreneur.

"And then my life partner left me, but that's a story for another time."

He asked to be excused and went to the restroom for fifteen minutes.

———

When David returned, he tried to smile. "Now you know why I'm such a failure."

"You're not," Angela said. "You had some bad luck and a bad partner, that's all."

"Yeah. I sure know how to pick 'em."

"You know," Rick said, "another famous saying from the guy you don't like is, 'Failure is simply an opportunity to begin again, but more intelligently.'"

David nodded. "You like Henry Ford, don't you?"

"He said some smart things."

"Even though he was a big anti-Semite," David said. "I

looked him up. He bought and published a bigoted newspaper."

"Oh, wow. Okay. No more Henry Ford then."

"Besides, I thought you were only a Tony Robbins kind of guy."

"I can be with more than one guy at a time."

"That can't be good for my diet," David said when the waiter brought sopaipillas with honey for dessert.

"All those books Rick gave you," Angela said, "and yes, I admit I read them, talk about being the best. Being *number one*. Beating everyone. Maybe not all of the books, but a lot of them do. Even though Rick likes to push us to our limits, I'm not sure it's for everyone." She wiped her clean mouth and took a sip from her water. "Don't get me wrong, the only way to be successful is to keep pushing all the time. Never surrender and never quit. That's the only way to beat depression. And anything else in life. *But* I'm not sure everyone's built for it. Not *all* the time. What you went through may have pushed you over the limit. Maybe you need to rest. Or maybe you need a different path in life. A more relaxed one."

David tilted his body toward Angela.

"I think Tony Robbins talks about being the best *you* can be," she said, "not beating everyone else. If you must push yourself, stick to that."

David considered what Angela said. She had a good point. He had a hard time relating to some of Rick's stuff, but once he got past his objections, Rick made sense. He saw himself *achieving*—in the future, at least. But Angela's point was important. Maybe he pushed himself over the limit. He should start slower for sure. His goal had always been to beat everyone else. Probably like Rick.

"Is it generally a man's problem?" David asked.

"Probably. Men are much more competitive than women."

"Maybe there would be no more wars if women ruled the world."

"Probably."

"I see she's the smart one in the family."

Angela smiled. Rick did not.

FIFTEEN

When David heard footsteps going down the stairs, he peered outside and saw Angela wearing a tight white tank top, black shorts, and running shoes. She had her hair tied up in a long, blonde, straight ponytail. The cord of her white earbuds trailed down from her ears, over her body, and into a phone she held in her right hand.

His hands tingled.

Was it her *hour of power?*

Maybe she would stop and ask him to join her.

I'd probably trail behind her the whole way.

She walked outside his view, and he sprang to the window, cracked open the shades, and kept staring. Her legs were long, smooth, and perfect. She accelerated out of his line of sight.

He didn't hear her return. *Maybe she'll come by later for dinner? Rick was at a conference. Or a seminar. Or whatever.* David showered and wore clean clothes, just in case. At dinnertime he wondered if he should text her. Was it appropriate? Then he remembered he didn't even have her phone number. Should he friend her on Facebook and ask her to dinner?

Just as a friend.

Am I becoming a stalker?

———

The following morning, he opened the door when she passed by in the hallway.

She stopped, almost startled. Then she smiled and took out one of her earbuds.

"Hey!" She wore a different pair of shorts and a different tight tank top. "How are you doing?"

"I'm good, thanks."

"That's great to hear." She came closer. "I don't think I ever heard you say that before."

His smile flattened, and he lowered his head.

"You want to join me for a run? Or a walk—"

"Yes! I mean, sure, if you insist. Can you give me a few minutes to get ready?"

"Of course."

They stood there for a few seconds.

"Do you, um...want to wait inside?"

"Sure." She entered.

He excused himself as he walked into his bedroom, closed the door, and changed his clothes. The thought of her being less than ten feet from him while he undressed gave him goose bumps.

When he returned, she was sitting on his couch, her back to him, earbuds back in. Her hand tapped her crossed legs in time with the music.

He stared at her long, perfectly tanned legs. She had the softest skin he'd ever seen.

When she turned and saw him staring, she froze, then stood. "Ready to go?"

"Ah...yes." He looked everywhere but at her.

Angela, like Rick, seemed to slow down to his pace. He wondered if she felt sorry he'd joined her.

"I hope you don't mind me saying," she said after ten minutes, "but you look much better these days."

"Why would I mind such a compliment? I'm flattered. Thank you."

They walked outside the gates of the complex on a sidewalk leading nowhere. When it ended, they made a U-turn.

"I hate the sidewalks here," she said.

"Why?"

"There aren't any."

"I haven't noticed that."

"They want people to walk and ride bicycles, but they hardly provide the infrastructure for it. In Chicago I could just step out of the apartment and walk anywhere."

"I never thought of that, but I guess you're right. It's a small city."

"That's no excuse."

"How about the river trail? I went there with Rick the other day. It's nice."

"Yes, I love that. But you have to *drive* there."

He nodded. "You know what Rick would say about that?"

"What?"

He deepened his voice. "Why are you looking at the glass half-empty? Look around you. Can't you see the green grass, green trees, and beautiful flowers?"

They laughed.

He wondered what to talk about. "Speaking of the devil —how's his seminar?"

"He's doing well. He's actually *learning* this time."

David breathed heavily as they reached his stamina limit.

"Do you want to go back?" Angela asked.

He nodded without looking at her.

They slowly returned and stood in front of his apartment.

"Thanks for the company," she said.

"Oh, no. Thank *you*."

He hoped she would invite him for coffee, or maybe want to come into his apartment for one, but she did not.

She suggested they go out for breakfast.

"*Yes*," he almost shouted.

"Great. See you here in thirty minutes?"

He nodded. "Won't Rick mind?" He wanted to joke but sounded serious.

"He's not the jealous type, especially not with *you*."

Did she insult or compliment him?

"I sometimes wish he was. Just a little." She checked her watch. "Besides, I have no classes today, and I'm bored by myself when he's really in a seminar."

"What do you mean?"

"I mean...um...this time he didn't come back in the *middle* of the seminar like he did last time."

David nodded.

We're going out for breakfast.

————

Angela needed groceries, so David drove her to Target. They sat at the Starbucks inside, and he did not look at other women. He remembered the girl he'd saved not long ago and contemplated telling Angela about it.

They ate muffins and drank coffee. It wasn't breakfast, but good enough.

"We can have fun when Rick's not around." She held the muffin high, smiling with her beautiful teeth.

"I won't tell him if you won't," he managed to say but almost peed his pants.

"Is there a special woman in your life?" Angela asked after they finished their muffins.

He shook his head and lowered his eyes.

Didn't she know this, or was she just making conversation?

"Oh, I'm sorry. Are you gay?"

"What? *No!*"

I thought she caught me staring at her legs this morning.

"I'm sorry." She made a puppy face and held his hand with both of her hands.

His blood pressure rose. He wished she would never let go.

"It's just that, um, you seemed weird when I asked you about a woman, so I thought..." She let go of his hand. "But it's not that I *thought* you were, um, gay. It—"

"Let's forget it." He sat upright. "There were a few women. The last one was special. But she broke my heart." He checked the clock on his iPhone. "But it's a long story. I don't want to bore you with it."

"I have all day."

"Are you sure?" He checked the clock again. "It could take a few hours."

"I have all day."

"Okay." He lowered his voice. "We're talking about the worst day of my life."

SIXTEEN

David looked outside and could almost see the girl he had saved, the truck almost hitting them, and the mother hugging him afterward.

"You want to talk about it?" Angela asked.

He sighed.

"A few weeks ago," he said, "the same day I met you, I almost got killed right here on this sidewalk." She followed his finger as he pointed outside. He told her what had happened and could see her eyes fill with empathy, then admiration.

"Amazing. You're a great person, David."

"Thank you."

After a few minutes, he said, "I moved to Tulsa three years ago from New York. I was between start-ups, doing mainly consulting. I moved because I met a great lady online. Her name was—*is*—Mia. It's funny 'cause we met by mistake. I researched online dating apps for a start-up I worked with. I registered with a few apps, and when I came across Mia's face, I froze. I sent her a message, and she responded a few minutes later."

Angela leaned toward him, eyes looking into his.

"We corresponded for a while. After a couple of weeks, we talked on the phone, and after some great conversations into the night, she said she would come to New York to meet me. I picked her up at JFK, and we immediately clicked. She planned to stay at a hotel, but we had such a great connection we decided she would sleep at my place. At first we said she'd sleep on the couch, but after a few hours, we decided it would be more comfortable if she slept in my bed."

Angela grinned.

He blushed.

"We didn't *do* anything. Well, maybe a little. But the following night we...never mind. I don't even know *why* I got into this." He tried to smile. "Anyway, she stayed for a week, and we had a great time. After a couple of months of a long-distance relationship, I ended up moving here, to Tulsa. I figured I would continue with my consulting business from here. We rented a nice big house. We even talked about getting married. It sounds stupid now, but we even started talking about having kids."

He wiped his eyes, excused himself, and went to the restroom. On the way back he ordered two more cups of coffee.

"I didn't believe in online dating before I met her. But Mia changed that. It wasn't relevant to the start-up I worked with—there were too many apps for dating—but I started to believe in the concept." He paused and glanced at Angela. "About a year later, she left me."

She covered her mouth with her hand.

He drank his coffee. "I hope I'm not boring you."

"Not at all. I'm sorry, though. What happened?"

"I worked with another start-up from Tulsa, but I traveled a lot. That's the start-up I told you and Rick about, where my"—he made air quotes with his fingers—"*partner* ditched me and told lies about me."

Angela nodded.

"At first, she supported me, but it only lasted a few weeks. When I started getting depressed and wasn't sure if I could find work, things started going south. I came home one day to find a note saying she'd left me. That's it. She took her stuff and left. I don't even know who helped her move. A few weeks later, I ran into her in a grocery store. She was smiling and laughing in the arms of another man."

"*Wow!* David, I'm so sorry."

"Thank you." He nodded. "I think it started *before* we separated. I'm not sure if it was before or after my start-up crashed."

He sipped his coffee. "Anyway, I later discovered this guy had a lot of money. A bestselling writer or something. I didn't run into her again for a long time. But the day I...you know, the day Rick *found* me was the day before her birthday, and I made the terrible mistake of looking for her on Facebook. I saw she'd gotten married." He lowered his eyes. "Maybe *that* was the worst day of my life."

"I'm so sorry, David."

———

"Did you ever consider dating again?" Angela asked after she finished her coffee.

"A million times. I'm embarrassed to admit it, but I even come here from time to time to look for women." He pointed at the store. "Pathetic, huh?"

Did I just admit that? I never told anyone that.

"Not at all," she said. "I think it's sweet. We all need

someone to love. We all want to be loved. I'm not sure *Target* is the best place for it, but you never know where you may meet your special someone."

He gave her a small shrug. "I think I lost faith in women —and in people in general, to be honest. Then I started looking like *this*—" he gestured to his body "—which didn't help much either."

"You look much better."

"Thank you." He swallowed.

"I'm sure you'll find someone soon. I wish I had some friends here for you to meet, but we just moved here." She sipped from her coffee cup, realized it was empty, and put it down. "There may be someone at school. She doesn't have a ring, and she seems nice. Would you like me to check?"

"Sure." He forced a smile. "Why not?"

"Great! You know, I think you're going through an amazing process with Rick. And alone. I think you'll continue getting better, and then you'll find someone special."

He nodded.

"Rick and I have a lot of differences in the way we think people should be coached," she said. "But I've seen him do an amazing job with people, helping them improve their lives."

As David finished his last sip of coffee, Angela checked her watch and said, "I'm sorry, I have to go soon."

He looked away. *Didn't she say she had the whole day?*

"Sure." He rose. "Thank you for today."

"My pleasure," she said and, of course, smiled.

Angela forgot to buy groceries.

Trever and Mark met their boss in his huge new black Mercedes.

"We found nothing in his apartment, boss," Trever said. "But I think he got the message."

The boss nodded. "Let's give him a little more time. The third warning will be the last."

Trever nodded. Mark grinned.

SEVENTEEN

"I heard you had a nice breakfast with my wife while I was gone," Rick said after their morning walk.

David nodded.

"She said you had a good talk. I'm glad."

"Good thing you're not the jealous type."

"I trust my wife. And you."

"How did you end up coaching?"

Rick sipped the stinky green drink he brought every now and then while David drank Coke Zero in his living room.

Rick sat back. "I guess it all started when I got depressed after high school. I knew I couldn't go to college—I had a bad case of ADHD and all that shit, and I couldn't sit in a class for more than an hour. I barely finished high school. I always looked for shortcuts. I'm the absolute opposite of Angela. And from you, I guess."

David nodded. "I can't imagine *you* being depressed."

"I was. I believe being depressed is sometimes an easy way out. You don't have to deal with anything. It can become somewhere to go to. I'm depressed, so I can't deal with life. You know what I mean?"

"I don't think people fake depression." David moved in his chair.

"I don't think that either. And I don't think most people *fake* or *choose* to be depressed. But I believe you can force yourself out of it. In many cases, not all. Sometimes you'll need help, but it *is* possible."

"But it's like a disease. You wouldn't judge someone for having cancer, would you?"

"I think a lot of diseases are also related to the mind. Mind and body are linked. It's not just me; it's been clinically proven. There's a lot you can do with your mind for all kinds of diseases as well as depression."

David finished his drink and reflected on what Rick had said. *Did I give in to my depression? For a long time, it felt easier not to deal with life. I couldn't deal with it. Watching TV and eating junk food was easy. Waking every morning and going for a walk take a lot of effort. Could I have forced myself to do it? Did I want to force myself?*

"I started listening to some tapes and books—the basics," Rick said. "I started with *The Secret*, then Tony Robbins, then went to seminars. Read more stuff, even psychology books—but don't tell Angela, okay?" Rick smiled. "Then I got myself up. Almost alone. I even went to a therapist. He said my progress amazed him. Said he'd never seen anything like that. Then, one day, I helped a friend and liked it. I took a course and started putting my name out there as a coach. It was after the trend started, so people found it easier to believe and understand it.

"It went well. I make a good living. But I have a lot of dreams. I wanna do seminars for hundreds of people. That's why I go to a lot of them. I'm learning how to do it and working on my network. You know my motto—*dare to dream!*"

"To be honest with you, I always thought those seminars were a scam," David said.

"Do you *still* think that?"

"After meeting you?" he asked. "Probably more."

They laughed.

"I gave up on my dreams," David said after a while.

Rick nodded. "I know. But we're working on getting them back. *Never* lose your dreams. You always have to get up after you fall. That's life."

"I'm not sure I can. You know? I kinda gave up."

"Tony Robbins always says, 'The past doesn't equal the future.' I love that quote. It's one of his best. It means that if you failed in the past, it doesn't mean you'll fail in the future."

David nodded and searched for something smart to say but could find nothing.

After a long silence, Rick said, "I had something I wanted to talk you about." He sipped the last few drops out of his glass.

"I don't have that green shit you drink, but I have some black *diet* shit, if you want."

Rick shook his head.

"I should get some of that green drink. For special guests."

Rick smiled.

"Anyway, you were saying?"

David filled their glasses with water. Rick sipped and continued, "I'm not sure if it's the right time to talk about it." Rick shifted in his seat. "But I...I had an idea for an app in my field."

"*Really?*"

"I would love to share it with you and see what you think. Maybe when you feel better?"

David nodded slowly.

"How did you meet Angela?" David asked after a while.

"She didn't tell you?"

He shook his head.

"What *did* you talk about?"

"Me, mostly. I told her about my love life," he said, "or the lack of it."

"Oh. I need to hear about that sometime."

David nodded. "Maybe. Sometime."

"We met at a marathon. I was faster, of course, but when I noticed her, I started running slower to try to talk to her. At first she ignored me, but then—"

A soft knock on the door made him stop. David opened the door and let Angela in; she kissed Rick and sat down. "What are you guys talking about? Women?"

"As a matter of fact, yes," Rick said.

"He was telling me how you guys met."

"Oh. Did he lie and say I chased him?"

"He said *he* chased *you*."

"That's not how he usually tells this story."

"Rick never lies to *me*." David grinned.

"At first she didn't want to go out with me," Rick said. "Only on my third attempt—when I suggested a quick coffee after the race—she said okay, just to get me off her back."

"That's true," she said.

"It was a short coffee date, then she said she needed to go. She made the mistake of giving me her number. I'm sure when she discovered I didn't go to college, she wanted to get rid of me, but I kept calling her and tried to get a second date. After that we dated for two years, got married, and eventually moved here."

"That's nice," David said.

"Let's toast!" Rick stood. "To success, love, and happiness!"

They all raised their glasses and smiled.

David tried to remember when his apartment was full and happy.

Never.

EIGHTEEN

Rick appeared a few days later with a huge grin on his face. "I have a surprise."

"A good one?" David asked.

"Of course."

"It's hard to tell with you. Your kind of a surprise would be to drag me to a marathon."

"No. But that's not a bad idea. This time we're going to New York City!"

"What? Why?" David almost jumped. "Wait. Is there a marathon there you want to trick me into doing?"

Rick sat on the couch. "I have a meeting there. They bought two tickets for me and Angela. But Angela can't come. And I know you like New York, so I hoped you'd join me."

David couldn't remember the last time anyone wanted to take him *anywhere*. The last time he had visited the Big Apple had been over two years ago. He had considered going, just to travel, but decided the flight and the hotel would be too expensive. "Are you serious?"

"It's only for forty-eight hours. If that's okay with you."

"That would be amazing. Thank you so much."

"Happy to do it, buddy."

"Wait," David said. "I'm not sharing a bed with you, right?"

"Heh, you wish," Rick said. "We'll just be sharing a hotel room. I only share a bed with Angela."

———

They took two flights to get to New York City, which lasted almost half a day. They freshened up at the hotel and walked together to the subway station where Rick took the train to his meeting, and David walked down Fifth Avenue.

He forgot how it felt to walk in the midst of a crowd, people coming and going, some in a rush, some just tourists admiring what the big city offered. Taxis flew around between a million cars, most of them sharing their feelings with their horns. Well-dressed, good-looking women and men walked, talked into a phone, or listened to music on their earbuds.

He'd missed the chaos of the big city.

After Rick's meeting, they met at the Columbus Circle entrance to Central Park and walked inside. After a while they sat on a bench.

"How did the meeting go?" David asked.

"It was okay. Could have been better, I guess. But never mind that. How was your day?"

"Great." David stretched his legs. "I walked the streets all day, looking at people. I missed that."

Rick turned to look at him. "You know, I never heard you use that word."

"Which one? Walk the streets? There aren't many streets to walk in Tulsa."

"No. I never heard you say you feel *great*."

David nodded.

"Maybe you should move back here? Looks like this city is good for you."

"I thought about it. Many times. Maybe I will, someday. I guess you and Angela would be happy to get rid of me."

"Of course not." Rick almost rose from the bench. "Well, maybe a little."

David slapped him on the shoulder as they laughed.

"But seriously, we want you to be happy. If that would make you happy, who are we to keep you in Tulsa? Hell, if it were up to me, I'd move here too."

"It's way too expensive to live here these days. I couldn't afford it without a good paycheck. And people are much nicer in Tulsa."

"You have a point. They smile at you all the time and say *thank you* and *excuse me*."

"And never honk their horns. I almost lost my hearing today."

A mother walked along the path in front of where they sat. She pushed a stroller with a baby in it. A boy ran past her, and when she called him, he ran back to her and laughed. She smiled at him, then bent over to kiss him.

"I'd love to meet someone and have kids," David said.

"You will."

David watched the mother and the kid walk away. "I'm sorry if it's none of my business, but...don't you and Angela want kids?"

"*She* does. I'm not so sure. Maybe in a few years. I feel like I'm too young for that right now. It's a big commitment."

David nodded. "Sometimes I feel like I've wasted my life."

"You can't say that. You made some mistakes, had some bad luck, but that's it. You remember we talked about how the past does not equal the future? Always remember that. I mean—look at you. You're light years ahead of where you were a few weeks ago. You almost ki—" Rick paused.

"It's okay. I understand what you mean."

"I didn't mean to upset you or anything," Rick said. "You should decide you *want* to, and *can*, do something and go ahead and do it. With everything you've got. Can you look back at a past success you had?"

David seemed to consider this. "My second start-up. We made a small exit."

Rick sat straight. "Small?"

"Yeah. It wasn't that small, but what I had left wasn't much."

"How come?"

"Investors took a big chunk, the partners took their part, and, after taxes, I was left with only a few hundred thousand dollars."

Rick inhaled and exhaled slowly.

"I also managed to spend most of it in the past couple of years. But it was an amazing time for me."

Rick nodded slowly and took a deep breath.

"There you go. Remember *that* moment. Remember how you felt back then. You did it once, probably more, and you can do it again."

"Okay, as long as you stop with your clichés."

"*Actually...*" Rick took out his phone.

"Oh, no."

"I have a new saying I thought of recently."

"You mean you didn't *steal* it from anyone?"

"Hey, I never steal. I always give credit."

"You do."

"You want to hear it or not?"

"Do I have a choice?"

"Not really." Rick stood and read from his phone with great importance, speaking slowly. "Guide your life as if a can't-go-wrong fortune teller told you what you will become."

It took David almost a minute to digest. He wanted to make a joke but could not. "That's not bad," he said.

"I know."

———

After they returned home, David dreamed of Angela. She came to his door again, this time wearing a robe. He let her in. When she started taking the robe off, he stopped her.

I'm sorry, I can't, he said. *Please go back home.*

———

"You *idiots* had the wrong apartment!" the boss yelled inside his Mercedes.

Trever and Mark stared at him.

"You scared some other poor idiot. Good thing the cops didn't come looking for us for no reason. *Idiots!*"

He was the only person in the world who could call them that and live. But they *were* idiots. They got his dirty work done but needed a lot of guidance. Muscles with no brains.

"How do you know?" Trever asked.

"I have contacts in the police. Some idiot made a complaint. A different idiot."

He handed them a note with the correct apartment number. "Wait a few days. Then think of something good to do."

PART 2
THE DREAM

NINETEEN

Two weeks later, after a fifteen-minute run, David and Rick sat on David's couch and drank green and black no-calorie drinks.

"I think it's time you told me about your app idea."

Rick straightened up. "It's basically a coaching app." He moved to the edge of his seat. "It's what I did with you but without me actually being there. It'll also be more structured. Every week there'll be a new lesson and exercises to help you learn and implement. You'd get exercises you'd need to complete, then get credit for your overall progress."

David nodded. "We call it gamification, which is when you make a game out of a process to make the user want to return to the app." He sat upright, faced Rick, and made big hand gestures when he talked. "It gets them more involved so they advance further."

"Makes sense. Anyway, that's the basic idea. What do you think?"

David considered Rick's words. "Don't they have apps like that?

"Not that I could find."

David would need to check. If he had a penny for each time a person with an idea told him they were the first, he would be rich.

"The idea sounds great. I guess I would be your first customer."

"I don't want you to be my first customer." Rick leaned in. "If you feel you're ready, I'd like you to be my partner."

David's mouth opened. A million thoughts raced through his mind. After his last partner had screwed him, he promised himself never to get another one. But Rick had become his best friend, and he trusted him. With his life.

Doing real work, and maybe getting paid for it, would be a welcome change. If it succeeded, he could run his own start-up again. He would not repeat the same mistakes.

Rick's questioning eyes stopped his thoughts.

"That's why you gave me all those free coaching lessons, huh?"

"You son of a bitch." Rick slapped him on the shoulder again and again while David laughed and hit him back.

"If Angela were here, she'd think we're acting like kids," David said.

"We *are*."

After they calmed down, Rick explained more aspects of his idea, showed him a few sketches he had made, and told him where he wished to take it.

"You know," David said after a while, "a vision without execution is just a hallucination."

Rick's eyes lit up. "Nice!" he said. "That's good. We should write it down." He reached for his phone. "I'll give you credit."

"It's from your racist friend again."

"It is? I didn't know that one," Rick said and typed it

into his phone. "Did you go out and buy more books without telling me?"

"I wouldn't betray you like that." David smiled, then waved his phone. "There's this thing called the internet. It has a lot of stuff in it. You should check it out sometime."

Rick tried to look grave. "Now seriously, are you with me?"

David considered it. "From my experience, there's always an app for anything you can think of. You wouldn't believe how many ideas I had or that people came to me with and we found something similar every time."

"And you gave up?"

"Usually when people have an idea, they're so in love with it and have a hard time giving up on it. As a consultant, I have the privilege of looking at it from a distance. It takes a lot of time, hard work, and money to pursue an idea, so I believe it's pointless to go after an idea with zero point zero, zero, zero—" he paused for the effect "—one percent success. Some would think I'm wrong, but I'm talking from my experience."

When he escorted Rick to the door, David said, "It's a great idea, and I'm flattered, but it's a huge step for me."

"I know. No rush."

"Did you think of a name for the app?"

"Of course."

"What is it?"

Rick smiled, raised his hands, and said, "Dare to dream!"

———

A few days later, David made Rick a disgusting green drink in his kitchen after their morning jog.

"Thanks for having my green drink here." Rick sipped it.

"No problem. Angela brought it around one day."

"I know." Rick said. "But she told me you asked her to get it."

They sat down and snacked on raw almonds David had bought at Target the previous day. He noticed they finally had those carts he could drive inside the store. The ones he had wished for not long ago. He looked at the carts, smiled, and walked inside the store. He contemplated telling Rick.

"No donuts?" Rick asked.

"I never had donuts. I had some other bad food here, but never donuts."

"Did you have a chance to think about my start-up idea?"

David turned the TV on and mirrored his iPhone to it. A presentation with the title DARE TO DREAM filled the screen.

David changed the slide using his iPhone. The second slide had "Competitors" written on it and a list of icons. "I found a few competitors but, surprisingly, not too many. Many of them are personal goal ones, which is nice, but it's not exactly what you had in mind. The goals might be a feature in it but not the main idea. Some are just app versions of magazines. I couldn't find anything that's exactly like what you described."

The next slide showed the business model. David explained that most of the other apps were free to download. "Free is a good model for us."

"I struggled with the price," Rick said. "I heard many apps were free, but how can free be good?"

"Many apps charge between three to ten dollars a month, which is great." David stood in front of Rick and looked down at him, his spine straight, shoulders pulled back. "I believe it should also be free to download but with a subscription to get more things. That means the users have no barriers to download and try the app. We can even give them some basic features for free, and if they like it, we get steady monthly payments, hopefully for a long time. Usually a small percentage of people pay for apps, but if you have a large install base and get enough people to stay and pay, you can build a great, viable business."

Rick looked up at him and leaned in, his eyes sparkling.

David felt a few inches taller.

"When someone pays you one dollar," he said, "or even a few dollars to get the app and you don't hear from them again, you don't have an ongoing revenue stream. You need to get new users all the time, which usually costs money. With monthly payments, you get money every month. You need to update the app every now and then, but you'd have to do it anyway. This way at least you get paid for it. The free model attracts many people to download the app to begin with. You give them seven days for free, maybe more, or some free features. That lets them try it, and if they like it, they'll pay."

Rick nodded.

"About ninety-eight percent of the people don't pay," he continued, "but we have to live with it. We aim for the remaining few."

David explained other business ideas and options he had gathered.

After the presentation, Rick said, "That was amazing. I appreciate all the work you did." He stood. "Would you like to be my *equal* partner?"

"What?" David sat down, glanced at the TV, then

looked back at Rick. "Fifty percent is a lot," he said. "Are you sure you're willing to give up that much?"

"I wasn't sure before I came here, but your *amazing* presentation made me realize how much I don't know about this business. I realized I can't do it without you. To be honest, I have no idea what you just talked about."

They laughed.

"You can be the vice president of business or something," Rick said.

"Business development," David said. "But why not CEO?"

"Leave something for me, will ya?"

"I was kidding. You *are* the brand. You *must* be CEO, even if you don't know the business."

"That's why I need you."

"You do." David crossed his arms. "You really mean fifty-fifty?"

Rick hunched over, and his eyes were almost at the same level as David's. "I do."

David seemed to consider. "I've put a lot of work into it already. I guess you have a deal." He extended his hand to shake Rick's, but Rick ignored it and hugged him.

After a few seconds, Rick said, "Was it too much? Should I have offered less?"

"Too late, *buddy*."

"That's *my* word."

"I used to get a lot of offers like that. I once got an offer for ten percent from a guy with an idea and nothing else. The idea excited me, so I started working on his business plan, and I even did some coding to get the app going. When I asked for a bigger percentage of the company, he consulted with other people and insisted on not sharing more. He wasn't even going to pay me. He didn't do anything with it before he met me. I rejected that offer, even though I put a lot of work into it."

"And what happened?"

"He ended up abandoning it, and it went down the drain."

"Why didn't you take the idea and finish the app yourself?"

"I'd never do that. He trusted me with his idea."

Rick nodded.

"I also had another offer for *ninety* percent, but I didn't like the idea. Didn't think it'd work. And I was right, of course." He grinned.

"That world is amazing."

"That's why I loved it."

"I hope you can learn to love it again."

"I never really stopped. I got burned. Hard."

"Have you seen *Pretty Woman*?" Rick held the door open.

"Of course, who hasn't?" David asked. "My generation saw it for sure. I'm embarrassed to say I saw it more than once. But *you*? You're young."

"We're not that much apart," Rick said. "Anyway, I wanted to say I would have given you sixty percent, if you'd asked for it."

David made a shocked face. "You know," he said, "I would have taken forty."

They laughed.

"Before you go, let's talk about action items," David said. "I'll continue to work on the business plan, and you'll work on a full-length design for the app. Every idea you have, every function you can think of—put it into a document, preferably with drawings or even mock-up pictures.

I'll send you some samples, if you want. That's your home-work for now. Let's meet again in two days?"

"I thought I was the CEO."

"I just made you think you were."

———

"You know, I've been thinking about the start-up thing you're doing with David," Angela said during dinner.

"And?" Rick asked.

"I don't think you should do it."

"Are you *serious*?"

"I don't think he's ready. He's fragile. If anything goes wrong, I'm afraid he'll break."

"I've been planning this for a long time. That's a big part of why I did what I did." He fiddled with his fork. "You should see him. It's like he's on steroids. He's stepped up like a man. I think it helps him become human again."

"I understand that, but I think you should take it easy on him." She held his hand. "Maybe just go slower?"

"I'll think about it."

———

FBI Special Agent Bob Alexis gestured for his partner, Agent Stuber, to sit in front of him in his office, but Stuber remained standing.

"We have to let him go. We have nothing concrete on him."

"This is the second fail to get a witness. We had to let the other one loose a few months ago," Stuber said. "This is not how you run an investigation—"

"Take it easy." Bob raised his hand and almost slammed

his desk. "I've been running investigations since you were a child."

"We have to make him talk. He won't do it with lame threats, we need—"

"What do you suggest?" Bob rose. "We beat a confession out of him?"

Stuber said nothing.

"This is not how we do things here." Bob said.

Stuber ran his hand through his hair, shook his head, and sat down in front of Bob.

"What are your plans?"

"We'll keep tapping all of his communications. We'll get him, eventually."

"What did he do again, exactly?"

Bob inhaled and exhaled. Stuber wanted to get a confession using rough methods, not even knowing what the case was about.

What an idiot.

"He mainly launders money for the mob," Bob said. "He does it through investing in innocent start-ups."

Stuber sneered. "I can't believe his real name is Guy Cash."

TWENTY

"Are you sure about this?"

"Of course."

"I appreciate it." David drove his car, Angela next to him. "I don't remember the last time I bought clothes. I could use a new wardrobe, especially after I've lost all that weight."

"I love to help," Angela said. "I usually pick out Rick's clothes as well."

David's eyes sparkled. If he could look a little like Rick, that would be something to write home about.

She stopped in front of the second store they passed inside the mall and stared at a dress in the window. He stopped and looked at her.

"Let me remind you we came here to shop for *me*."

"I know. I'm sorry. It won't happen again."

She stopped next to the fifth store.

He cleared his throat. She apologized again.

"Do you want to try it on?"

"What? No. It's okay."

"Are you sure?"

"I can come here again some other time. We came here to get *you* some clothes."

He nodded, and they continued. "So the myth is true," he said.

"What myth?"

"That women can't go to the mall without shopping for clothes."

She laughed and stopped next to the tenth store.

"I promise I'll let you look for clothes *after* we buy some for me, okay?"

She smiled.

The sight of a familiar woman made him freeze. *Is it Mia?* His heart stopped for a second.

Then he realized it was someone else. Mia liked shopping and dreamed of going to the mall all day instead of working. If Mia came to the mall and saw him with Angela...

She'd be jealous. Nothing would make me happier than her thinking Angela was my girlfriend.

Angela stopped and noticed he was behind her. She looked back at him. "What are you smiling about?"

He considered telling her. "Oh, nothing."

They stopped in American Eagle, where he tried on a few pairs of jeans while Angela made funny faces and said they did not sit well on him, whatever that meant. Probably her polite way of saying they did not look good.

He'd almost given up when one pair of jeans made her say, "Those look great!"

"I agree," the saleswoman said.

He thanked the attractive, too-young-for-him saleswoman.

He couldn't tell the difference between this pair and the previous ones. They bought three pairs of jeans and a few polo shirts. He felt a little more comfortable with his body and loved the way Angela looked at him while he tried on clothes. It had been a long time since a woman did that.

"I think we did enough shopping for one day. For one *year*, actually," he said. "Are you ready to go?"

"You promised me I could go shopping after we were finished with you."

"Oh, right. I did. But I didn't mean it."

"You have two choices. You can go to the video game store you were staring at before, or you can join me and get bored. What will it be?"

Join her?

The thought of watching her try on clothes made him shiver.

"I'll go to the game store."

"Okay. See you soon."

After thirty minutes, he got bored. *Are you done?* he texted her.

After a few minutes, she replied, *Not yet. I need some more time. Do you mind?*

Of course not, he replied.

Thanks! she wrote back. *There's a bench here if you want to sit and wait.*

He had never been in that store. He couldn't remember the last time he had entered a women's clothing store. A saleswoman greeted him and asked if she could help him. "I'm with someone." He pointed to the middle of the store.

He sat on one of the benches next to the fitting rooms. He figured men would sit on them while waiting for their ladies. They should be called *man-benches*. He had seen funny pictures of men sitting on those types of benches, waiting, looking bored, playing with their phones, or falling asleep.

He envied those men.

Men who did not take *other* men's wives shopping.

After a while, Angela stepped out of the dressing room, barefoot, wearing a long, red dress that showed her cleavage.

He almost choked.

"You found me," she said.

He tried to nod.

"I see you got comfortable." She checked herself in the mirror.

"Yes." He sat upright. "I guess they make these for men. I think Steve Jobs invented the iPhone for men waiting on their wom—well...for men on benches."

"I'll be done soon. I promise. What do you think?" She gestured at the dress.

She forced him to look at the dress. To look at her *body*. He had no choice. She made him do it. He looked at it for the shortest time possible.

"It's...it's amazing," he said finally.

"Thank you." She went back to the fitting room.

Angela came out every few minutes to show him the clothes she tried on and to ask for his opinion. She tried different dresses and some shirts and pants. Everything looked amazing on her.

Was it appropriate for us to do this? Did she want to tease me, or did it not mean anything to her?

He forced himself not to imagine her undress in there. One of the shirts she tried on was tight, and it must have been cold in the store, which made him move on the bench with unease. He did his best not to stare, but she made him critique the shirt. *Mission impossible.* He hoped to God she didn't notice how awkward he felt.

When she asked him for his opinion about a short dress with flowers, he said, "That one looks great."

"You say that about everything."

Everything looks great on you, he wanted to say, but she was not his wife. He wondered if Rick gave her compliments.

Thankfully, the saleswoman came to ask how they were doing. She seemed more excited than both of them.

"Does your husband like it?" the saleswoman asked.

David raised his eyebrows, not sure whether to laugh. He glanced at the saleswoman, then at Angela. As he opened his mouth to correct her, Angela said, "I think he loves it." She winked at him and grinned. "Right, honey?"

He almost choked again but managed a nod.

Being her pretend husband combined the best and worst feelings in the world.

After the saleswoman left, Angela, still in the amazing dress, sat next to him on the small bench. He could almost smell the flowers.

"I hope you didn't mind."

"Of course not. Why would I mind?" He checked the floor.

Eventually, he normalized his breathing. "It's okay." He nodded. "I don't mind playing into your fantasy world."

———

David helped carry Angela's bags when they left the store. Two older women wearing sports gear passed by them, doing a mall walk. They seemed to wonder what a woman like Angela was doing with a man like him.

David imagined him and Angela walking hand in hand.

"You remember the woman I told you about, from the university?" Angela asked.

He had forgotten about her but nodded.

"She said she may be interested in meeting someone special. Would it be okay if I hook you up?"

After a while, he said, "Sure, why not?"

They went to a men's clothes store and bought him a nice button-down shirt, just in case he had a date.

———

When Angela said she was hungry, David realized he didn't want it to end. For the first time in his life, he enjoyed shopping for clothes.

The food court was noisy and smelled like the inside of a frying pan. Even though it was warm outside, someone had decided to light the gas fireplace. They ate chicken salads without cheese and dressing on the side. Many people filled the food court, most of them ate, and some searched for a table. *How can so many people have so much free time?*

Every second man who passed by turned to look at Angela.

"I can't believe it's your first time in this mall. It's the biggest one in the city."

"There's more than one?"

"I'm not sure."

"You'll find it hard to believe, but I'm not a big shopper," she said. "Rick appreciates that."

"The perfect woman," he said out loud.

"I *wish*."

You are, he did not say out loud.

"Where *is* Rick, by the way? I haven't heard from him in the past couple of days."

"He went out of town to meet potential clients."

"He didn't tell me," David said. "He should also report to me, now that we're also married."

"I wanted to talk to you about that," she said. "How do you feel about all of this?"

He considered making a joke but didn't. "I like his idea. And I think we have a good chance of getting an investment." He sipped his Coke Zero. "I also trust him, you know? It's been a long time since I trusted *anyone*."

"I wanted to tell you to take it slower, but hearing you now, I'm starting to think it may be a good time for it."

"What do you mean? Why wait?"

"I thought you might not be ready."

"No," he said, "I feel good. I can do this. I *know* I can do this."

"Good to hear," she said. "You know, you impressed him. He said your knowledge and abilities are amazing. He said he sees a lot of potential in your collaboration."

It had been a while since he felt appreciated. "Thank you," he said. "We complement each other, which is a good thing to show investors. We make a great team."

———

"There's something I've been meaning to ask you for a while."

"Go ahead."

"What happened with your father?"

She wiped her mouth, stared at David, then lowered her eyes.

"I'm sorry." He wanted to hold her hand. "It's okay if you don't want to talk about it."

"It's fine. I needed a minute." She looked around, examining who might hear them. "What did Rick tell you?"

"Nothing."

"So how did you know?"

He sat up a little straighter. "He just mentioned you went to your mom's, so I figured your dad is out of the picture. I'm sorry. I never meant to upset you."

"It's fine." Angela grabbed a piece of lettuce from her plastic plate and put it in her mouth. She wiped her mouth again and said, "You know, it's funny. It took Rick a long time to notice my dad was out of the picture."

Is she complimenting me at her husband's expense, or is she stalling for time?

After a few minutes she said, "My *father*—" she inhaled, then exhaled "—was a son of a bitch. I have some memories of him...most of them bad. He...left me and my mother when I was six or seven. I haven't seen him since, and I don't want to see him."

David nodded. He had never heard her curse.

"He..." Tears burst out of her eyes. He had never seen her cry before. "He...did...bad things."

"What do you m—" David started to say. His jaw dropped as he let it sink in. He looked around at the food court, which was now almost empty. His hands stiffened into fists. He wanted to hit the table. He wanted to hug her.

He didn't know what to do.

"I'm so sorry, Angela."

She nodded. She had a long tear coming down from her right eye to the side of her mouth. He wanted to wipe it off. "It's okay. It's always hard for me when I think about him. That's why I try not to."

"I'm sorry I brought it up. I didn't mean to upset you."

"It's okay."

"Can I..." He rose, then sat back down. "Can I give you a hug?"

"You better." She smiled through her tears.

He stood, walked over to her side, and as she rose he hugged her.

———

"He asked me for more time, and I agreed," the boss said inside his Mercedes. "I'm giving him a couple more weeks."

Trever raised his eyebrows but said nothing.

"We have more urgent issues. If he doesn't come through, we can always grab his *fine* wife."

TWENTY-ONE

The default iPhone ringtone woke David up. "Can you come meet me for coffee?" A woman's voice. "At the university. In thirty minutes?"

"What? Who is this?"

"Your shopping buddy. Are you still asleep?"

"Yes." He checked the time on his phone. "It's the middle of the night, you know."

"It's *nine thirty a.m.*"

"That's what I said."

"Some people have to *study* in the morning. Can you make it?"

"What?"

"Even for *you* nine thirty is late these days. Why aren't you out on a jog?"

"Some people *work* all night. I worked till three a.m. On your *husband's* stuff. So stop harassing me."

"Call me when you get close. I'll tell you exactly where to meet me. See you in twenty-seven minutes."

"What—"

"And wear the clothes we got together yesterday. Not

the fancy shirt, just one of the nicer ones. See you soon."
She disconnected before he could protest any further.

She can't get enough of me. He giggled.

The sound of a text message startled him. He unlocked his iPhone and checked the screen.

Don't forget to shave, the text read.

Another text read, *And comb your hair. With gel.*

He almost stumbled getting out of bed.

He shaved his three-day-old beard and combed his hair. With gel. He hated gel, but Angela had said it held his hair nicely.

When his brain started working again, he figured it out.

She set me up.

Oh my God. With the woman she mentioned yesterday? A real woman?

I'm not ready for that.

He paced in his bedroom, then checked himself in the old mirror. He looked much better these days. It may work. And he had been looking for it for a long time.

Too early. He was not ready.

Sorry, Angela. I can't make it, he texted her.

She texted him right back. *Nononono. You must come. I'm waiting for you.*

I'm sorry. I'm not ready for this. Maybe some other time?

A few seconds later, she replied, *Okay. I understand. Talk soon.*

———

Angela knocked on David's door the next morning.

"Oh." She said as he opened the door. "You're awake."

"Funny. You're skipping school?"

"You should know me better than that." She walked in. "I'm starting late today."

She sat on his couch. "She's very nice. You'll like her."

"*Very nice?* Isn't that what they say when they're ugly?"

"She's not ugly!"

"Okay. Don't hit me like your husband."

"I wasn't going to."

He sat in front of her. "I appreciate your efforts, but I'm not sure I'm ready. I haven't been out with a woman in years. I wouldn't know what to say or what to do or—"

"You'll be *fine*. Stop worrying about it. You can talk to a woman. You're funny, good-looking, and fun to be with. You have a lot to offer a woman."

He swallowed. "Thank you," he mumbled.

"We'll do it together. We can meet her for coffee. That's what I had in mind. Another option is to go on a double date, but I figured the three of us having coffee would make it less official."

David went to get two glasses of water, gave one to Angela, and sat back down.

He wanted to meet a woman. He wanted to get married and have a family. He had made an effort to find one, but the actual thought of going out with a woman—talking, laughing, *touching*—made him nervous.

"I don't know."

———

David met Nancy Cartwright and Angela at the university's cafeteria a few days later.

Nancy was not ugly at all. She had blonde hair—not as pretty as Angela's, but still fine. She had dark roots, which made him think she dyed her hair. He liked blonde hair on women. He didn't know why. He read somewhere that men are attracted to their mother's type, but his mother had dark hair.

She wore a pink shirt (or was it a brown shirt?) and tight black jeans. She wore short brown boots, which covered part of her jeans. She was skinny, but not as skinny as Angela.

She had makeup on her face, lipstick, and some more color he didn't know what to call.

"It's nice to meet you." David shook her hand. He noticed only six students in the cafeteria, but it reminded him of his days at the university. When he had studied computer science there was only one woman in his class. They still called them *girls* back then. When he got his MBA, the number of women in his class jumped to seven—not nearly as many as he would have liked, but then he didn't have much time to socialize.

She didn't rise to greet him. On the other hand, Angela smiled, stood, and hugged him.

If he had seen Nancy somewhere else, even at Target, he would have considered talking to her. She was studying for her master's, same as Angela. She was a few years younger than him and a few years older than Angela. Right in the middle.

How come you never got married? he wanted to ask.

He had always thought there must be something wrong with a woman who had not gotten married at that age.

They could say the same thing about me.

They probably did.

He decided he should give her a chance. Unfair to judge her. Maybe she didn't want to get married. Maybe she had a boyfriend for many years and it hadn't worked out.

A new thought occurred to him, one that he had not considered for many years: Was *he* a bad catch?

———

David picked up Nancy in his old Honda and took her to a local Mexican restaurant for their first date.

As he opened the door for her to get out of the car, he noticed her hair was blonder and had fewer dark roots. When they sat to eat, he got a better look at her face. She wore more makeup than when he first met her.

They drank Diet Cokes and had as-much-as-you-can-eat chips and dips.

Do these have a million calories in them? Are they trying to kill us?

Who said that? he almost said out loud. He wanted to laugh but couldn't. Angela and Rick would have understood the joke. It was too early to talk about diets on a first date.

He stopped after ten chips and stuck to the red dip. He figured it had tomatoes in it, and it had to be better than the cheesy one.

He considered it a personal achievement. In the past he would have stopped only when the main food arrived. Maybe after a few hundred chips?

Who cared back then?

"I was born and raised in Tulsa," she said. "I only left the city twice in my life, with my parents. The first trip was to Disney World. I loved it. A few years later, we took our first trip to New York City. But I didn't like it."

Who doesn't like New York? Is it a sign she isn't for me?

"How come?"

"I dunno. It's too weird. People there are not so nice. Not as polite as I'm used to."

"I'm from New York," he said. "I'd love to go back there."

An awkward silence filled the air. The worst thing he could wish for on a first date. He never had awkward silences with Angela.

Why did I have to say that? Idiot!

"But I can understand what you mean," he said after a while. "I visited again not long ago, after living here for a couple of years, and it's much crazier. Much less polite. But you get used to it. It's very much"—he held his fists up—"*alive*. You know?"

He told her about Mia, his ex-girlfriend. He wondered if it was the right thing to talk about on a first date. He figured if he told her about himself, she would open up as well.

Nancy seemed sympathetic. Her face seemed surprised and caring, and she nodded at all the right places.

"I only dated one guy," she said, and he tried to keep a straight face. "I met him in college. We dated for over five years. It took him four years to get the courage to ask me to marry him. My girlfriends told me I should do it myself, but I couldn't. Besides, I felt he wasn't ready, and I didn't want to push him. Even when we got engaged, we couldn't decide on a date for the wedding. I mean *he* couldn't decide. *I* was ready to elope."

She sipped her soda and had a few more chips. He didn't want to rush her.

"When I finally told him we either get married or I was leaving him, he told me we should separate. I tried to change his mind, but then he...then he told me he had an affair. For over a *year*."

She had tears in her eyes. He wanted to touch her, but it felt inappropriate.

"I don't know why I'm telling you this." She wiped her tears, trying to hide them. "The worst part was that the son of a bitch had an affair with *my* best friend."

"I'm sorry, Nancy." He put his hand on hers, but only for a few seconds.

She nodded. "That's a lot to handle on a first date, isn't it? I'm sorry."

"It's okay," he said. "We both have a similar story, I guess. We both chose bad partners. I hope we choose better next time."

"I don't think I ever told that story to someone I just met. The difference between us is that it happened to me almost ten years ago."

His jaw dropped. He pulled it back up fast, hoping she hadn't noticed. He tried to maintain a sympathetic look.

"I didn't think I could trust anyone since," she said. "Even women. But Angela is different. From the little time we've spent together, she seems like an amazing person. Beautiful inside and out."

His eyes sparkled. "She sure is."

"When she first told me about you, I didn't want to meet you."

"That's okay. The same exact thing happened to me."

They smiled.

"But she said so many good things about you that I decided to give it a shot. I hope you won't disappoint me."

Isn't it too early to talk about this? What did I get myself into? We're starting to get to know each other. Will she start talking about marriage soon? What did Angela get me into?

Or is it the best compliment Angela could have ever given me?

David told Nancy about his travels around the world, about his start-up adventures, and even more about other women he had dated. When he told her about his current job, the one he did with Angela's husband, it made him feel good. He used to dread when people would ask him what he did for a living. What would he tell a potential wife? That he was unemployed?

I'm unemployed, and I live with my parents. He remembered George Costanza's line from the sitcom *Seinfeld* he loved.

They don't make good comedies anymore.

The only difference between him and George was that he didn't live with his parents.

His parents were gone.

———

When David dropped Nancy off at her house, she didn't ask him in. He wondered if he could have said no if she had. He had not been with a woman in ages.

Should he give her a kiss on the cheek?

Should he ask her?

God, it's like being seventeen again.

No one needs to know I got my first kiss just before I turned eighteen.

When he leaned in for the kiss, she turned to open the car door, and his nose hit her head.

It probably looked like a scene from *Seinfeld*.

But it hurt.

"I'm sorry!" She sprang out of his car like a woman running from a stalker.

Driving home, he thought the date went well. They

talked a lot, she laughed a little—less than he had hoped. He thought they hit it off. But maybe she felt he didn't like her?

Maybe she didn't like *him*?

The important thing was that he'd gotten back in the saddle.

I can go on a date and have a nice time.

TWENTY-TWO

The following morning, David and Rick met for a morning
walk.

"How did it go? You *dog*," Rick said. "Did you screw
her?"

"*No!*" David almost stumbled.

"Don't lie to me."

"We didn't even kiss. I'm not even sure we'll go out
again."

"What?" Rick stopped walking and stared at him.

"Don't stop," David said and kept walking.

Rick ran up to him. "Did you blow it?"

"I'm rusty, and I'm not sure I even know *what* to do on a
date. And she's—" Not sure how much to share with Rick,
he said, "She's *complicated.*"

"I know. Angela told me." Rick put a hand on his shoulder
and grinned. "Let me know if you need some lessons."

David's phone vibrated in his pocket. It rubbed against
his leg when they walked, so he welcomed the opportunity
to take it out. He considered getting a runner's armband for

the phone, like real runners did, but decided to wait until he became a serious one. It would be a status symbol. It would mean he was a real runner.

He was not ready for it yet.

He wondered why Rick didn't have one.

He took out his phone and peeked at the screen. *Call me ASAP*, Angela wrote.

Is she mad at me? I didn't do anything wrong.

David called her after the walk when Rick went to take a shower.

"What happened?" she asked.

He told her.

"She thought you were making a move on her. I knew you would never do that. Let me talk to her."

Why is she so sure I wouldn't?

Trying to kiss her on the cheek at the end of a date was such a big deal? Why did Nancy take it so hard?

A few hours later, as the men worked from Rick's apartment, David received another text message.

"That's the second text you got today," Rick said. "You *dog*."

"Unfortunately, it's just your wife."

"Oh?"

I explained everything. She wants to see you again. Call her this evening, the message read.

A few seconds later, Angela texted again. *Call her. Don't text her.* She added a smiley.

"Your wife's fixing things." David sat up. "God, I feel like we're kids all over again."

"Yeah, you're totally reminding me of middle school. I had a friend, a girl, who I didn't find attractive, so we never hooked up. She was in love with me, so she'd hook me up with all the other girls in our class." Rick grinned. "And other classes."

"That's mean, man."

"I know. I was a real SOB back then."

———

David took Nancy to AMC Theaters to watch a romantic movie. He liked the theater because of the huge recliners, which made him feel at home.

Does she have a car? He didn't see one in the driveway, and she never offered to meet him anywhere. *Do men still need to pick women up?* Her house seemed small but well kept from the outside. *Does she live there alone?* He wondered how it looked from the inside. Probably nice and tidy.

After the movie they had dinner, and when he dropped her off at her house, he didn't try to kiss or hug her. They didn't even shake hands. They said good-bye, and she left his car and walked to her house—much slower this time.

———

During Christmas, David hoped he wouldn't be alone, but Angela and Rick traveled to her mother's for the holiday. David hoped they'd invite him, but no one talked about it. Nancy traveled with her family, so he ended up abandoned.

As usual.

In the following month, David and Rick worked from their apartments and coffee shops. David preferred to work outside of his home—he enjoyed looking busy and valuable around other people. After completing a full business plan and a working prototype, he said they should look for investors.

"How do we do that?" Rick asked.

"I'll try to arrange meetings for us in Silicon Valley and New York with investors. We'll go on a little road trip and *beg* them for money. It would have been much easier if we had paying customers, but we can't afford to acquire users by ourselves. I'll get in touch with some of my old contacts."

"Will they talk to you?"

David raised his eyebrows, making sure Rick saw it.

"I'm sorry, but, you know...after what happened with your old partner and all."

"I'm sure *a few* of them will return my calls. One of them will probably help me find others if he's not interested. We'll be fine."

That evening, David thought about Rick's doubts. Did Rick not believe in him? Why would Rick work with him otherwise? Could Rick be right? Would they get rejected because of his past?

They had a good idea, a good business plan, and a nice, solid prototype to show investors. His professionalism should do the job.

Wouldn't it?

———

It took David two weeks to arrange meetings with seven different potential investors in New York City.

"Most of them are small investors," he told Rick, "called *angels*. A lot of them made their money selling their own start-up, and now, because they have nothing else to do with their time or money, they get to abuse people by making them beg for their money."

They flew to New York for five days, in which they met with all seven. A few recognized David and were friendly. They all seemed interested in the idea; some of them thought they asked for too much money, especially for a product with no users yet.

"I'm amazed you can walk up to people who've never heard of you before and ask them to give you three million dollars," Rick said as they went to a sports bar not far from the hotel.

"When you put it that way, it does sound crazy," David said. "But some of them have heard of me, they do due diligence before investing, and—"

"What do you mean?"

"They check our business plan and the product and compare it to their own research on the market and the competitors. Many of them do a background check on both of us—"

"Really?" Rick blinked rapidly.

"Don't worry about it. It shouldn't be a problem for us." David paused. "As far as I know, anyway. You don't have any skeletons in your closet I don't know of, do you?"

He laughed. Rick smiled.

The bar was filled with people laughing, drinking, and cheering to a baseball game on the big TVs. David used to enjoy those bars when he was younger. It felt good to be there with a friend.

"They also check how we get along, which shouldn't be any problem." David winked. "They'll ask about our intellectual property, but we know we have a problem in that area and should be honest about it. They'll figure it out before we can tell them." He put his hand on Rick's shoulder. "That's most of it. For now, anyway."

"What do you mean we have a problem with our intellectual property?"

"We don't have a patent. You can't patent an idea like that."

Rick nodded, still gazing at David.

"Besides all that, we sign papers and give them a big chunk of our company."

"We're giving them twenty-five percent of it."

"It'll probably be more than that," David said. "Unfortunately."

"What do you mean *more*? That's not enough?"

"It's part of negotiation."

Rick looked at the floor. After a while, he raised his eyes. "I think we worked hard enough, don't you? Let's get you a beer and go find some ladies." Rick called their waitress over.

"I thought we couldn't have beer. What about all the wheat and sugar and stuff? Isn't that illegal in your book?"

"Not *tonight*." Rick smiled at the waitress. "Hello. What was your name again?"

"Stephanie." She smiled at him. A big smile.

"*Ste-pha-nie*." Rick touched her arm, still smiling. She didn't retract. "Great name. It's nice to meet you, Stephanie. I'm Rick, and this is—" he pointed at David "—what was *your* name again?"

"I'm David." He blushed at the waitress.

"What do you do besides being our lovely waitress?" Rick asked. "Let me guess, you're an actress or a model. Am I right?"

Stephanie smiled and nodded. "I'm trying to get onto Broadway."

"I could tell. I think you should be a model. *A top model*."

Was Rick hitting on her? I thought he'd do it for me, to help me get started. But now I see he isn't making any effort in that direction.

Rick's smile left no doubt. He wanted her and was slick —and even sleazy—about it.

Did that work with women? *Did I get it wrong all along?*

Maybe it worked if you looked like *Rick.*

Did Angela fall for that crap? It wouldn't make sense.

David missed a few of the sentences they exchanged. When Rick touched her arm again, David kicked him under the table.

Rick looked at him, startled.

"Could we get two beers, *please*?" David asked Stephanie.

"Sure." She nodded and left.

"*What* are you doing?"

"What?"

"Are you *hitting* on her?"

"I'm just having a conversation. For you, mainly. To get you started."

"It didn't look that way. And I'm kinda taken, you know."

Rick burst out laughing. "I'm sorry, but I don't think it's going anywhere, is it?"

"What do you mean?"

"Are you even still seeing her?"

"We went out three and a half times."

Rick couldn't control his laughter.

"Half?" he asked, after relaxing.

"She didn't feel well on our last date, so I took her home early."

They were quiet for a while.

"How come you didn't mention that?" Rick asked. "We've been together for almost a week."

David stared at him.

"I bet Angela's up to date," Rick said.

David nodded.

"You don't trust me anymore?"

"It's not that." David looked anywhere but at Rick. "I didn't want you to make fun of me and ask about sex and shit. I'm not like you, you know. I take it slow, and so does she, which is good. Angela understands."

Rick nodded. "Man, I'm sorry. I've been a jerk. You're right. I do wish you the best. You know that, right?"

David didn't know how to reply. He believed Rick, but talking to him about matters of the heart made David uneasy. Rick always changed the subject to sex, which made David feel nauseous. As far as talking about feelings, Rick was as supportive as a piece of string keeping a car from rolling off a cliff. David always had a hard time talking to men about feelings. Men were less sensitive. Women were much better at that. Especially Angela.

The waitress returned with their beers. She smiled at Rick but didn't look at David.

No tip for her, he thought. *Maybe just from Rick.*

They had a few more beers while Rick continued asking the waitress personal questions. She answered all of them, smiling and giggling. Rick talked about himself, their start-up, and his work as a coach.

But nothing about Angela.

David searched for Rick's wedding band, but Rick buried his left hand under the table.

Rick was hiding Angela.

Before leaving, Rick asked the waitress to come to their hotel room when she finished work.

The good-looking waitress who wanted to be an actress said yes.

"*What?*" David yelled, but they ignored him. The waitress focused on Rick and saw nothing else.

After she left their table, David asked, "Are you crazy?"

"Are you jealous?"

David rose, pushing the chair back. "How can you do this to Angela?"

"She doesn't care. She doesn't need to know." Rick wrote something on a napkin. "And what she doesn't know won't hurt her. Right?"

David considered taking a picture and sending it to Angela. Or texting her. Or calling her.

When the waitress returned, Rick handed her the napkin. "That's my number. Call me when you get off work."

"I'm off now."

"That's great!" Rick stood. "But I have a tiny problem. I'm sharing a room with my friend here in the hotel. We're a start-up with no money. I never thought I'd meet *you* here."

Stephanie giggled like a teenager in love for the first time.

Rick rubbed his hands. "Unless you have a friend for my friend here, we should go to your place."

David's jaw dropped and his eyes opened wide as he watched them leave the bar together.

———

David walked back to the hotel. The wind froze his face, but he needed time to digest what had happened. The New York cold wrapped his bones like tight nylon stockings. In the room, he lay on his bed and turned on the TV. He texted Rick a few times but got no reply. He kept checking his phone clock—over two hours and no word from Rick. What the hell did Rick do?

Had sex, probably.

God.

He picked up the phone a few times to call Angela but couldn't go through with it. He typed her a message but deleted it. He tried a few different messages, but none of them enabled him to press send.

How could Rick hurt her like that?

What she doesn't know won't hurt her. Right? Rick had said.

David considered calling Nancy and asking her what he should do.

Having the option to call a third person made him feel good. To talk to *someone* other than Rick or Angela. A potential life partner. He could get used to it. He saw her contact information on his iPhone and realized he had not spoken to or texted her in over a day. His iPhone showed the time was 11:00 p.m., and even though it was an hour earlier in Tulsa, he didn't feel comfortable calling her.

He texted her a short summary of the day—the business part of it—and asked her about her day. She took a few seconds to reply, congratulated him and said she was okay.

For a few minutes, he forgot about *Rick the creep.*

Should he talk to her? *She probably won't know what to tell me. And I couldn't be sure she won't tell Angela. Women stuck together like that. Once the cat's out of the bag, there's no way to get it back in.*

Should he stick up for Rick? As *men?*

He couldn't help but think of poor Angela, in their apartment, all alone. Not knowing what her asshole idiot of a husband did. Did she know? Did she have a clue?

Had it happened before?

Angela didn't deserve this. She deserved a good man. Someone who would love her. Someone who would respect her. Someone who would never, ever hurt her.

———

The following morning, David awoke to his iPhone's alarm. He had fallen asleep with the TV on, which tried to sell him a new ab-sculpting machine he would never use.

Rick's bed had not been slept in.

David checked his phone. No messages. He checked his text history with Angela. His heart sank when he saw a message to her, in which he'd cursed Rick and told her she should leave him.

Thankfully, he had not sent the message.

He erased it as fast as he could.

The last thing in the world he wanted to do was to hurt her.

———

On the way to the hotel, Rick texted them that he was ready, entered Central Park in the dark, taped the envelope under the second bench, looked around, and left.

TWENTY-THREE

David tried to call Rick a few times. He didn't reply. David texted him a few times. The last message ended in too many exclamation points, but Rick didn't reply.

He decided he would go alone to the next investor meeting. He would explain that Rick was sick and couldn't make it. He would apologize. It wouldn't look good, but it would be better than not showing at all.

He shaved, donned his suit, and had grabbed his bag to leave when Rick stormed in.

"I'm sorry." Rick breathed heavily as if he had run up the stairs. "I didn't wake up in time. I'm sorry."

"*Hurry*." David's jaw tightened. He wished he could slap him. "You need to shave and change your clothes. We'll take Uber."

They didn't speak in the car. When they were late to the meeting, David said, "I hope it was worth it."

"Oh, it *was*." Rick grinned.

David wanted to punch him. The beer from last night came up his throat. He didn't want to hear that or see his smug smile. "I can't believe you did this to Angela."

"Oh, come on. All men do that."

"Not *all* men."

"Men who—"

Rick didn't finish his sentence.

After they apologized a few times for being late, they didn't give a good presentation. They were both off. David noticed the investors were mad and uninterested.

When they left, he wondered if he had made a mistake choosing Rick as a partner.

Again?

————

Next, they met a Japanese investor who kept nodding his head all the time.

When they left, Rick said he had wanted to leave after three minutes.

"It's a cultural thing," David said. "Don't worry about it."

But David did.

————

"I need to apologize," Rick said while they drank coffee in a midtown Starbucks. "I know you're friends with Angela, and I shouldn't have done it in front of you. It's just that we've been having some...issues lately. I didn't tell you this, but we argue a lot. And we don't have sex as often as we did in the past. I don't know what to do."

Trouble in paradise? How the hell could that have happened? David tried to dismiss the thought of them having sex.

136

"I didn't know that," David said. "I'm sorry. But you should work on it. I'm sure you'll be fine." He drank his coffee slowly. "I can talk to her, if you want."

How did he turn this around? Now I need to feel sorry for him? It wasn't his fault anymore?

"Maybe you could give us couples' therapy." Rick smiled. "The high-tech dude giving couples' therapy to the shrink-to-be and the famous life coach. *That* would be funny."

David didn't want to, but he smiled.

"Seriously," David said, "go to therapy, both of you. Please. I heard it works."

"You're absolutely right. We should."

"And promise me you won't ever do it again. I'm sorry I didn't stop you yesterday. I was close to talking to Angela."

"You didn't, right?" Rick grabbed the sides of the table, fingers turning red.

After a minute, David said, "No. I didn't. But I wasn't trying to help *you*. I didn't want to hurt her."

"I promise," Rick said. "Won't happen again." His foot shook a little.

———

After returning from New York City, the two men didn't meet or speak for a few days—not even for their morning jogs.

David had to force himself to work, something he had not experienced in a long time. He went out to coffee shops, alone, and tried to work but was unproductive. He wanted to walk and jog next to the Arkansas River but had a hard time getting out of the car.

He had lost his passion.

Rick talked about passion. *You have to have passion for what you do*, Rick had said. Tony Robbins always said you should *live with passion*.

But it was gone.

How can I trust someone who cheated on his wife? Will he cheat on me the first chance he gets?

Or was it something most men did and should mean nothing to him as a business partner? He cared about Angela, which made it bad, but he had to separate the two things.

He researched online and found a lot of different information. Seventy percent of men cheated, so maybe Rick wasn't that different. He could have any woman he wanted. Maybe most men couldn't settle for being with just one woman.

But it's not any woman. It's Angela.

Maybe seventy percent was conservative? Would people admit they cheated when they were asked? Would cheaters tell the truth to begin with?

He read that half of all women also cheated. He found that surprising. He didn't think Angela could cheat. She was too good of a person.

———

Nancy invited David to her place for the first time on their fifth date.

Would they finally progress in their relationship? Did she want that? Did she invite him in for that?

He wanted to. He had a hard time admitting it to Rick or Angela, but he was horny. Would they finally do it?

God. Nineteen years old all over again.

She made lasagna and Caesar salad for dinner.

"The food's great," David said. "Thank you for having me over."

He hated lying to her. The food was only average. It looked good, so he thought she had gotten takeout—but it was even worse than a fast-food restaurant.

He realized he didn't know if Angela cooked.

He should ask her sometime.

Poor Angela.

"How's work coming along?" Nancy asked.

"Could be better, I guess."

"Was it that bad in New York? You've seemed a bit off since you got back."

Was it obvious? Should he tell her? It would be nice to get it off his chest.

"Yeah, it, um..." He played with his lasagna with his fork. He only ate half of it. "It went badly. I'm not too sure we'll be able to raise money anytime soon."

Did he lie to her? It was the first time he mentioned, or thought about, the problems with raising money. He had been sure they would raise money. He knew it would take a long time, but he never doubted it. The last few meetings, and Rick's lack of professionalism, made him uncertain. Who knew if Rick could be trusted professionally?

"I'm sorry to hear that," she said and ate the last piece of her lasagna. She checked his plate. "You didn't like it?"

"Oh, no. The lasagna was good. I'm just—" he glanced at his plate, then at her "—I'm trying not to eat too much. I'm watching my weight, you know."

She nodded and checked his plate again. He wondered if she was insulted or if she wanted to eat his lasagna as well.

"Rick came late to a meeting, which is why we blew our chances there," he said.

Sharing felt good, especially when he needed to change the subject. Besides, he couldn't talk to Rick or Angela about it, and there was no one else he could talk to.

"That's weird. Angela always says he's good at what he does. And committed." Nancy took away their plates, and when she returned, she stood in front of him, one hand holding the back of her chair. She looked at the living room, then back at him. "What do you think you're going to do next?"

"I don't know. I haven't been able to work much in the past few days. And we haven't talked at all since we came back."

She raised her eyebrows.

"Please don't tell Angela. I don't know if he told her, and I don't want her to get hurt."

She nodded. After she seemed to consider his remark, she said, "Why would she get hurt?"

Oops.

"I mean, I don't want her to get mad at him. You know, for screwing things up."

She nodded again. After a while, he asked if she wanted to move to the living room.

"You go ahead," she said. "I'll be right there."

He offered to help with the dishes, but she dismissed it.

"You should get comfortable in the living room," she said.

He sat on the couch and heard her moving dishes around in the kitchen. The couch seemed old, with flowers on it and some tears on the sides. The living room had three big windows with long drapes, decorated with flowers matching the couch. The table in the middle of the room and the chairs next to the couch were made of old wood. They were in better condition than the couch.

In the middle of the hardwood floor lay a white, slightly worn rug, full, surprisingly, with little flowers.

He looked back at the dining room but couldn't see Nancy. He heard a toilet flush somewhere in the house.

She could have said something.

Maybe she would surprise him and come back wearing a shimmery nightgown?

She said I should make myself comfortable in the living room.

He crossed his legs, spread them, then crossed them again. He stood and walked around the living room. He sat back down and checked his phone for messages. After ten more minutes, she returned, still wearing her damn buttoned-up dress, which covered most of her body.

She apologized and sat next to him on the couch.

Even though she had a lot of makeup on, getting a closer look at her face revealed imperfections in her complexion. He hadn't noticed them from farther away.

Not that bad. Still nice looking.

Not every woman can have perfect skin like—

"Angela said Rick thought highly of you. She said he thinks you're a real professional."

"She did?" He smiled. "She's amazing, isn't she?"

Did I say that out loud?

Nancy drew back, but only for a moment. When she moved closer, she examined his face. If it had been any other woman, he would have had the courage to lean in for a kiss, but after what happened on their first date, he couldn't take the risk.

Her face tightened. Did she not like what she saw, or was he unable to believe a woman could find him attractive?

Maybe both.

Maybe I should call Angela and ask her if it's okay to kiss Nancy.

He almost laughed.

"Do you trust Rick?" she asked.

"What?" He drew back a little. "What do you mean?"

"I don't know. He seems too sleek for me. He doesn't seem like Angela's type. And your story about what he did in New York makes my suspicions stronger."

She's a great judge of character. If she only knew what Rick really did in New York.

"Sometimes I don't understand what someone like *Angela* is doing with him, but in general I would trust him with my life. He saved my—" *Am I ready to talk about it? Not yet.* "I would trust both of them with my life. They're the best friends I've ever had."

Nancy nodded. She examined his face again.

After a while he realized they had not spoken in a long time.

"Would you like to kiss me?" she asked out of nowhere.

He nodded.

He leaned in and kissed her. It took only a few seconds, and they drew apart. She had bad breath, which bothered him more than it should have.

She had a lot of time in the bathroom to fix that.

He wondered if he should tell her. With Mia they reached the point in the relationship where they felt comfortable asking each other to brush their teeth, but saying that after a first kiss seemed almost illegal. He should probably keep it to himself.

Didn't she like the kiss, or did his breath stink as well?

"Is everything okay?" he asked.

"I don't think you're fully here."

"I have some things on my mind, but there's nothing more I'd like to do than be here with you."

He took a different approach. He smiled at her and put his hand on her left breast.

It felt nice.

She didn't resist or cooperate.

His hand went for the back of her dress and he unbuttoned it. Slowly. He never stopped making eye contact with her, making sure she approved.

He dropped her dress on the floor, and his hands went for her bra.

His phone vibrated in his pocket. He reached for it, then noticed her surprised face. "Sorry," he said.

She pushed his hand away. "Let's take it slower," she whispered.

"Sure." He drew back.

She suggested they watch a movie.

A movie?

He agreed. She put her dress back on and stared at him. He tried to hide his disappointment. Did he suck?

As if she read his mind, she put his arm over her and lowered her head to his chest.

Nineteen years old again.

Or in Rick's case—*twelve?*

When the movie ended, David said he should go. She walked him to the door. He thanked her for a lovely night.

As he leaned in to kiss her, she stopped him and said, "I think we should break up."

"*What?*" He didn't see that coming. "Why?"

"Look, you're a nice guy. I believe you tried to like me. And maybe in some other time and some other place—it

143

could have worked. *Maybe.* But I don't think you're ready for a relationship."

"Why do you think that?"

"Because I think you're in love with someone else."

"Mia? I'm over her—"

"Not Mia."

TWENTY-FOUR

David lay down on his couch, staring at the ceiling. Did he lose another friend? Did he move from having three friends to one?

He wondered what Nancy would tell Angela and how Angela would react.

He remained awake for most of the night, staring at the ceiling. He didn't feel like watching TV. He wanted to go to Target the next day, buy bad food, and get back to his old life in his comfortable recliner.

I don't need that crap. I did fine alone. People are too hard to handle. Partners, of all kinds, are too hard to handle. Who needs them?

He awoke, startled, to a loud knock on the door.

He sprang to a sitting position, stared at the door, and rubbed his neck.

The knockings were too soft to be Rick's but too hard to be from Angela. Could it be Nancy? He had never heard her knock on his door.

He opened the door and saw Angela. She wore baggy sweatpants and a T-shirt. Not the nice ones she wore when she jogged. Maybe those were the ones she slept in? She didn't wear any makeup (did she need it?), and her hair was messy.

She had tears in her eyes as she stared at him.

Oh my God.

He let her in. She thanked him and sat on the couch.

His heart beat fast. What did Nancy tell her? Did she tell her she thought he was in love with her? Did she come to tell him she loved—

"I'm sorry to barge in like this, but I need your help."

He wanted to ask a million questions.

He wanted to hug her.

Oh my God.

Did Nancy get it right?

Am I in love with her?

No. No way. He had a crush on her. That was obvious. Maybe. She looked exactly as he ever dreamed a wife should look like. He dreamed about her—he couldn't help it —but he didn't want to make love to her.

Or maybe he did?

But she was just a *friend*. His best friend's *wife*. He couldn't be in love with her. Besides, she was out of his league. She would never go out with someone like him.

He sat next to her on the couch. When she said nothing, he asked, "You talked to Nancy?"

"Not recently. Why?"

He exhaled slowly, hoping she didn't notice. "It didn't go well last night. I'll tell you all about it later. What's wrong?"

"I think I'm in trouble, and I can't find Rick. I'm scared."

"I'm sure he's fine."

Where is that son of a bitch?

"I've tried calling him all morning, but he's not getting back to me. It's not like him."

Is he with another woman? He promised me he would stop. That son of a—

"Have you heard from him?" she asked.

"No. We haven't spoken much in the last few days."

"He's been weird since you two got back from New York. What happened there?"

Oh, nothing much. He just cheated on you. And fucked up our meetings.

He didn't know what to say when he noticed her hands shaking. "Angela? What's wrong? What happened?"

Did she find out Rick cheated on her?

This could devastate her. Would she hate him for not telling her?

She should.

"I got a text message this morning. It scared the hell out of me."

"From who?"

She took her phone out of her pocket, unlocked it with her thumb, and showed him the phone. It had a text message from an unknown number, which read, *We're coming for you unless you pay what you owe us.*

"The only one I can think of is my—" She started crying. He put his hand on her shoulder. She looked back up at him. "My *father*."

"Your father? What would he want from you?"

"Could I please have some water?"

"Yes. I'm sorry."

When normal people were upset, they would drink alcohol or eat ice cream, but with Angela it would mean water or maybe even something stronger, like green tea.

Or maybe she *was* the normal one.

She thanked him for the water and sipped it. "After my father left, my mother found an envelope with cash under one of his drawers. It was money he'd hidden from us. She used it to cover some of their debts. Most of them were *his* debts. After a few years he contacted her and told her he would come back for the money. The son of a bitch claimed *she* stole it from him. He said he would chase us both into the grave. My mother told him she paid off some of his debts with it and that there was no money left. She told him she needed *more* money to pay his other debts and for raising *me*." Angela took another sip. "We even had to move so he wouldn't find us. We thought it worked, and I even forgot about it over time, until this morning." She raised her phone. "I think now that the message on your wall was for *me*."

That made sense. Who'd want to threaten me?

Is it better or worse that it was directed at her?

"This text confirms it." She stared at him, still shivering. She held his hand. "David, I think he might be coming after me now."

He held her hand tight. "Let's call the police."

"I already did," she said. "They told me there's nothing much they can do unless he makes specific threats."

"Wow. I thought they did more."

"Me too."

"They could probably trace him, look him up or do *something*," he said. "If they can't arrest him, they could at least scare him into leaving you alone."

She nodded. "Would you mind if I stayed here until Rick came back?"

He looked into her eyes. "You can stay as long as you like."

An hour later, they heard a loud knock on a door. Not on David's door. It seemed to be from the apartment upstairs. Someone shouted in the distance.

Angela jumped.

"Is that from our place?" she asked.

"I think so."

"What are they saying?"

"I don't know. Do you want me to go look?" He rose.

"No." She grabbed his arm. "But thanks. I don't want you to get hurt."

"Should we call the police?"

"And say what? They aren't knocking on *our* door, and we can't hear what they're say—"

Loud footsteps going down the stairs startled them. David peered outside but missed them. He pointed at the windows, and they sprang over to them. They crouched as he moved the shades slightly. They were close together, their thighs touching. She didn't seem to notice. He wondered if he should move away a little, but he wouldn't be able to see outside.

They saw two big men, about Rick's age but much bulkier than him. They seemed like professional body-builders. The two men went to the parking lot.

"I'm guessing neither one of them is your dad." She was closer than he had ever seen her. "You think he'd hire two muscle men for this? They look like professionals. They look *expensive*. How much money was it?"

Angela shrugged. "I don't know." She looked back outside.

They drove away in a white sedan, no license plate on the front of the car. David couldn't recognize the car brand,

and by the time he thought to get his iPhone and take a picture, they were gone.

"Good thing I didn't go out." He grinned.

Angela nodded slowly, mouth a little ajar.

They moved back to the couch.

"What the hell was that?" he asked.

"I have no idea."

———

A little while later, Angela's phone startled them. Rick texted her: *I'll take care of it. Don't worry. Stay with David.*

Then another text from Rick. *I'm boarding a plane now. I'll be home in a few hours.*

Eyes open wide, she showed her phone to David.

"As I said, you're welcome to stay here for as long as you want."

Angela thanked him and stared out the window, her hands still trembling.

He wondered where the hell Rick was. *Does he really go to conferences? Does he really have meetings? Clients? Or is he having sex with every woman on the planet?*

"How did Rick know about them?" David asked. "How did he know you're here?"

She shrugged. "I probably mentioned it in one of my messages."

She tried to call and text Rick, but he didn't reply.

"You know, even though I hated him"—for a second David thought she was talking about Rick—"a small part of me wanted him back in my life. I wanted to have *a father.* Even for a few minutes. Even a bad one."

"I think I understand."

"What about your family?" she asked. "You never talk about them."

"*My* family?" His voice pitched. "You don't want to hear about them now, do you?"

"I could use the distraction."

He nodded. "Not much to say. My parents died a few years ago. I was their youngest, so they were relatively older. My mom died first. She had lung cancer. She smoked a lot when we were kids. She quit when I was in my twenties, but it was too late. My dad took care of her until she died. He died a few months later of a broken heart. They were a great couple. Did everything together. They were my role model for the perfect couple. I guess I've been looking for that kind of relationship all of my life. Maybe it was too much to look up to."

He expected her to give him some psychological bull-shit, but she nodded and smiled with understanding. "I'm sorry, David."

He nodded. "They sucked as parents, though. They were too busy with work when I was growing up, and when they had time for us, they preferred going out with their friends. When we got older, I'd only see them once a year. It's funny, but I still miss them. I regret not having more time with them. I wish I could have shared more. I wish they *cared* more."

She leaned in closer. "Do you have brothers or sisters?"

"Do I look like someone who grew up with sisters?" He laughed. "I have one brother. John. Almost three years older than me. But we don't talk at all."

"How come?"

David exhaled. "In high school I was in love with a girl named Amanda. I wanted to ask her out for ages but couldn't get the courage. My brother knew I loved her but asked her out anyway. I didn't have a chance against him—he was better looking, and she preferred older guys. When I confronted him, he said she was interested in *him*, not *me*, and that I should learn an important life lesson." He swallowed. "John dumped her a few weeks later and never even apologized."

Angela looked at him with sympathy. "Have you ever considered contacting him?" she asked. "It's been a long time."

"I have—usually when I get lonely, which used to be *a lot.*" He looked down. "But I had too many people betray me in my life. I could never get myself to forgive him."

"Maybe you *should*. Maybe he's changed. He's family, after all. And it could be good for you to have another friend in your life. You know, for rainy days."

"Maybe." He nodded and looked away.

———

"Let's look for a movie on Netflix," David said after Angela tried calling Rick a few more times. "What do you say?"

She picked a romantic comedy. He brought them each a blanket, and they sat next to each other, covered. For most of the movie, Angela hugged one of his living room pillows and laughed a lot. Every time she laughed, he moved his eyes from the TV to her. Only once did she notice David looking at her, and smiled at him.

Was Nancy right?

He stood periodically and peered outside the door and through the window shades to make sure they were safe.

To make sure she was safe.

When the movie ended, he suggested they watch another, but Angela's phone rang and she jumped.

"It's Nancy," she said after looking at the phone.

"She probably wants to bad-mouth me."

"Don't be *stupid*. There's nothing bad to say about you."

He almost choked.

"You never told me what happened."

He shrugged.

"Would you mind if I answered?" Angela asked.

"Of course not."

David raised his eyebrows when he noticed Angela neglected to mention she was with him. She listened, said "Ah-ha" a few times, and twice she almost laughed. At one point she stared at David and touched her throat.

Did Nancy tell her what she thought?

"I'm sure that's not true," Angela said into her phone. "He's not like that. I promise you."

Then she listened some more, and they ended the conversation after Angela promised they would meet the next day for coffee at the university.

"What did she say?" he almost yelled as she ended the call.

"She said she decided to leave you, but she took it hard. Even cried a bit. She said you were like all other men. She said you left her because she didn't want to sleep with you."

"What?" His chin dropped. "You know that's not true, right?"

"Of course I do."

"I didn't hear you defending me so much."

"I did."

"Just a little."

"She's hurt. There's nothing I could have said that would have helped. She'll be okay in a few days. I may have made a mistake trying to fix you two up. I'm sorry."

"Don't worry about it."

"Are you okay?"

"I think so," he said. "I don't think she was the one for me."

———

David suggested they go out to eat or that he would bring dinner, but Angela didn't want to leave the apartment or stay alone. She taught him how to make pasta and salad. Even though he usually hated cooking, he loved every minute in the kitchen with Angela.

Is this what it would feel like making dinner with my wife? A future wife. He smiled a lot and even whistled as she made him cut the vegetables.

They had dinner and talked about what had happened in New York and about his last date with Nancy. On both topics, he couldn't be totally honest.

David had too many secrets from her. He hated hiding things from his best friend.

When it became late and there was still no word from Rick, David suggested she stay the night and use his bed.

"I'll sleep on the couch," he said. "I have a folding bed in the spare bedroom, but it's broken. I need to get it fixed."

"I can't let you do that. I'll sleep on the couch."

Did she agree to spend the night here? She must be terrified of her dad.

"No way. I'm used to sleeping in my recliner."

They argued more, but he won. He changed the sheets, and she slept in his bed. He watched TV in his recliner, taking a long time to fall asleep.

A loud knock on the door awoke him. He crept to the door, stopped, and went back to the kitchen. He grabbed a knife, then peered outside.

Rick.

David put down the knife and opened the door.

They stared at each other for a few seconds until Angela stepped out of the bedroom, covered with his blanket. David wondered if it looked bad, but only for a few seconds. She yawned and seemed half-asleep, but when she saw Rick, she dropped the blanket, ran into his arms, and kissed him.

David turned and picked up the blanket from the floor, folded it, and put it on the couch. When he sensed they had pulled apart, he turned.

Rick thanked him and explained he'd met with her father—without his muscle men—and scared him enough so he would leave her alone.

"How did you know to contact her dad?" David asked as Rick opened the door.

"Her dad called me, after his men were here. He told me he sent some people to look for Angela. I started threatening him, but it didn't seem to help." Rick shifted his weight from one foot to the other. "I promised him I'd send him some of the money by the end of the week."

"You did *what*?" Angela yelled.

"I'm sorry, Angela, but that's the only way to get him off our backs. *Please*, let me take care of it. He won't bother you again. I promise."

Angela nodded. David wondered if she agreed with Rick or if she was too tired to argue. She thanked him, and they left.

David examined his apartment, which seemed lonely.

He went to sleep in his bed without changing the sheets.

They smelled better than they ever had.

TWENTY-FIVE

The following morning, Rick arrived, sat down on the couch, and asked David to sit in front of him. Rick put a big white shopping bag between his legs and rubbed the back of his neck.

"I hope you're not going to propose," David said, but Rick didn't smile.

"I need you to listen to me, okay?" Rick scratched his leg. "First of all, I want to thank you for yesterday. You helped Angela, and I appreciate it. You're probably the only person in the world I can trust who'd help her and not even think of taking advantage of her."

David stared at the floor. His eyes moved from the carpet to Rick's bag.

"And you're probably the only one in the world *she* trusts," Rick said, "besides me, of course."

David nodded.

"I also wanted to apologize for what happened in New York." Rick opened the bag, then closed it. "Something happened right before our trip, and I totally lost it. My last trip gave me a lot of time to think. And I realized I need to clean up my act. I promise I won't ruin meetings like I did in New York, and I won't cheat on Angela ever again. I shouldn't have done it. I know how much you care about her. And you were right. I'm lucky to have her. She's an amazing person, and I love her."

David scratched his temple and nodded slowly. After a moment he said, "Rick, what happened before our trip to New York?"

"I...I can't talk about it."

"*What?*"

"I'm sorry. I can only say that...that it had to do with what happened yesterday."

"With Angela's dad?"

Rick nodded.

"How *did* you fix it?"

Rick rubbed his hand through his hair and looked behind David. "I wasn't completely honest yesterday. It wasn't the first time I had to pay them. And I paid a lot of money to keep them off our backs. It ate up most of my savings."

"*Them?*"

"Those goons that they...that *he* sent. But I think it was the last time we'll hear from him."

"Why not involve the police?"

"We can't prove much, and he's a violent man, so I decided it was best to pay him and get it over with. But I don't want Angela to know."

David nodded.

They were quiet for a while. Rick's phone rang twice, but he silenced it.

"I got you a gift. To show you how sorry, and thankful, I am." He opened the bag and pulled out a long white box, which looked a little like a brick.

But it was not a brick.

"An Apple Watch?" David rose from the recliner, almost jumping. "Are you *crazy*?"

"A little." Rick showed a long line of teeth with his famous smile. "I knew you wanted it, and I got a...a nice bonus from one of my clients, so I figured I owed you at least that much."

David had mentioned to Rick that he wanted one but never expected him to buy it for him.

"I can't take this. It's too expensive." He grabbed the box from Rick's hands.

"Sure you can. It's the cheaper model." Rick looked at the box. "I remember you mentioned you needed it to test our app."

"But you need every cent you have."

"I got it at a discount. Don't worry about it. And besides, I have no receipt, so I can't return it."

"I hope it didn't fall off the back of a truck."

They smiled.

"Thanks, man."

"What are you waiting for?" Rick said. "Open it and start playing."

"It's not a toy."

"Sure it is," Rick said. "Although I hear it tracks your workouts, so I'd need to see those reports."

"You got it, sir."

He opened the box, examined the inside as though it were a beautiful woman, turned it on, and paired it with his iPhone.

"How's Angela doing?" he asked, eyes still on his new watch.

"She's better. She said you were great. She said you

helped her calm down. I sent her to her mother's for a few days to help her relax."

Rick watched David as he put the black watch on his wrist and smiled.

"When are we getting back to business?" Rick asked.

David's eyes sparkled. "ASAP."

"That's what I like to hear. But first, let's test this baby out. Let's go to the River Walk and jog to start this day on the right foot."

They met a few minutes later, both wearing their running gear.

"Where's your car?" David grabbed Rick's arm.

"Um...it's in the shop. Had some issues with it. Do you mind if we take yours?"

"Sure." They walked to David's car. "What kind of issues?"

Rick slipped his hands into his pockets. "Um...it made some weird noises when I turned on the AC."

"Oh. I'm sure it's nothing. You should let me drive it one of these days like you promised."

"Of course." Rick nodded and bit his lower lip.

It took David a few more days to discover that the black Camaro Rick had loved so much was gone forever.

TWENTY-SIX

They had contacted over a hundred potential investors in the past few weeks and met with less than a fifth of them. A handful said they would think about it. No one said yes.

"I'm giving up," Rick said when they switched from running to walking.

David stopped walking. "After all the work we've put in? That's nuts."

"We can't do it. It's impossible." Rick continued walking. "We've been all over the US and met with a million investors. They don't like my idea. *Our* idea. This is frustrating. I can't wait that long. We should give up."

"You're right."

"What?"

"You know, a great man once told me, 'If you say you can or if you say you can't—*you're right.*'"

Rick stopped walking. "*Touché!* I almost believed you there."

"Maybe we should try a new tactic," David said as they stretched.

"I'm listening."

"We should find some way to get you better known. If you were Tony Robbins, we wouldn't have a problem getting funded."

"If I were Tony Robbins, we wouldn't *need* to get funded. The man's got millions. Or billions."

"It would be nice if we could get his support," David said. "I tried contacting his company, but they weren't cooperative. I'm assuming you don't know him, right?"

"I saw him once at a seminar, but so did a million other people. That's the closest I ever got to him."

"It may be a good idea to get to him at a seminar. When's the next one?"

"You're a harsh businessman."

"I'm doing my job. If he supports us in any way, he could have his name on it and sell it to his followers. Win-win."

Rick checked his phone. "The next seminar is a couple of months from now. We can't wait that long. Besides, I think it's nearly impossible to get close to him. He has bodyguards."

David nodded. "Maybe it's a good time for you to try to do a seminar or maybe a book. It'll give you—us—the publicity we need."

"I wish. I looked into it once. Getting a book out is almost as hard as getting money for a start-up. Probably harder."

"I didn't know that. I'm not too familiar with the publishing business."

"I tried it, contacted a lot of publishers and agents. No one would even consider my idea. I even wrote a few chapters. They said there are too many self-help books. They also wanted me to have a base of followers who'll buy my book first."

"We're back to square one."

Rick nodded.

"What about a seminar? Same problem?"

Rick swallowed. "I did it once. Almost went door-to-door to get the word out. Handed out flyers. Even had Angela hand out flyers, which a lot of men were happy to take," Rick said. "We did it for a few months, some days even sixteen hours a day. After all that effort—only eight people showed. They all used the fifty percent coupon we gave them. Obviously, I ended up in debt. That's when I came up with the idea for the app. I thought it would be easier and would get me the publicity I needed for a book and seminar. I heard everyone made apps and made a lot of money."

"People outside the business have that misconception. Last time I checked, one out of ten funded start-ups is able to make any kind of money." David checked his watch. "We're in a pickle."

Rick nodded.

After they were done stretching, David asked, "When do I get to read those chapters you wrote?"

———

"New tactics," David said. "We must get the app out there and try to get users."

"Didn't you say we need an investment for that?" Rick asked.

"It would help, but we don't have much of a choice. Things have changed in recent years, and it's much harder to get an investment without paying customers. The MVP is nice, but it's not enough."

"What do we do?"

"We need to get it into the app stores. If we get users—especially paying subscribers—we have a much better chance of getting an investment."

"Don't we need money for that?"

"I checked my savings, and I can put in a few grand for marketing. What about you? Can you chip in?"

"Hmm...I'm sorry, but no."

David nodded, then touched Rick's hand. "Don't worry about it."

————

A few weeks later, the app was in the store and almost a thousand people had installed it.

"We've got over sixty percent returning customers." David raised his head from his laptop, mouth open. "*Paying* customers."

"Is that good?"

"That's amazing! Now we can update the investors, show them we have traction and can make money, and explain we need most of the money to get more users."

He emailed all the investors they had previously contacted with the new information.

A day later, he received a call from the twentieth investor who said he liked the idea, the team, and the traction. He wanted more information.

"Ironically, his name is Mr. Cash," David said to Rick, and they laughed.

————

David sent the investor all the requested materials. Cash—usually through his assistant—asked for a lot of documents. He made them work hard for it. They exchanged a lot of emails and phone calls.

A few days later, Mr. Cash called and congratulated them.

He wanted in.

David ended the call, put the phone on the table, and turned to Rick.

After a few seconds of silence, the two men jumped in the middle of his apartment. They yelled, danced, and laughed.

"I can't believe it." Rick caught his breath. "I was ready to give up a few days ago."

David was still celebrating, punching his fists in the air.

"How does it work now? Do we get all the money right away or what?"

"You *are* clueless." David laughed. "It doesn't work that way. They give it to us in bits and pieces. We get part of the money for each milestone. Usually we get the first part for the development, and only after the product is ready do we get the money for marketing—which is usually also split according to our needs. From what he told me, I gather we'll get the money in at least three segments, a million dollars each time. The last million may also get split."

"Oh." Rick dropped his shoulders and stared down at his hands.

"What's wrong?" David said. "It's a great offer. You should be excited."

"You're right. I am." Rick rubbed his hands.

David put his hand over his friend's knee. "And, as you know, that's the *only* deal we got."

"You're right." Rick nodded and looked up at him. "I guess I got overwhelmed." He forced a smile. "A million dollars should be fine. How do we get the money? A check?"

"I'm not sure. He's an angel investor, so there should be less formality. It'll probably be easier and faster than a VC. We'll know when we meet him, I guess."

Rick nodded. "I love his name. So appropriate."

"Yeah. *Mr. Cash* is going to give us a lot of cash."

"Let's call Angela and go celebrate."

———

Rick called Angela on speaker, and they laughed and screamed. They dressed nicely and went out to celebrate at a local Mexican restaurant.

"I have even more great news," David said.

"What can be better than landing this investment?"

"You remember I told you we'd need someone to help with the programming?"

Rick nodded.

"I got off the phone with an old friend who wants to join us. He's tired of his job and needs a new and interesting challenge. He said he would love to come work with us as CTO."

"As *what?*" Angela asked.

"*Thank you,*" Rick said. "He speaks French sometimes and makes me feel stupid."

David smiled. "Chief technology officer."

"Sounds good," Rick said.

"Yes. I want you to meet him. He's great."

"I'd love to meet him, but I trust your judgment. If you say he's good, that's all I need."

David nodded. "He can start as soon as the money comes in."

"What happens now?" Angela asked.

"We'll have to open an office, get an additional two or three programmers and maybe one person to help with design. They want us to open the office in New York, and we have to decide if we need it now or when we start marketing. Which brings me to my next question for you two—how would you feel about moving to the Big Apple?"

"*What?*" Angela jumped. "We got here a few months ago. I'm still studying."

"You could travel back and forth," David said. "At least one of you."

"I'll do it," Rick said. "I don't want you to travel all the time, honey. And I want you to finish your studies. I can rent an apartment with David in New York, and I'll come here every weekend. You'll come visit us from time to time. I'm sure David won't mind."

"Of course not."

David wondered why Rick seemed eager to leave Angela alone in Tulsa and move to New York. Did he plan on cheating on her? *I'll have to tell her if it happens again. I promised myself I would. But Rick assured me it won't, so maybe I have nothing to worry about.*

"I don't understand why you have to move, both of you," Angela said. "I thought today, with laptops, smartphones, and the internet, you could work from anywhere."

"They want us close so they can keep track of their money."

Rick nodded at Angela and said, "It makes sense."

When they were ready to leave, Angela stopped them, told them to stand close to her, and pulled out her phone.

"Let's take a celebration selfie."

The men joined her, smiling. She ducked a little to get David's face in the frame.

"You better send it to me," David said.

"I'll do better than that. I'll post it on Facebook."

––––––

When David arrived home, a Facebook notification mentioned Angela tagged him in a picture. He couldn't remember the last time anyone had tagged him—or the last time he *wanted* his picture posted.

He opened the app and saw the three of them smiling in the restaurant. Angela named the picture *The Celebration Selfie*.

They appeared happy.

David had not seen a picture of himself in a long time. He had removed the full body mirror from his bedroom over a year ago so he wouldn't have to look at himself. Looking at his picture, he looked much better than he had in a long time. The picture showed only their upper bodies and faces but enough to see the improvement. He couldn't remember himself looking like that. Ever. Having Angela next to him made him look even better.

He hoped Mia, his ex, saw the picture and felt jealous.

Before going to sleep, he checked the picture again on his phone. The picture had received a few likes and a few "you look great" comments from Rick and Angela's friends. He thought he almost looked good enough to be their friend.

––––––

David dreamed they sold the start-up for two hundred million dollars only a year later. After the investor's cut, they were left with tens of millions of dollars. Each. In the dream, he found the woman of his dreams and moved into a huge apartment overlooking Central Park.

When he awoke, he wondered if the money would be enough for such an apartment.

TWENTY-SEVEN

As soon as Rick got out of the shower, a loud knock on the door startled him.

Is it David?

Rick put a shirt and shorts on and opened the door with a smile, but a huge fist struck his face, thrusting his body a few feet inside the apartment and down to the carpet.

Two men, much larger than him, entered the apartment and slammed the door. One of them kicked him in the ribs, enough to make him scream—which made the big man put his large shoe on Rick's face.

The other man kneeled next to Rick and said, "We've been looking for you for a long time now. We left you a message and even came knocking on your door. Those visits will add to your cost. But you knew that, didn't you?" He didn't wait for Rick to reply. "Where's the money?"

Rick knew they were not burglars.

Not the ordinary kind, anyway.

He knew they were looking for him but had never met them. David and Angela had seen them and called them the muscle men.

They weren't kidding.

He struggled to talk but could only gasp for air.

"You know I'm not gonna ask again."

"It's—" Rick tried to push the foot off his face, but the huge shoe didn't even budge.

The kneeling man nodded to his partner. The shoe came off.

Rick breathed heavily and held his ribs. *Did they break them?*

"I have—" he gasped. "I talked to your boss. I paid him part of it. In New York. Twice." He paused for more air. "He told me I'd have until next week."

"He changed his mind. You cost us too much."

Rick sighed with pain. "I have some of it now. I'll have the rest by next week. As I promised him."

"Let me see what you have."

Rick pointed at the console table next to the door. "In the drawer."

He looked at the clock on the cable box. Angela wouldn't return for a long time. Could David hear the noise? Would he do something?

Could he do something?

I don't need him here.

The man took an envelope from the drawer and opened it. He extracted the cash and counted it.

"There's only fifty thousand dollars here," he said.

"I sold my car and some other savings. I'll have the rest next week. I have money coming in. I prom—"

Like a well-trained robot, the bigger man forced his foot back onto Rick's face.

The slightly smaller man kneeled next to him again. "No," he whispered. "You'll have it by the end of *this* week.

If you don't, the next time we come will be when that beautiful wife of yours is here."

Rick's teeth clenched under the big shoe. He tried to push it hard and to fight back, but it was no use.

The smaller man grinned at Rick's efforts. "And we won't be as gentle with *her* as we were with you."

The man with the foot on Rick's face raised it, allowing Rick to move a little. As he thought they were about to let him go, the bigger man kicked him in the face.

His entire head burned.

The two men left the apartment, slamming the door behind them.

Rick stared at the door. He breathed slowly, trying to get air into his body, but each time he did, his ribs hurt even more.

He rose after a long time. He covered his aching face with one hand and his broken ribs with the other. He limped to the couch and fell on it.

———

David came to Rick's apartment the following day.

"What the hell happened to your face?" David asked as he walked in.

Rick looked back at Angela, then turned toward David. "I got into a fight at my last seminar. Drank a bit too much at the bar. It's stupid, I know, but—"

"We're going to meet the investors in *two days*. We can't go like this. What will they think?"

"I know, man. I'm sorry, buddy. I was...I'm sorry."

Angela smiled at David. He tried to smile back, but she turned away.

"Maybe I'll go there alone. I'll tell them you're sick."

"No!" Rick said. "No. We'll be okay. Angela will help me hide it with some makeup. It'll be okay."

"You can't hide it."

Angela showed no signs of agreement or disagreement.

David sat on the couch, then stood. "Maybe we should postpone it. We can go next week."

"No!" Rick yelled. "We'll go this week. We'll be okay. I'll be okay. We must do this. Trust me."

"I don't know, man. You screwed up again." David looked at Rick out of the corner of his eye. "Maybe I chose the wrong partner again."

He walked to the door and opened it.

"David!" Rick and Angela both said, but he slammed the door shut behind him.

———

An hour later, Rick knocked on David's door. He let him in but didn't look at him.

"Listen. I'm sorry again. I know I screwed up, but it's not what you think."

David raised his eyebrows but said nothing.

"I didn't want Angela to know. She *shouldn't* know about this. I need you to promise me." Rick waited for David to agree, but when he said nothing, Rick continued. "I didn't get into a fight in a bar. I'm not *that* stupid. And I wouldn't do that to you. You have to believe me."

David jerked his head back. "What happened?"

"You remember the goons who came looking for m—for Angela a few weeks ago?"

David nodded.

"After I thought I scared-slash-paid her father off, he

sent them *again* yesterday. This time for me. They came to my apartment. They beat the crap out of me."

David's eyes widened, his mouth opened, but he said nothing.

What if Angela had been there when they came? He shivered.

Rick had tears in his eyes.

After a while, David said, "We have to go to the cops."

"No!" Rick said. "We can't. They threatened Angela. I gave them the rest of the money for her dad. He promised he wouldn't hurt her *or* us. It's over."

"Why do you keep paying that scumbag?" David said. "This shit will never end."

"We're leaving for New York soon. Angela will stay here alone. I couldn't risk it. I needed to get this over with before we go."

David considered it, then nodded. "How much did you give them?"

"Total?"

David nodded.

"Thirty thousand dollars."

"That's *sick*. How did you get that kind of money?"

"I had to sell my car."

———

David came to Rick and Angela's apartment on the day they were supposed fly to New York City.

Rick opened the door, looking better.

"I don't usually have a soda, *obviously*," Rick said, "but to celebrate, I bought one especially for you. We'll celebrate with beer in New York." Rick winked.

"Great. Thank you." David sat down. He tried to see if

anything had changed in their living room since he knew the thugs had been there. Nothing had changed. He always envied their modern furniture. Their apartment had a woman's touch.

"Are you ready for our jog?" Rick asked.

"Are you sure you're up for it?"

"Maybe we should just walk today. It'll be our last workout in Tulsa for a while, huh?"

"We'll be back to get our stuff. We have to find a place in New York, and I need to give my one month's notice. We're just going to get the first check and start talking business."

After they drank and discussed their travel plans, David asked, "Where's Angela, by the way?"

"At the university," Rick said. "But she'll be back to give us a good-bye kiss."

"That's good." David drank his Diet Coke.

"After our walk I'll take a shower and finish packing. We're leaving for the airport in a few hours, right?"

"Yup."

———

David could hardly open the door when Rick and Angela arrived.

"What happened?" Angela asked. "You're whiter than your wall."

"I don't know. I have a high fever, I'm shaking, and I can hardly breathe. It started a couple of hours ago. I think you should go without me. I can't fly like this. I'm sorry."

"Oh, no," Rick said.

"Maybe you should cancel," Angela suggested.

"No way. It won't be professional. You go today, start without me. I'll come as soon as I feel better. Okay?"

"Are you sure?"

David nodded.

"You're right. I'll do that. See you tomorrow." Rick kissed his wife and headed for the door. He stopped, turned, and said, "I think you needed to sign some stuff for them, didn't you?"

"Yes." David let them in. Rick printed a few documents from the investor on David's printer and gave them to David to sign.

Rick thanked him, kissed Angela again, and looked at David. Rick looked as if he was about to hug him but patted his shoulder instead. "I'm sorry."

"For what?" David asked.

"That you won't be with me on that special day."

"I know. I hate it."

Rick shook his hand and walked with a suitcase toward his old car.

"I'll make you soup," Angela said. "Do you need anything else?"

"You don't have to bother. I'll be okay."

"Nonsense. I'll be back soon." She checked his face. "You look bad."

"Thank you."

She touched his forehead. "You're burning with fever. You're sure you don't want me to take you to the doctor?"

"No. I'll be fine. Thanks."

"Okay," she said. "Lie down here." She pointed at the couch. She put her arm around his back and put his arm on her shoulder.

David examined her. He could feel her breathing. He hoped she didn't notice how bad he smelled.

175

Angela helped him lie on the couch, went to his bedroom, returned with a blanket, and covered him. She brought him a glass of water and a bottle of Advil. She gave him two pills and put the bottle next to him on the living room table. She looked at him, looked back at the pill bottle, and then took it back to his medicine cabinet.

She left the bottle of water next to him and brought the TV remote closer.

She checked her watch. "I'll be back in an hour with a great soup. I'll take your key so you won't need to get up. Okay? Call me if you need anything. Where's your phone?"

He stared up at her as she searched for his phone.

I love you, he almost said out loud.

"What?" She turned back to him.

"Nothing," he said and dozed off.

TWENTY-EIGHT

When David woke an hour later, a model sat on his couch, reading a magazine he had never seen before with more beautiful women on the cover.

"You're here," he whispered.

"Hey! You're awake. How are you feeling?" Angela bent over him and touched his forehead. "Your fever is down. That's great."

She went to the kitchen and came back with a bowl of soup and a towel on her right shoulder. She helped him sit up, put the towel in his lap, and helped him sip the soup with a spoon as if he were a child.

"Thank you so much for doing this," he said. "I don't remember the last time a beautiful woman took care of me when I was sick."

Did I say that?

Her cheeks blushed as if it were the first time she'd ever received a compliment. She thanked him and moved to the other couch.

"It's always nice to hear a compliment," she said. "But I don't feel beautiful."

"*What?*"

She shrugged.

"I usually don't say stuff like that to women I'm not dating," he said. "It was probably the fever."

"Too late. It's out now," she said. "And you don't have a fever anymore, so you can't blame it on that."

"I'm a bit embarrassed." He didn't look at her. "It always felt cheesy to me. Like a cheap come-on."

"It could be. But it depends on the situation and the people involved. We're good friends, and I know you're not flirting with me, so that's okay."

"I guess you're right. And you know I usually don't compliment married women."

"It's okay. Rick doesn't compliment me much these days."

"He's been preoccupied lately." *If she only knew the beatings he took were for her.*

"Yeah." She shrugged. "Anyway"—she pointed at him— "*you* will find someone special. I promise. Especially now that you're doing well, look great, and are about to be rich."

———

The following morning, Angela came in with her huge smile. "How are you feeling today?"

"I'm much better, thank you. All thanks to the miracle soup of yours," he said. "I didn't know you cooked so well."

"You just assumed I couldn't?"

"I knew you could cook, but not *that* good."

"There's a lot you don't know about me. But I'm glad to hear you liked it." She walked in. "Do you need anything else?"

"No. Thank you. I'm doing well. Probably a twenty-four-hour flu."

"I thought you said the soup made you well."

"It would have been a *forty-eight*-hour virus without your soup."

They smiled.

"Have you heard from Rick? I want to catch the flight later today."

"We spoke last night. He told me he landed and asked a lot about you. I think he's nervous going there alone today."

"I would be too. But I'll join him this evening, and we'll do most meetings tomorrow together. If we had direct flights to New York I could have been there earlier and maybe we could have met with them today. I'm sure he'll be fine."

"Are you sure you can go? I mean, you were almost *dead* last night." She seemed as if she regretted her choice of words but said nothing.

"I'm fine. Besides, I don't want Rick to run away with our money."

They smiled.

———

Two hours later, he knocked on Angela's door. "I can't reach Rick, and he's not responding to any of my texts. Have you heard from him?"

"Not since I saw you earlier. Why?"

"Angela, is everything okay?"

"I'm sorry. Please come in." She let him in the apartment. He could see luggage on the bed when he glanced into the bedroom.

"Are you going somewhere?"

She looked at the bedroom. "No, I just didn't finish unpacking from my trip to Chicago. I'll let Rick know you were trying to reach him. When's your flight?"

"In two hours."

"I can drop you off at the airport on my way to the university," she said.

———

When David landed at JFK, the cold air made him shiver. He forgot to check the weather and didn't bring warmer clothes. When he checked his phone, he saw that the weather would improve the following day but found no messages from Rick.

He always loved returning to New York, but this time he had a bad feeling.

The front desk agent told David that Rick had checked in the previous day, but when David entered the room, there was no sign of him.

I hope he didn't screw up with the investors. The idiot's probably fucking around with someone he met last night. I shouldn't have let him go alone. Damn it. And I can't even talk about it with Angela.

Or maybe it's time?

———

The following morning, David noticed he had a text from Rick.

I'm sorry, something came up. The meeting went well yesterday. I'll meet you at Cash's office and explain, the text read.

He exhaled slowly. They would get some of the money today and would get to work. And for the first time in a long time, he would get a paycheck for his hard work.

He couldn't shake the feeling that something was wrong.

PART 3

DON'T DARE TO DREAM

TWENTY-NINE

Day 1

David walked to the meeting but didn't want to ruin his only nice suit, which he had bought at Burlington Coat Factory a week earlier. He had enough time to go through Central Park, admire the green trees, and listen to the birds whistling for him. For a few seconds he felt like dancing in the street. When he left the park, he felt tired, so he took a taxi downtown.

The elevator took too long to arrive, so he used the stairs to get to the seventh floor, climbing two steps at a time. He forgot how tall the buildings in New York were and wondered if choosing the stairs had been a mistake. He burst into Cash's reception area, breathing heavily.

On the most important day of their lives, Rick was late.

David smiled at the receptionist.

"Mr. Pascal?" She stared at him. "We weren't expecting you."

"What do you mean? We have a meeting."

"Let me check." She pointed at the waiting area. "Please have a seat."

He sat on the leather couch and texted Rick. No reply. After a few minutes, he called him again. When he got Rick's voicemail for the millionth time, he left another message.

"Where the hell are you?" When he noticed the receptionist looking at him, he covered his mouth with his other hand. "I'm here at Cash's office, but you're *late*. I swear to God, I'm gonna kill you! Call me—ASAP." Before pressing the end button, he added, "Or better yet, *be* here."

He had grown to like Rick, maybe even to love him. As much as a straight man can love another man. Rick helped him. Had been there for him. Rick turned out to be one of the only two people he could trust.

But the previous time Rick pulled a stunt like this, the meeting ended badly.

"Mr. Pascal?" The receptionist startled him. "Mr. Cash will see you now."

He entered the big conference room for the fourth time in his life. The big mahogany table was spotless and shiny, the leather seats looked as if no one had ever sat in them, and a huge, top-of-the-line TV was mounted inside the far wall. He could see part of the Empire State Building from the big window.

He sat and stared outside at the famous landmark. He loved the view, but the sky turned gray.

David rose when Cash opened the door and they shook hands.

"I'm sorry Rick isn't here, he had to—"

"David"—Cash shook his head—"Rick *was* here yesterday. He told us you were sick and couldn't make it."

"We were supposed to have another meeting today."

Cash shook his head again. "Our next meeting is next week. He told us he was going back to Tulsa and that you'd both come back to New York on Monday."

"*What?*"

Cash nodded. "He had your signature on the papers. He took a million dollars and left."

David almost fell back into the chair. His heart raced, and he could hardly breathe.

"Are you *sure?*"

Cash nodded.

"You just *handed* him the money?"

"It's more complicated than that."

David's phone vibrated. He took it out of his pocket.

I'm sorry man. I'll be there in a few minutes, Rick wrote.

THIRTY

David shook his head and looked at Cash. "He texted me he'll be here in a few minutes. I'm sure there's a good explanation."

His heartbeat slowed almost to its normal rate. *There must be a good explanation for this.* Rick probably screwed up again, in a weird way this time, but he couldn't have stolen the money and fled. *No way.*

Cash seemed to consider, then checked his watch.

"I'll be back," he said and left the room.

Cash called Jason Walker, his lawyer, and explained what happened.

"I'll be there shortly," he said.

"Should we call the police?"

"I don't think they'll respond to something like this." The lawyer cleared his throat.

Cash returned to the conference room exactly fifteen minutes later.

"Any news from your friend?"

David shook his head. *Surely Cash will give us more time. Rick will show up. Late as usual, but he won't screw me over.*

Cash left again.

David tried to breathe, forcing himself to inhale through his nose and exhale through his mouth, like Rick had taught him.

The secretary came in with a glass of water. David forced himself to drink.

He tried to text Rick again.

An hour later, Cash returned, accompanied by an older man wearing an expensive suit and tie. David had met him before but couldn't remember his name. Cash and his lawyer sat in front of him.

David could hardly hold himself up in his seat.

The lawyer took out a stack of papers from his briefcase and tossed them in front of David.

"Are those your signatures?" he asked.

David nodded as he flipped through the pages. He saw his initials on every page and his full signature on some of them. At first, he thought Rick had faked his signatures, but then he remembered.

Rick asked me to sign the papers in case I couldn't make it.

He screwed me over.

"I was sick and didn't think I'd be able to make it, so I signed it for him." David held his head between his hands. "But I don't remember writing initials on every page."

Then David thought of a way out. He raised his eyes to them. "You just *gave* him the money? How? Why?"

Cash glanced at his lawyer, then back at David. "He convinced me you guys needed a third of the money immediately. He can be...*persuasive*."

David nodded slowly.

Cash seemed a few years older now than he was an hour ago. When they'd met him previously, Cash had the appearance of a wise, older gentleman. A confident man. Now he seemed afraid—even of his lawyer.

Is he afraid or furious?

"He said you guys needed to pay an advance on a two-year lease for an office you found nearby. I should have known. Anyway, I gave him three hundred thousand dollars via money transfer, and the rest was deposited into the account."

"I can't believe this." David shook his head. "Can you cancel both of them?"

"I called the bank. They can hold the money in the bank, and it'll take a few days to get it back. But the money transfer"—he glanced at his lawyer again—"he already withdrew that. Two minutes after he left our office."

"This can't be happening." David shook his head again.

No one replied.

"How well do you know Rick?" the lawyer asked.

David told them about getting to know Rick and about becoming friends. He left out the part when he tried to commit suicide. He also minimized the coaching part of the story.

He told them about their plan to get the start-up going. He emphasized it was Rick's idea. He told them about looking for investors. He told them about getting sick and that Rick had gone to NYC without him.

Cash and the lawyer took notes.

They told him not to leave the city.

"We haven't involved the authorities yet, but we might," the lawyer said. "Can we ask you not to leave town in the next twenty-four hours?"

David nodded, apologized to Mr. Cash a few more times, said he would figure it out, and left.

Trapped in New York City.

A few hours earlier, it could have been a good thing.

————

David called Rick again as he left Cash's office. After a few times, he tried Angela.

She didn't answer.

Could she be a part of this? No way.

There must be a good explanation for this.

When David left the building, the streets were darker than a usual New York evening. He wanted to walk back to the hotel, but it was cold and rainy. He entered the nearest subway station, added money to his subway card, and waited for the train. After a while, he realized he was standing on the wrong side of the tracks, so he crossed the station to go uptown. The next two trains were too full to fit him in comfortably. He didn't feel like squeezing in with other people.

He decided to walk to the hotel. He didn't mind getting wet, and there was no reason to hurry—no one waited for him.

He used to love walking in New York. Maybe it would help him think. When he left the subway station, it had stopped raining. He closed his jacket, which helped little against the cold, and marched.

Walking could be good for him, but there were too many people in his way, and some of them bumped into him. He was not used to it anymore. Cars honked their horns, sirens screamed, and people talked loudly. The tall buildings felt taller than ever.

David had missed New York, but now it felt gray, noisy, and dirty. The people seemed like ghosts. He took a longer way to the hotel and went through Central Park. He used to take walks in the park twice a week when he lived in the city.

He sat on the first available bench, not caring if it was clean or not, and stared at the trees, the grass, and the people. Assuming Rick wouldn't be back at the hotel anytime soon—or anytime at all—he had nothing better to do.

A good-looking younger woman ran past him in tight pants and a tank top. David wondered how she could take the cold. Another beautiful woman walked past him with a laughing baby in a stroller. She smiled at the baby but not at David.

People don't smile at strangers in New York City.

A boy played with a ball, going back and forth, not sure where he was headed. The boy picked up the ball and left David's sight.

It rained again, lighter this time. David didn't mind. He looked up at the trees, which closed in on him from above. He kept trying to text and call both of his friends. Neither one answered. He didn't even get a read receipt from Angela's iPhone.

His phone's battery drained.

He didn't know what to do.

He wished he would wake up back at the hotel and see Rick in the other bed, right before the meeting with the investor.

Rick had helped David a lot. He had saved his life. Rick

helped him get his life back together again. David had lost hope before Rick came along. He had given him hope.

Had Rick planned this all along? Had he manipulated him with his stupid coaching techniques?

Rick's betrayal felt bad enough, but Rick was a smooth guy. A slick guy. A snake. A gold digger. David had considered him a great friend, but he could see, maybe, in some way, his reasons for such a crime.

But *Angela*? Was it even possible she had been in on it? Did she fake all her good-heartedness?

The drizzle stopped after a while. He took off his soaked jacket and walked back to the hotel.

There must be a good explanation for this.

———

He sat in the lobby of the hotel and decided to get a grip on himself. *What would a real man do?*

What would—*oh God*—Rick do if David had stolen his money?

Rick would probably find David and kick his ass. Then Rick would return the favor and stab David in the back. That's what Rick would do.

But can I do that? How do I stab him in the back? How the hell do I even find him?

What would a good detective in his favorite crime TV show do?

Start investigating.

David's battery was dead, so he took the elevator to his room. He opened the door, hoping to see Rick apologizing and explaining it had been a mistake.

But the only sign of anyone being in the room was from the cleaning staff.

David plugged his iPhone into the charger and went to the bathroom.

I'm smart, and I'm doing well these days. I should be able to do something.

He had an idea, but it meant breaking the law. He had practiced it in the past and, in theory, could do it again.

David could try and get access to Rick's phone. He knew Rick had not updated the operating system on his phone for a long time, which made him more vulnerable to hacking. He had nagged him to update it, but Rick didn't listen.

Thank God for small favors.

David downloaded an infected file, emailed it to Rick, and wrote, *Open this file. It'll give me access to our bank account. If you do this, I'll take a third of the money and I'll leave you alone. I set it so you can monitor what I do. I won't tell the police. I promise.*

Rick wasn't stupid, but it might just work. Rick didn't think David could lie.

He set it so he would get a notification on his phone if Rick opened the file, and he waited.

———

David's phone charged to almost fifty percent. He couldn't wait for Rick to open the file and decided he needed to investigate more. He went through all the correspondences with Rick but couldn't find anything about this trip. David's job had always been to book the flights and the hotels.

"You always find better deals," Rick had said.

Right.

David searched for the hotel reservation, which was under his name. He couldn't remember sending it to Rick and couldn't find the email in the sent box. It meant he hadn't forwarded it to Rick.

How could Rick have gotten the room without having his name on it or without having the confirmation number?

Maybe Angela sent the email to Rick from my phone? She could have done it when she pretended to take care of me.

And she deleted it from the sent box afterward? Unlikely.

How did she unlock my iPhone? He looked at his hand. *She could have used my thumb while I slept.* This was a major disadvantage of the finger recognition technology.

Maybe Angela had texted Rick the number from her phone.

The room was under David's name, which meant it would be easy to get information.

He went down to the lobby and charged ahead of an older couple to get to the reception desk first. Cutting in line was something he had not even considered in the past few years. The nice front desk agent told him a man under the name of Rick MacMillan had been there the previous day, checked into their room, gave an ID and a credit card, but didn't check out or return the key.

"The room's under *my name*. How could you give him the room?"

"I'm sorry, sir, but I'm not sure." She checked her computer. "I can only assume he had the reservation number and your name."

When David first entered the room, it seemed as if no one had used it. There had been no sign of Rick. David rushed to get to the meeting and had no reason to suspect anything was wrong. He figured Rick had been with the waitress.

Or some other woman.

Rick's cheating on Angela didn't seem that bad anymore. He wished he had told Angela. Or maybe she knew. Maybe this was all a well-planned scam. Maybe the waitress was in on it as well.

"Is there anything wrong?" the front desk agent asked.

"Never mind. Thanks."

David sat again in the hotel lobby and tried to think of what else he could do to sort this out.

His phone buzzed. He looked at it. Startled.

He hoped for a message from Rick or Angela.

But it was not.

It was the next best thing.

Rick had opened the file.

Bam! I got him.

David ran up the stairs to his room, opened the laptop, and after less than a minute got into Rick's phone. The first thing he did was check Rick's location.

The tracking took forever to return a location. When it stopped, he discovered Rick was nearby. He was in Central Park, about a fifteen-minute walk away.

The hacking tool could give David more information from Rick's phone—which could be valuable—but his top priority was to find the asshole. David would be able to snoop inside Rick's phone all he wanted later.

David contemplated taking off his suit and putting on his sports gear—Rick made him take it anywhere they went —but decided it would take too long. He took a screenshot of the location and rushed out of the hotel.

When David stopped inside the park where Rick should have been, his head and eyes bounced everywhere as he looked for the tall man. David was close to tackling anyone who resembled Rick. After twenty minutes of frantically looking for his partner, he gave up and sat down on a bench to breathe.

Did Rick trick me somehow? How could he fake the location?

Or did he just drop the phone and run away?

Even though David had made huge progress in recent months, Rick could outrun him anytime.

David wished he had his laptop with him so he could look inside Rick's phone. He figured there should be a way to do it from his phone, but he didn't have time to learn how.

He looked on the ground, under the benches and water fountains, behind rocks and trees. Nothing.

He noticed a trash can nearby.

Yuck.

But the trash can was in the radius.

He looked at the people walking and enjoying the park. What would they think of a grown man in a suit looking through trash?

It was New York. They wouldn't even notice.

After diving through rotten food, dirty diapers, and dog feces in nylon bags, he found a phone.

Rick's phone.

David yanked it out and started walking toward a nearby bench, but when he saw a police officer he put the trash back in. He went to the nearest bench and held the phone up with shaky hands. He looked around, searching for Rick or anyone else who might be watching.

No one cared.

David wanted to clean the phone somehow but decided there was no time. The phone had been turned off, which was a bad sign.

When David turned it on, the phone looked like someone had erased it.

———

David showered and changed clothes. He stared at Rick's phone lying on the table in front of him. He wanted to wash it as well. He wanted to smash it against the wall.

But the phone could be useful.

There must be a way to recover the messages and history on it, but that was out of his skill set. He should look for a company to do that.

Or should I give it to the police? How will I explain I got it? By illegally hacking it?

They could arrest me for that.

He lay on the bed and stared at the ceiling. He thought of the day's events. How the hell could this have happened to him? How did Rick know David wouldn't come with him to meet Cash?

Then it hit him.

I got sick right before we were supposed to fly.

THIRTY-ONE

Day 2

The following morning, Cash told David they needed him and Jason Walker, Cash's lawyer, in the office again. David dressed slowly, didn't shave, and took the longest route there. The three men sat together in Cash's meeting room.

"We've never had a case in which an entrepreneur ran away with the money," Jason Walker said. "We needed more time to decide how to proceed."

David nodded.

"In one of the contracts you signed prior to this one, we—"

Cash stopped him with his hand. "Look, David, I'll be honest with you. Before we continue with the lawyer talk. I need to confess that we—"

It was Jason's turn to stop Cash with his hand. Cash glanced at him, nodded, and said, "I just want to say that from stories I've heard, I had doubts about *you*, not Rick."

Is he trying to hurt me now? Why?

"I wasn't worried you'd *steal* the money, but I was

worried about your performance. I decided to trust you. The two of you together seemed perfect, and our due diligence found nothing to worry about." Cash inhaled, then exhaled slowly. "Rick walked away with three hundred thousand dollars of my money. And if we can't get the rest back from the bank, it's going to be one million dollars."

Cash gestured to his lawyer.

"After reviewing the contract you signed in the past"— Jason handed him papers with text on them—"according to clause 7A in this contract, each partner is responsible for the return of all the funds not used to promote the project. That means both you and Rick are responsible for the money, but since Rick's MIA—*you* are responsible for that money."

David tried to inhale, but it was too hard. Rick had stabbed him in the back again, in the same open wound he'd had since yesterday.

Now I owe them the money Rick stole.

"You have thirty days to return the money. If you are unable to do that, we will have to sue you *personally*."

David stared at Jason, then at Cash, who stared at the table.

David didn't remember reading such a clause in the contract. Who thought of such an option? He had gone over the contract twice. *With* Rick. Did Rick go over it and remove it before letting David read it? Or maybe David read it and dismissed it.

They even had a lawyer go through it. A cheap one they found online, but still.

Then he recalled that Rick had found that lawyer.

Who thought anything like that could happen?

How the hell did Cash and Jason think about it? They had the time and the sense to cover themselves in case only one partner stole money from them but didn't have enough brains to check with *both* partners before giving away money?

David wanted to share his thoughts but decided against it.

The room grew bigger and darker. They were stronger, had more resources and the law on their side.

And they were right.

"One more thing," Jason continued, "the thirty days started *yesterday*, so you have twenty-nine days to give us our money back."

———

David took a taxi to the hotel. He hated the city at this point. He considered looking for Rick on the streets, but there were ten million people in NYC, and to find Rick would be like finding a needle in the ocean.

Rick had probably gotten out of the city anyway. David exhausted the ways he could find him there. Maybe he could break into their apartment in Tulsa and search for more clues.

Halfway into packing his suitcase, he remembered he was not supposed to leave the city. He lay down on the bed next to his suitcase and stared at the ceiling. How would he pay for a few more nights here? What the hell would he do?

A loud knock on the door made him jump. The knock sounded similar to Rick's.

David sprang to the door and, without peering through the peephole, pushed it wide open.

Instead of Rick there were two men, slightly bigger than him, wearing suits and a tie, but they didn't look like lawyers.

Nor did they look like the muscle men, thank God.

But who knows?

"Can I help you?"

"David Pascal?"

"Yes."

Police?

"We work for Mr. Cash. Can we come in and talk to you for a few minutes?"

Not the police. Should I let them in? If they wanted to hurt me, they wouldn't ask politely.

"What do you mean you work for him?"

"We're private detectives. We're helping him find Rick. It's in your best interest to help us."

He let them in, but when they started searching the room, he got annoyed.

"Rick isn't here."

"We needed to make sure."

He recalled he had put Rick's phone inside his suitcase. He looked for it, but thankfully it lay hidden underneath his clothes. He had cleaned the phone and put it in a Ziploc bag.

He didn't think he should share it with them. He didn't know if he could trust them.

"Are you leaving?" The investigator pointed at the suitcase on the bed. "As I understand, you were told not to leave the city."

"You can't tell me not to leave the city. You're not the police. And I have nothing left to do here. I want to go back to Tulsa and see if I can find anything there."

The investigators looked at each other.

They asked him some personal questions, then asked him to tell them what happened from the beginning and took notes.

"I told all of this to the lawyer in Cash's office."

"We need to hear it again. It'll help us with our investigation."

David figured he had nothing to hide. Maybe they'd give him some slack if he cooperated. He told them about getting to know Rick, becoming friends, their plan to get the start-up going. He told them about looking for investors and about getting sick.

He left out Angela, even though he was sure by now she was involved.

But she took care of me so well, like a mother to a child.

They took more notes, confirmed his details, and left. They told him they'd be in touch.

———

The flight back was the longest flight of David's life. It felt like days. He almost missed his connection. He sat in the gate area, but only when he realized they were calling his name on the airport speakers did he rush to the airplane. The passengers seemed mad at him, but he didn't care.

When he arrived at Tulsa International Airport, he remembered he didn't have a car.

Angela had taken him to the airport.

Oh, Angela.

THIRTY-TWO

FBI Special Agent Bob Alexis was walking to his car when his cell phone rang.

"Bob?"

He knew the voice. He knew the tone.

"What?"

"Great job solving the Santiago case. You did great. We're proud of you here at HQ." His boss always sounded as if he had a cigar in his mouth.

"What do you want?"

"Can't I just call and give you a compliment without wanting anything?"

"You never do."

"You got me. I have a great lead for you. It's a development in the Cash case."

"Cash? The investor from New York?"

"That's the one."

"Can't you send someone else? I was supposed to go on vacation with my kid. You know that."

"I do. But you'll have to postpone it for a couple of days."

Bob didn't reply.

"I need you on a plane ASAP. There're no direct flights where you're going."

"*China?*"

"No. I actually think they have direct flights to China."

"So where?"

"Tulsa."

"*Where?*"

"You know, where Chandler went when Monica was upset with him?"

"Are you talking about *Friends*?"

"Yup. But unfortunately, he's not there anymore. You'll meet a hardened criminal called David Pascal. A geek who may have stolen some money from Cash. His partner certainly did. I'm sending you more information right now."

"No way. Send someone else."

"You're all I got, and you know this case by heart."

———

An old, dirty taxi took David to his apartment complex. A strong Oklahoma wind shook the car on his way home. The driver tried to talk to him but gave up after a few attempts. David plugged earbuds in his ears and listened to nothing but his own breathing.

As they drove through the apartment complex gates, he thought he had grown to like the place in recent months.

When the taxi stopped, David saw his car waiting for him. Angela's car was nowhere to be seen. He searched for Rick's Camaro, but then remembered Rick had lost it. He had to sell it.

Maybe Rick owed them more money. Maybe it's why he stole our money. It could explain why he did what he did.

David imagined the two muscle men walking into Cash's office with Rick, waiting for him in the waiting area, guns ready to shoot.

Would it make it any easier?

Probably not. Rick should not have done it.

"Sir? It's fifty dollars." The taxi driver acted as if he had said that a few times already.

"I'm sorry." It seemed expensive, especially now that he owed a million dollars and every cent counted. David paid the driver and exited the taxi.

He couldn't recall which car Rick had gotten instead of the Camaro. He only remembered it was old. He couldn't see any familiar car.

It won't be here anyway.

The trees were gray, and the grass was dead.

No glass half-full anymore.

He entered his apartment and saw nothing had changed. The blanket Angela had covered him with lay lifeless on the couch—the only reminder he had of her taking care of him.

They poisoned me, and then she took care of me. Her job was probably to make sure I was still sick and couldn't leave for New York.

David left his luggage unopened in the middle of the living room, climbed up to Rick and Angela's apartment, and knocked on their door. No reply. He knocked louder and louder. He knocked loudly and continuously until an older woman walked by and glared at him as if he were a serial killer. She didn't say hello, but he didn't care. Who needed friendly neighbors? He didn't even remember seeing her before. She entered her apartment across the hall, and he continued knocking on the door every few minutes. He tried the door handle, but the door didn't budge. He tried to push the door, first by pressing the handle and then by pushing it with his whole body. Eventually he tried to kick it in.

It wouldn't cave.

He wished he had asked them for a key.

Would they have given it to me? Apparently, they didn't trust me.

He sat down on the floor, his back leaning against their door. He hoped it would open suddenly, causing him to fall in. He hoped they would both hug him and tell him it had all been a misunderstanding.

A few tears fell from his eyes. They joined other tears, and all of them ran down his cheeks and wet his shirt as if he had jogged on a warm summer day. He didn't try to stop the tears. He looked down at his shirt and recognized it as one of the shirts he had bought with Angela.

When David heard a door open, he wiped his face with his hands and rose, but it was the same neighbor who hated him for making noise. He tried to smile at her. The neighbor nodded, examined him, and headed outside to the parking lot. She didn't ask what happened. She didn't care.

Maybe I should have searched for more friends in the building. Maybe some of them wouldn't have stabbed me in the back.

Eventually, he went down the stairs and into his apartment. He opened his refrigerator to get a drink, but when he saw the pot of soup Angela had made him, he took it out and dumped it violently into the kitchen sink.

He sat in his recliner, pulled the blanket from the couch, and covered his whole body and head with it.

What should I do now?

What could I do?

He considered going for a run. It could help him change his state of mind.

When you work out, the body releases endorphins, which trigger a positive feeling in your body, Rick had said.

There's no way in hell I could go for a run. I can't even get out of this chair.

Tears gushed from his eyes and wet his blanket.

He cried until he fell asleep.

———

A loud bang on the door woke David.

It threw him back a few months, to when Rick had done it for the first time.

Who the hell can it be? The knock was even too loud for Rick.

Could it be any one of them?

He wanted to jump out of the recliner but couldn't.

After a few knocks on the door, he noticed someone trying to peek inside the apartment through the window.

What the hell?

The muscle men again? What the hell could they want from me?

They can kill me for all I care.

He opened the door and found two men wearing suits and ties.

"Mr. Pascal?" one of them asked.

David had not been called "mister" in a long time, but he nodded.

"I'm Special Agent Alexis, and this is my partner, Special Agent Stuber. We are with the FBI. Do you mind if we come in?"

The talking agent showed him a badge with an FBI logo.

Agent Alexis seemed to be about David's age. He resembled an older Brad Pitt with a mustache. The other one was younger, about Rick's age. They were about the same height. Agent Alexis appeared more muscular in his tight suit. In the picture, the agent looked much younger.

What's the FBI doing here? Is this case so important they had to involve the Feds?

Are they here to arrest me?

David let them in and invited them to sit on the couch. They both shook his hand, and he sat in the recliner without moving the blanket away. He didn't offer them drinks, even though it crossed his mind.

The older Brad Pitt agent put a big folder on the table. They asked him personal questions, about his work, studies, and the woman he almost married.

Why all the personal questions?

Then they asked him about what happened with Rick.

Both agents took notes as he told them the story, but not at the same time. One of them examined the apartment or David's face while the other one took notes. They alternated with each other as if they had been trained to do that. They didn't interrupt him while he talked, and when he finished the story, they both stared at his unopened luggage in the middle of the living room. They seemed relaxed and almost understanding.

"Angela had some problems with her dad. He sent two huge muscle men to look for her. He thought she owed him money. Rick paid them off so they'd leave her alone. He had to sell his car for that. I thought maybe he owed him more money, but he said he paid them off. You should look into that."

"Do you know how much money he paid his father-in-law?"

The term *father-in-law* seemed odd. Angela's dad was no one's father. "I think Rick said thirty grand."

The talking agent leaned in and looked David in the eyes. "And you say you had no idea about what they were planning?"

"Of course not."

Agent Alexis nodded and wrote in his notebook. "Did *you* help them in any way?"

David's throat dried. "You don't seriously think I had anything to do with that, do you?"

"Everyone's a suspect until we can prove otherwise."

A suspect? Me? Isn't it enough I got stabbed in the back, lost my two best friends, lost my start-up, and owe the investor a million dollars—now this agent wants to twist the knife inside my back even more?

"So?" Agent Alexis said. "Did you?"

"*I* got scammed. If I'd helped them, you think I'd stick around to talk to you?" He stood, his hands flying all over the place. "I'm liable for the money! They want *me* to pay it back. I don't have that kind of money. I lost my friends, my job, and now I owe them a million fucking dollars!"

The two agents looked up at him. Only when he stopped talking did he notice how aggressive he must have seemed, hovering above them, shouting and waving his hands. He feared they would reach for their guns, but they didn't seem alarmed. He sat back down and tried hard not to cry.

"We understand how hard it is for you, sir, but we have to check every angle," Agent Alexis said. "I don't think you were in on it. I think you got conned by scam artists. I don't understand how you didn't suspect them, but I think you're innocent."

Did he call me stupid?

Better stupid than a thief.

"Didn't you think it was strange"—he checked his notes —"that *Angela's* dad came to look for her and her money, that an older man would send two professional muscle men, which cost a lot of money, just to collect thirty thousand dollars?"

David nodded. "It crossed my mind. I thought her dad was a maniac. They were my friends. They helped me get my life back. They could probably have taken money out of my pocket and I wouldn't have noticed."

He couldn't stop the tears anymore.

The two agents looked at each other. Agent Alexis rose from the couch, and the younger agent stood right after him. "Is there anything else you can think of?"

The phone!

David nodded. He opened his suitcase, fished out Rick's phone in the Ziploc bag, and put it in the middle of the coffee table, where Rick's books had been not long ago.

"What's this?"

"Rick's phone." David looked at the floor.

"How did you get that?"

After he explained, he couldn't tell if the agents were angry or relieved they had a lead. They said they would check the phone. "Make sure you don't pull any more stunts like that again."

David nodded. He was happy he wouldn't go to jail for that.

"Here's my card," Bob Alexis said. "Call me if you remember anything else. We'll be back later today or tomorrow morning. We have to ask you not to leave town. Do you understand?"

David checked the card, then the agent, and nodded.

He had nowhere to go.

———

An hour later, David heard footsteps coming down the stairs. He jumped to the door and peered outside. He saw nothing, so he sprang to the window and looked outside through the blinds.

He saw the neighbor from earlier that morning get into a car. He breathed in deeply and exhaled.

Where the hell did she come from? He couldn't recall ever seeing her before that day, maybe because she was too old to be a potential wife. Maybe she was spying for Rick and Angela.

He wanted to laugh, but at this point, anything seemed possible.

Just before he turned to go back to his recliner, he saw an unfamiliar car parked next to his. The big black SUV with tinted windows faced his apartment. The front window was not as tinted as the ones on the sides, but it took him a while to recognize the familiar face behind the wheel.

The non-talking younger agent from this morning sat there and stared directly at David.

What the hell's going on? Are they following me?

He considered going out to confront the agent but decided not to bother.

They could be waiting for Rick and Angela to come back.

That made more sense.

Maybe they were waiting for him to go meet them. It made sense to follow him—if he was a suspect. He wondered if the talking agent lied about believing him. Maybe the agent was waiting for him to relax and make a mistake. There were no mistakes to make since he had nothing to hide.

He couldn't go to jail. He had seen in the movies what they did to nerds like him in jail. He wouldn't survive a single day.

He knew what to do. He had to do it.

He walked to the kitchen and took out a knife from the drawer.

THIRTY-THREE

"Do you believe him?" Agent Stuber asked.

"I think so," Agent Alexis said, peering at David's apartment through the windshield. "He doesn't look like he could pull this off. Not the type. Besides, I see no reason for him to stick around if he had. At first, I thought the three of them had planned this to slow us down, but he seemed genuinely devastated by all of this, and, unlike the couple, it looks like he has nothing to hide."

"I see what you mean." Stuber turned on the engine. "But I find it hard to believe they could fool him that easily. He seems too smart for that."

"He is, but he trusted the coach. He trusted both of them. He was a lonely, depressed man with no work or friends." He opened the folder and looked at the couple's picture. "Suddenly this perfect-looking couple becomes best friends with him, help him, and get him a job. Anyone would have fallen for it. Besides, I think the whole coaching thing helped Rick twist this poor guy's mind."

Stuber nodded. "I don't trust coaches."

"I want you to return here and stick around. If he goes

anywhere, I want to know about it. There's always a chance the lovely couple will return. We need to be here if they do."

"Can't one of the locals do that?"

"We'll get someone on loan tomorrow, but today we're on our own. Drop me at the local sheriff's office; I have more work to do."

Stuber nodded. "Why would anyone be stupid enough to steal money from an investor who works with the mob?"

———

Later that evening, a local detective replaced Agent Stuber, who brought two cups of coffee from Starbucks to the local sheriff's office.

"I got them early. But we won't have them twenty-four-seven." Agent Alexis took one of the coffee cups, nodded, and drank.

"We'll take what we can get." Stuber sipped from the second cup. "What's new?"

"I checked David Pascal's bank account, bills, flights, etc. He has less than five thousand dollars in the bank. He had a small exit from a start-up he was part of, but he's been living off his savings for the past two years. No income at all during that time. He spent some money on ads for their app, which gives him credit, but it could also be a tactic that helped them get funded. His flights and credit card records check out. It looks like he told us the truth regarding his whereabouts. A couple of years ago he had problems with another start-up partner. I talked to the partner, and he said David fucked up professionally, but not legally. He said that, looking back, he was much too harsh on David."

"I see a pattern here."

Bob nodded. "To make things worse, around that time he almost got married to a"—Bob checked his notes—"Mia Belkin, but she dumped him for another guy. We'll talk to her tomorrow, but I think it's a dead end."

"This guy can't catch a break." Stuber rolled his eyes. "What about the couple?"

"I can't trace their phones, cars, or any kind of credit card activity. They know what they're doing. They seem professional. They must've planned it months in advance, maybe even before they met their poor victim. Angela had no income in recent months, but Rick did well with his private coaching business, and I'm assuming there's a lot more money he didn't report." Bob took a long sip from his coffee. "All three didn't have any priors. No one changed their names, besides Angela when she married Rick."

"Education?"

"Rick MacMillan hardly finished high school, David has an MBA, and Angela MacMillan was studying for her master's in psychology. I checked with the university, and it looks like Angela did extremely well. She was on her way to getting her degree with honors. I don't understand why she would quit in the middle."

"A good cover, maybe?" Stuber said. "She could probably make a lot of money as a shrink. She gave up *modeling* for that."

Bob stared at him. "Based on my talks with other investors, I think they had a good idea and a good chance to succeed. Why run away with only part of the money? Why now?"

"I think Cash is in on it. Another way for him to launder his money. We've been on his tail for a long time, with no luck. He didn't even report the money stolen. We only found out about it by tapping his phone."

DON'T DARE TO DREAM

"Why would the couple be a part of it? They both had the potential for good careers, even without the start-up. Why become fugitives?"

"Maybe the whole father thing scared them. Maybe he's connected to Cash's side businesses."

Bob nodded. "That would explain the muscle men they sent."

"Either that or the father found Rick in New York, forced him to get the money, and fled."

"Why would they disappear, then? Why not call the cops?"

"Another option is that the father took the money and killed them."

———

David stared at the knife for about an hour and considered the consequences of what he wanted to do. It would solve all of his problems. Rick and Angela would feel bad when they found out what they made him do.

If they ever found out.

Would they be sorry? Maybe not. Maybe just Angela.

If he killed himself, it would mean they won.

He didn't want those fuckers to win.

———

"He could have killed Rick in New York," Agent Alexis said, "then came here, killed Angela, and got rid of the bodies, respectively. Or used his goons for Angela."

"It's a good theory." Stuber sipped his coffee. "The father has a history of violence. It sure would explain some of the stranger things. The only issue is that it looked like

DAN FRIEDMAN

the couple planned to screw David for a long time. Maybe they even targeted him to begin with. How do you figure that in?"

"It sure looks that way. Maybe they planned to steal the money, and the father learned about it and got in the way."

"Or maybe they were in on it with the father."

"That could also be the case. Anyway, we should get the warrant tomorrow morning, and we'll be able to search their apartment. There *must* be something there that'll help us find them."

"And what about David?"

"We should keep him in the loop. It looks like he wants to find them as bad as we do. We should keep him close just in case we were wrong about him. I know it's not professional, but I feel sorry for the guy."

"He looked like he was ready to kill himself when we left."

Alexis nodded, then his eyes slowly widened.

He tried to call David.

———

David turned the knife in his hand.

Maybe pills are a better way. I have experience.

This time there would be no one walking into his apartment and saving him.

His phone rang, startling him. David didn't recognize the number. He let it ring.

If he killed himself, he wouldn't have a chance at a great career, at a wife, at a family.

When the phone rang for the third time, he thought it may be important.

"David? This is Agent Alexis. I wanted to make sure you're okay."

Why does he care?

Alexis also wanted to let him know that they officially didn't consider him a suspect anymore. But they wanted him to stick around. They would need his help.

David ended the call and put the knife back in the drawer.

Day 3

David fell asleep late the previous night in the recliner in front of the TV, which forced the agents to knock hard a few times to wake him. He hadn't shaved or taken a shower, and he could see the agents looking at him as if he was homeless.

"I tried to call you all morning." Agent Alexis clenched his fists as they walked in.

"Yes, I'm sorry. I fell asleep late and turned off my phone."

They refused his offer of drinks and told him they had a warrant to search the couple's apartment. They wanted him to come with them to check if he could see anything out of the ordinary before they started.

"Were you able to see anything on Rick's phone?"

"We sent it to the lab. They couldn't recover anything. It looked as if it had been professionally erased."

Professionally? Rick didn't know enough about technology to do that. Did he pay someone to do it?

The agents wore nylon gloves and gave him a pair. They told him to wait outside, drew their weapons, and cleared Rick and Angela's apartment. When they let him in, they told him not to touch anything. When he entered their apartment, his legs almost failed. He couldn't find anything out of the ordinary.

At first.

Then he noticed Angela's iPhone thrown on her bed, forgotten. He walked to it as the agents yelled at him not to touch it. They would take it to the lab.

As he turned to leave, he remembered something. "The day I left for New York, Angela had a suitcase open in her bedroom. Right here on the bed. When I asked her where she was going, she dismissed me. I didn't think much about it at the time, but now I can't see the suitcase anywhere."

The two agents stared at each other.

———

"May we come in?" Agent Bob Alexis asked.

David saw more agents walking around outside behind the two familiar agents. He nodded and let them in.

"We're finished here for today." The agent pointed up. "I wanted to update you that we found a large amount of rat poison in their house." He was as expressionless as a cow on its way to the slaughterhouse. "My guess is they used it to get you sick, maybe even tried to kill you. A little more of this, and it would have killed you."

David lost his balance; Agent Alexis grabbed him and helped him to the recliner.

THIRTY-FOUR

Days 4–6

David stayed in bed all morning, listening to the storm outside. *Even a real storm siren wouldn't get me out of bed. Getting carried to the sky by a hurricane would be a welcome change.*

David hadn't even gone to his recliner to watch TV.

After twenty hours in bed with no sleep, he decided he needed to do *something*. He turned on his phone, but there were no messages from Rick or Angela. No messages from the agents either.

But there were ten messages from Albert, the company's chief technology officer.

The dead company.

Oh my God. I totally forgot about him.

David didn't read the messages. He called him back.

"I got a call from private investigators," Albert shouted, forcing David to move the phone away from his ear. "You lost all the money? You didn't even tell me about it? I have to hear it from investigators?"

"Albert, I—"

"How the hell did you manage to do that? Huh? I left my job because of *you*, you *idiot*! I should have known. You're nothing but a loser. You always were and always will be. People told me not to trust you. I should have known better. *You fuckin' loser!*"

"I—"

But Albert ended the call.

———

David awoke after a few hours, startled by a loud thunderclap. When his pulse retuned to almost normal, he decided he should try to put Albert behind him. He had done nothing on purpose. He got scammed. By professionals. Even the FBI said so.

You fuckin' loser! Albert had yelled at him.

David felt hungry, and when the rain stopped, he forced himself to drive to Walmart, bought a lot of bad food, but didn't look for women.

"Hello." A voice came from behind him when he returned home.

David turned swiftly but saw his neighbor, old man Barton, in his doorway.

David opened his mouth to talk, but nothing came out. He just nodded.

"You know, you and I never got a real chance to talk. Would you like to come in for a beer?"

Does he know what I'm going through?

"Thank you. But I...can't right now."

"I see. If you change your mind, feel free to come knocking."

"Thank you." David entered his apartment.

He ate most of the bad food and fell asleep in his recliner.

When he awoke, he watched boring news on the TV.

Any news? David texted Agent Alexis.

Bob replied a few minutes later: *I'm sorry for not getting back to you sooner. We're busy. No updates at this point, but I'll keep you in the loop.*

A few seconds later, Bob added, *How are you doing?*

Could be better.

David planned to go for a jog—or at least a walk—and to do it every morning. He postponed it till later that day, then to the day after. At that point, his old food habits and his beloved recliner seemed much more appealing.

He'd reached his peak a few days ago. He was back on his way to becoming a Steve Jobs again. The only thing missing was a woman, but he had been optimistic. He had a chance of obtaining his dreams again. All of them. He would have made millions. Hell, he didn't even need the millions or even the respect. Going back to work every day felt great. He had started building a new thing, which could have changed the world, even if only a little.

The best thing in the past few months had been his friends. For the first time in years, he had friends. *Real* friends.

But, as all humans do, they betrayed him. He should have known better than to get a new partner. Partners always cheated. Always stabbed him in the back.

Not only had he lost his friends, his start-up, and his respect, he also owed a lot of money. *A million dollars.* How the hell would he come up with a million dollars?

His best friends had brought him back to life...only to try to kill him.

Day 7

Bob sat with Stuber in a small office inside the police department in downtown Tulsa, both drinking cafe lattes Agent Stuber had brought.

"The poison changes things."

Bob nodded. "I'm not sure anymore that the father was in on it."

"Maybe they planned it but then the father screwed up their plans."

"Most of the evidence points that way, but we can't rule out the possibility that the three acted together."

"Why would the father send muscle men to hurt them?"

"You have a point. It's too expensive and complicated just to fool David. And David said Angela looked genuinely worried."

"Okay, so we're sticking with the theory that they were in on it, but the father killed them and ran away with the money."

"Did you update David? It may help him cope a little."

Bob called David a few times, but he didn't answer.

"I think I'll go there," Bob said.

"Again? Why don't you just have him come here?"

"He annoys me like hell, but I'm worried about him," Bob said. "Besides, I can always take another look at the couple's apartment."

———

David planned to go for a walk but didn't. When the talking agent came to visit him again, he barely opened the door.

What does he want from me?

"I tried to call you all morning." The agent clenched his teeth. "I can't come here every time I need you. If you want to help us find them, I need you to be more responsive. Would that work?"

David nodded. "I'm sorry. I don't feel so good. I slept in."

He couldn't tell him what he suffered from, even though the agent could probably guess.

Bob sat down. "We couldn't locate them, their cars, or their cell phones."

"What about Angela's iPhone? The one I found in their apartment."

"It isn't easy to crack an iPhone, even for us."

"What about the Israeli company that cracked the terrorist's iPhone for you?"

The agent raised his eyebrows but lowered them promptly. "I forgot who I'm talking to. Yes, they did, but it's way too expensive for a small case like this. Probably more expensive than what Rick and Angela stole."

David's problems were nothing compared to homeland security.

"That's why I'm here," the agent said. "Would you be able to guess, by any chance, her passcode?"

Did she ever unlock her iPhone next to me?

"She always used her thumb to unlock it in front of me."

"You know her better than we do. We tried her mother, but she had no idea. If you have any ideas, please let me know."

"Her mother doesn't know they stole the money?" David cocked an eyebrow.

"That's what she says."

"And you believe her?"

"We don't have a reason not to."

"They were close. She's lying, or something bad has happened to Angela."

The agent's mouth opened slightly.

Is it possible something happened to Angela? He shook the thought away.

"I can try the iPhone if you want," David said. "You have it here?"

The agent nodded.

"Let me see it. I can try using stuff I know about her."

The agent took out her phone from his bag and handed it to David.

"I can give you *four* tries."

David nodded. "How many did you try?"

"Our technicians tried three. No luck."

"So I get *seven* more."

"If you hit ten tries, it'll get erased, and I can't risk it."

David nodded. "What did they try?"

Agent Alexis opened his notebook and read. "Her birthdate, her mother's birthdate, and their wedding day."

David held Angela's iPhone, which had been a part of her, like most people and their smartphones these days. But it was locked now, and she was gone. Why did she leave it behind?

Probably to prevent the police from tracking them. *Smart.*

I could never imagine leaving my phone behind.

But he didn't have to; he wasn't a runaway criminal.

He tried Rick's birthday. Bob wrote it down, but it was the wrong passcode. He tried the beginning of Rick's phone number. It didn't work. He tried their building and apartment number.

Wrong passcode.

One last try.

The agent bit his lip.

David considered trying her father's birthdate but dismissed it. He needed to be more creative. He opened his iPhone and launched the Facebook app. He could no longer avoid their profiles. He tried not to look at their faces and scrolled down through all of Rick's stupid clichés.

Then he found something. Rick's first seminar, the one Angela helped him get attendees for. There was a picture of Rick with his hands in the air. He appeared happy.

Angela stood behind him, smiling.

That could be it. Last try.

David tried the seminar's date on Angela's iPhone.

Wrong passcode.

The agent reached for the phone, but David stopped him.

"Can I try one last thing?"

"You had your chances. I can't risk it."

"Come on. One more. You'll still have two more. I have an idea."

The agent considered it, then gave the iPhone to David and bit his lip harder.

David remembered Angela had asked him to fix the email on her phone. People always asked him to help with technical stuff, even after he bought a T-shirt that read, *No, I will not fix your computer.* He didn't mind helping Angela. Not back then.

She had to tell him the password for her email. He didn't remember what it was, but he recalled she said it was a combination of the people she loved. He thought it was either their names or their birthdates.

Who are the most important people in her life? I thought I was one of them, but I guess I'm not. The remaining two significant people are her mother and her husband.

Her mother had to be first because she was first in her life. He entered the beginning of her mother's birthdate, which he had gotten from the agent, and then the beginning of Rick's.

Like a miracle, the passcode screen disappeared and the home screen icons appeared.

The iPhone unlocked.

Both of their faces brightened. They yelled, laughed, and almost hugged each other.

David wanted to look inside her phone, but the agent stopped him.

"Let me write down the passcode and get it to the technicians. I need it untouched."

The agent held the doorknob but then stopped and looked back.

"Good work, David. Thank you. This could help us. I hope I'll have more info tomorrow."

David nodded.

"I asked you this before, but if there's anything else you can think of—maybe places they liked, places they talked about, etc.—let me know."

"Okay."

Bob held up Angela's iPhone. "My bosses are getting tired of this, and they're starting to pull out resources. Do you understand? I need some more breakthroughs here."

"I understand." David tried to smile.

"Let me know if you ever want to go for a walk or something."

David almost smiled. "Maybe after I get my shit back together. Thank you."

Bob reached for the door again, then turned back. "One last thing. You said that if her mother didn't hear from her, you think something bad may have happened to Angela."

David nodded.

"One of our theories is that her father caught up to Rick, made him steal the money, then took out both of them and ran away with the money."

David stopped breathing for a few seconds.

Just when he thought it couldn't get any worse.

———

Good news or bad news? Could they both be dead? If they were threatened and killed, it means they were innocent. They didn't betray me.

After all the hatred he had felt in the past few days, he couldn't grasp the idea that they could be innocent. It would mean he hated them for nothing.

They would still be his best friends.

They didn't betray him.

But it would also mean he would never see them again.

He imagined Angela buried alone in the woods. He shook his head and tried to dismiss the horrifying vision.

A new wave of feelings surfaced through his chest. He felt mad, then sad, then almost happy. He couldn't deal with it. He wanted to go to sleep, but his heart pumped too fast.

An urge he had lost in the past few days returned again. He wanted to go for a walk.

It could be a great way to celebrate their lives. They taught him the importance of exercise.

He changed into the clothes Rick had bought him, even though the weather was too cold for shorts. He didn't care.

They didn't betray him. He laughed uncontrollably. If someone could see him right now, they would think he was crazy.

Was he?

But they tried to poison me. What does that mean? Maybe Angela's dad made them do it.

David needed them to be his lost friends.

Then he cried.

He washed his face and got out of his apartment. As he stared at the stairs leading to his old friends' apartment, his iPhone rang.

He examined it and saw Agent Bob's number.

So fast?

"Can I come back for a few minutes?"

"Sure. What is it?"

"We found Angela's dad."

"What did the son of a bitch say?"

"Nothing," Bob said. "He's been dead for almost ten years."

THIRTY-FIVE

"They lied to me about that too," David said, his eyes to the ground.

"Apparently."

"But those muscle men were real. I saw them myself. You think they paid them just to put on a show for me?"

Bob seemed to think for a moment. "That could be one explanation, even though it would have probably been expensive."

"Angela seemed genuinely afraid. She was *terrified*. She stayed the night—well, part of it—"

"She stayed the night with you?"

"It's not how it sounds. I wish. Uh...I...never mind. Nothing happened. I slept on the couch. She was too scared to go back to her apartment until Rick showed. He came here in the middle of the night, and they both went back to their apartment."

Bob took out his notebook and jotted down this new information.

"But she lied about the poison and the soup, so I guess I was wrong about her," David said into the still air.

He waited for Agent Bob to finish writing, then said, "He sold his car to pay them. They found him and beat the money out of him. I saw the marks. They were real. He told *me* he lied to *Angela* that he got hurt in a bar fight."

"He could have sold the car to get ready for their escape."

"What about the beatings? He hit himself?"

"Maybe he did get into a fight in a bar. Maybe the first story was true, and his confession to *you* was a lie."

David nodded slowly. "Why did it take you guys so long to find him?"

"The father?"

David nodded.

"After he ran away from Angela and her mother, he changed his name so they wouldn't find him. It took us a few days to find his new identity and the fact that he'd died. He didn't have a new family, and no one cared about him. That made it harder for us to trace him."

"This whole story was just another lie?" David asked. "Why am I even surprised?"

Day 8

David awoke late and decided he needed more food. He didn't feel like going out, but he had to. He dressed, put his shoes on, and put the Apple Watch on his wrist.

He stared at it.

Rick had given him the watch. Apologized for wrongdoing.

How would he apologize for what he did now? With a Ferrari?

It wouldn't help this time. *Nothing* would.

David had grown to like the watch but had not worn it for the past few days. It reminded him too much of Rick. He took it off, opened the kitchen trash can, tossed it in, and closed the lid.

He didn't want to see it ever again.

He stared at the trash can. He opened it with his foot and stared down at the watch.

On second thought, it was a nice gadget that cost a few hundred bucks.

He fished it out of the trash and cleaned it. A loud knock on the door made him drop it. He cursed, picked it up, searched for scratches, and then cleaned it again.

When he peered out, he saw his next-door neighbor, Barton.

He didn't feel like having company. What did the neighbor want from him, anyway?

After a few minutes, Barton left.

Now David couldn't go to the grocery store. The neighbor would see him.

He decided to look at the Facebook app. He had been planning to do it for a while. There must be something else to help him find *Barbie and Ken*. He examined both of their profiles. Nothing had changed since their disappearance. Not surprising. What could he find there? Probably nothing. The FBI had already searched their profiles.

David saw their celebration selfie again. He hated it. He wished he could delete it. He needed Angela's Facebook account for that, but the FBI held her phone.

He wondered if he could guess her Facebook password but decided the FBI would be upset with him if he did.

He'd loved that picture a few days ago.

Now he hated it.

He untagged himself. Nothing left to celebrate.

David examined Rick's picture for a few minutes. *How could you do this to me? You son of a bitch. And to think you came to my door and asked me to forgive you for scratching my car.*

Or did he do this only to get to me? To hit on me, in a way? Had he planned this all along?

I was a wreck back then. Why would he want my help? Had he planned to get me back into shape and then screw me over?

Facebook was no use. He closed the app and stared at the ceiling.

He hoped they were dead.

———

Barton knocked on his door again an hour later, two bottles of beer in his hands. "May I come in?"

What did he want? David felt he'd had enough of knocking neighbors for a while.

He moved aside and let him in. The move he had for Rick.

Barton entered and sat on the couch. "I'm sorry to barge in on you like this, but I felt I had to talk to you. I saw the FBI fellas and put two and two together."

David nodded.

"We haven't had a chance to talk properly, but when I was young, about Rick's age, I had a roommate who lived off of me. He stayed with me in an apartment I rented, promised he'd pay half the rent but never did."

What does he want from me?

"One day I came back and my apartment was empty. I discovered he flew off the handle."

"He what?"

"He took my furniture and sold it," Barton said, "even stuff that came with the apartment. I ended up owing a lot of money and almost living on the street, but I pulled myself together and forgave him, paid my debts, and moved on."

Was that supposed to help me? Will I end up lonely like my old neighbor?

"I got married and had kids," Barton said, as if reading David's mind, "and the reason I'm here alone has nothing to do with what happened to me back then."

Barton nodded. His Southern accent seemed heavier than David had remembered. When he first moved to Tulsa, he had a hard time understanding the older people with heavy accents. He noticed he'd gotten used to it.

"The guy who ripped me off reminded me a lot of Rick. I wanted to tell you this for a while now, long before he disappeared. I should have said something but didn't think you'd want to listen."

Barton stayed for an hour. They drank beer and watched TV. Barton wanted to switch channels and asked for the *clicker*. When David didn't understand what he meant, Barton explained that clicker meant remote control. Before leaving, Barton said David could call him whenever he wanted.

Why are people being nice to me? Do they think I have money? Could I ever have new friends, like Barton or Bob?

David didn't need more friends. He thanked Barton and went to get snacks.

Day 9

In the middle of the night, someone knocked on his door.

235

Probably the FBI, he thought. *Maybe they have some news.*

They found the money?

They found them?

But the knocking sounded familiar. He had heard it before, many times.

The gentle knock. Not the strong, loud one.

Could it be...?

No way.

David shuffled to the door like an old man walking through deep water. He peered outside and couldn't believe his eyes.

THIRTY-SIX

"You have to let me talk to her," Bob said on the phone outside the police station in downtown Tulsa. "You can't do this to me."

Stuber exited the station and motioned for Bob to come in. Bob gestured *just a second* with his fingers and turned his back.

"Okay. Please have her call me when she wakes up." Bob paused, listening. "I'll try to be available." He looked back and saw Stuber still there. "I've got to go."

I'm a good father, he wanted to say but hung up.

"They finished searching her iPhone. There were no traces of any plans to steal, poison, or flee," Stuber said. "Unlike Rick's phone, nothing had been erased."

"That's odd. Why did she leave it like that on the bed for us to find?"

"Maybe they thought we wouldn't be able to crack it. Or maybe they wanted to throw us off track."

Bob nodded.

"Are you going to update your new friend?"

Bob rolled his eyes. "Not yet."

Day 1

The morning after Angela had dropped David at the airport, she received a call from her husband.

"You have to listen to me," Rick said. "We're in a mess. I can't explain right now, but I need you to do exactly as I say. Am I clear?"

"You're not making any sense. You're *scaring* me."

"Just do as I say. David double-crossed me. *Us.* I can only tell you now that he helped your *dad* find us. I'll explain when we meet, but we're in danger."

"*What?* This is crazy! Are you sure about this?"

"Of course I'm sure, Angela." Rick raised his voice. "Don't you trust me?"

"Of course I do, honey. But it's just...it's too hard for me to believe. What should we do? We have to call the police."

"I already did. They won't help because I don't have proof. I'm working on it. *Trust* me."

"Rick?"

"I gotta go. I'll call you in a few minutes. Start packing a small bag. Whatever you do, don't talk to David."

"Rick?"

He hung up.

———

The carry-on suitcase from her last trip to visit her mother lay half-unpacked in Angela's bedroom. She stared at it for a few minutes, mouth trembling. Usually she would unpack the day she returned from a trip, but this time she didn't. She couldn't explain why.

The phone rang, suddenly breaking the silence. "Did you pack?"

"What? No. Rick, you're scaring me."

"Angela!" Rick yelled at her like never before. "I need you to do as I say. Don't think. Just trust me. Our lives are in danger. Please, Angela. I love you. You have to trust me."

After a few seconds, she said, "Okay."

"Good. I have a spare phone in my drawer. Take it. There's an old barn about a twenty-minute drive from where we live." He gave her the address and general directions. He told her to memorize it, not to write it on paper or use a GPS. He told her to flush her iPhone down the toilet.

Angela turned her iPhone off and dropped it on her bed. She would hide it later. She finished packing her suitcase and found the flip phone Rick had left in his drawer.

She rushed out of the apartment. The way to her car was long and dark, even though the car was parked close and the sun still shone. Her hands were shaking, and tears filled her eyes. She looked at David's apartment as she passed it. She knew he wouldn't be there, but she tried to be quiet anyway. Was it possible David had double-crossed them? He had been a good friend. Maybe the best friend she had had in years, besides Rick. A great human being.

Or so I thought.

She drove in the direction Rick had told her as fast as she could, but not fast enough to get a ticket. Her man was in trouble. *They* were in trouble. Her heart raced.

Rick's in trouble because of me. He tried to protect me from my sick father. But what did David have to do with it? Rick will explain later.

It took her over two hours to find the barn he had mentioned. She couldn't remember Rick's directions precisely, so she had to search for it street by street. She entered the adjacent woods, as Rick had instructed her, and parked her car as deep inside as she could. She saw the barn from her parking spot and walked almost ten minutes to it, dragging her suitcase and clearing a path through the trees and bushes.

It looked old and damaged by time and rain and never repaired. Half of the building was closed and the other half open in three directions, like a gazebo. Most of the original white paint had peeled off, and the unpainted parts were gray. Black mold decorated some parts of the barn. As Angela got closer, she saw the remaining paint wouldn't last long.

All the windows of the closed part of the barn were boarded up. Bushes grew from inside the building through the cracks, trying to find their way to the light. She tried to peek inside and could see only darkness. It seemed as if someone wanted to protect it from a storm or to block anyone from looking in. She walked to the door and tried to open it, but it was bolted shut from the inside.

The door was partly red, which reminded her of blood. *Blood doesn't stay red after it dries*, she reminded herself.

A car passed on a road nearby. It was the closest thing to a human being she could hear. She went back to the open part of the barn and found a spot next to the wall, between two stacks of hay. She sat down and leaned against the wall.

Rick told her to make sure she couldn't be seen from the main road.

No one could see her.

When she felt cold, she opened her suitcase and took out a sweatshirt. It helped a little.

Angela sat there for a few hours. She couldn't call, text, or browse the internet. She forgot how dependent she had become on her smartphone to pass the time and to communicate. She wished she had brought a book or a magazine. She took out the old phone Rick had left her and examined it. She flipped it open, and a gray screen greeted her with little options to choose from. There were messages, contacts, and recent calls, all of which were empty. No one had used the phone. She missed the touch screen on her iPhone she had grown to like. The battery was half-full, and she hoped it would last until Rick got there. She wanted to call him. She wanted to call *someone*.

Rick had told her not to call anyone.

He also told her to get rid of her iPhone.

Shit, I forgot that!

Did I do it unconsciously? I hate losing my phone and everything on it. I love that phone.

From where she sat, she could only see the woods. Her car was parked inside there somewhere. A few hours after she had arrived, she heard a second car. Every once in a while, she could hear airplanes overhead, probably flying in and out of a nearby airport.

What on earth could David have done? Why the hell would he help her father? David was such a sweet man. Could he have stolen Rick's idea? How? Why? Did he tell them Rick wasn't a part of the company? Did he steal the money? Nothing made sense anymore.

I wish I could call David and ask him what the hell happened. What has he done to my husband?

She could talk to David and knock some sense into him. She knew him. They were friends. *Good* friends. She trusted him. They both trusted him.

She couldn't take it anymore, and despite Rick's orders, she tried to call her husband. It took her a few minutes to remember his phone number. She had been too dependent on her iPhone to remember anything.

But Rick didn't answer. It went straight to voicemail.

When the sun disappeared, it got colder. She took a scarf from her purse and covered herself on top of the sweatshirt. She hugged her shivering knees, not sure if they were more cold or scared.

Rick wouldn't just leave her like that, alone in the cold.

Maybe David had hurt him?

Oh my God!

David was a good-hearted soul. He wouldn't hurt anyone. He—

A branch cracked somewhere close to her. She almost rose but decided it would be better to stay low. If it was Rick, he'd know where to find her. He would call her name. He would call her phone.

But what if it was another man? A bad man? What if he wanted to hurt her? She couldn't go through it again.

The sound didn't seem to come any closer. Maybe it was just an animal. *A small, friendly animal.* After some time—she didn't know exactly how long—the cold became much worse. She rubbed her legs and arms. She tried not to make a sound. She remembered hearing it would be a cold night. She had planned to stay home, under a blanket with a warm drink, and watch TV.

Angela stopped caring if anyone was out there, so she stood and walked. She saw nothing. She jumped up and down, trying to get warm. It helped a little. She considered going for a run, but she might be seen from the road. She should not have listened to Rick. She should have taken a coat.

Or stayed at home.

Where the hell was he?

Did David really hurt him?

Did Rick leave me?

———

It felt like an hour later—maybe more—when a loud noise woke Angela and brought her to her feet. Even though she tried hard not to, she had fallen asleep on the cold floor. She rose slowly, almost stumbled, and peered into the dark.

She couldn't stay still any longer. She grabbed a stick she had found earlier, walked around in the dark, and waved it in front of her. She knew it wouldn't help much, but it made her feel safer. She wished she had her iPhone's flashlight.

She walked slowly, trying not to make any noise with her feet, ready to fight for her life if needed. She would kick and punch and scream if someone attacked her.

But no one would hear her in the middle of nowhere.

No one knew her location.

Except Rick.

Finding nothing, she returned to her hiding place, stick still in her hand, tears running down her cheeks.

After a while, Angela couldn't take it anymore. *Screw it.* She considered calling the police but couldn't explain where she was. She should go back home. She would call Da—*Damn!* She couldn't call David. But she would call the police. She needed help.

She picked up her small suitcase and walked toward the woods in her car's direction. The first time she fell was not so bad, only a small scratch on her hand, but the next few falls were worse. Each one hurt more as the bushes and trees she couldn't see scratched her legs and arms. They went through her clothes. When she thought she was close to her car, she hit a tree head on, banging her forehead hard. She lost her balance and fell onto a bush. She felt blood running down into her eyes.

Angela sat on her suitcase and for a few minutes couldn't stop crying.

She reached her car. Or at least where she thought she had parked it.

But her car was gone.

She kept looking for over an hour, one arm stretched out, trying not to hit another tree, but it didn't stop her from hitting a few branches and falling again. She found nothing. Either she was way off or someone had stolen her car.

Who could have found my car in the middle of nowhere?

If someone found my car, they could find me. She shivered.

She could go to the main road and ask for help.

She couldn't betray her husband. She tried calling him again with no luck. She would give him another chance.

If she hitchhiked, with her luck, she would probably get kidnapped by a murderer.

Or worse, a rapist.

————

Finding the barn again took a long time. When Angela finally saw it in the distance, she almost ran. She parked her suitcase and sat back in her hiding place. She wanted Rick to come get her. She wanted *anyone* to come get her. *Maybe even David.* She only wanted a shower and a warm bed.

She decided she would wait until morning and then go to the road and ask for help—from a woman—or call the police from the old flip phone and try to explain to them where she was.

Day 2

Angela must have fallen asleep again because someone—a man—woke her.

She jumped like a wounded lioness defending her cubs.

She pushed him away and searched for the stick. She couldn't find it.

"Angela! *Angela!* It's *me!*" he shouted.

He knew her name.

She knew his voice.

Thank God.

Rick.

"Where the hell have you been?" She hit him in the chest with both hands but not much force. She burst out crying.

"I'm sorry," he said. "I'm sorry." He hugged her. "Come on." He took her hand.

Rick helped her walk to the other side of the barn; his other hand grabbed her suitcase. Part of the sun appeared somewhere. She'd waited all night, outside the barn, in the cold, alone. Rick took out a set of keys and unlocked the door. They went in; he closed the door and locked it.

"What time is it?"

"A little after six," Rick said after looking at his phone. He had switched to the same old-model flip phone.

"You left me outside the barn the whole night."

"I know. I'm sorry." Rick hugged her again. His muscular body made her feel safe.

Angela examined the cabin. The floor was constructed of old wood, uneven with many bushes and other unidentified plants growing out of the cracks. She had already seen the big ones, which grew outside the windows.

In the corner, she could see an old desk and chair next to it. She also saw a small sink and an old, small twin-sized bed. Rick helped her walk to the bed. She sat on it, trembling.

"Go to sleep. We'll talk when you get up," he said.

"No! Talk to me *now*. What the hell happened?"

"Okay. But at least lie down. You need the rest. Please."

She felt exhausted, so she did as he said. Rick covered her with an old, dusty blanket, which had been on the bed for a long time.

He sat down next to her, glanced at her, at his feet, then at the rest of the cabin. He examined the walls, the ceiling, and the floor. Only when she touched his hand did he look back at her.

He crossed his legs, his right foot shaking. "When I reached New York, I went to the investor. When I got there, they told me David had already taken the money, and they were surprised to see me there."

"He was half-dead in his apartment when you left. I made him soup."

"He must have faked it, which is why he didn't go with me to New York."

"It doesn't make any sense. I dropped him at the airport the next day."

Rick seemed to consider this. "He went to the investor a few days before I arrived. He must've fled the country when you dropped him at the airport."

"But why? How? I don't get it. He *loved* you. He *adored* you. You were his ticket out of his miserable life. Why would he do such a thing?"

"*Money*. He didn't have much savings left, and it was a way to make quick money and get away with it. I called him and he confessed. He even laughed at me."

"I can't believe it."

"I couldn't believe it either. He also said he would kill *you* if I went to the police."

"*What?*" she screamed. "David would never hurt me."

"That's what I thought. But he swore he would. He told me the poor woman he almost married had to get a restraining order against him." He looked at her feet.

"Mia? He told me she betrayed him."

"He's a pathological liar."

Angela coughed hard and almost choked.

Rick stroked her hair and then her back. "Get some rest, honey. We need to disappear. I'm afraid he'll come looking for us."

He helped her lie down again, and after a few minutes, she fell asleep. She dreamed they were locked in the barn by a snowstorm.

She woke later that day to see Rick sleeping next to her on the floor.

Day 8

After a week, which felt like a month, Angela said they must go to the police.

"Angela, I told you a million times already. We *can't*."

"But we didn't do anything wrong."

"He's crazy. We don't know what he'll do to us."

"The police will protect us. They'll put him in jail."

"We can't."

"What do you mean? Why not?"

Rick stood and, with a swift move, kicked the only chair in the room. It fell with a loud crash.

Angela jumped.

Rick picked it up. "I'm sorry. It's just...he has something

on me," he said. "If we go to the police, he'll tell them. I'll go to jail too."

Angela's eyes opened wide. "What would he have on you? He's the sweetest guy I ever met!"

Rick turned his head and stared at her. His eyes were furious. He raised his hand in the air as if to hit her.

Angela drew back.

"Your sweet *guy*," he said, "is not the guy you know. He's a maniac. Maybe he's bipolar. He had it planned since he met me. He—"

"*You* had the ulterior motive ever since you met *him*!"

"*I* only wanted to help him get in shape and open a business with him. He took advantage of me the first chance he got."

Angela held her head with her hands. "I need a shower, a proper bed, and a toilet. I can't wash my armpits in the sink anymore. I can't go to the bathroom in the bushes outside anymore. *Please*."

They had developed a daily routine. Rick encouraged her to work out with him. They went for walks around the barn every night. It helped a little, but she felt as if she had fallen into a garbage truck. She felt like an animal in a cage.

"You're right. I'm sorry. I'll take care of it. *Today*. I promise. We've laid low long enough. We'll go to a motel tonight."

She hated motels, but at this point, it felt like going to a castle.

"Then we'll leave the country. Maybe go to Mexico. You remember we always said we wanted to go there?"

"For *vacation*. I don't want to *live* there. I can't leave my mother, my studies. I want my life back." After a while, she said, "Rick, be honest with me. What does David have on you?"

Rick checked the floor. "You remember when I got home with a black eye?"

She nodded.

"It wasn't a bar fight. I had a fight with your dad's goons. They overpowered me, but eventually I found a knife and stabbed one of them. The other one ran away, but the one I stabbed...Angela, he *died*. I hid his body in the woods next to our apartment building."

She covered her face with her hands, then she rubbed the back of her neck. Even though she wanted to, she couldn't cry anymore. "I don't believe this."

"Me neither. I feel like I'm in a dream."

"You *killed* a man?"

"He was a professional killer, Angela, no one to cry about. It was self-defense. I protected *you*."

She tried to nod. "What's David got to do with this?"

"He saw me digging. He knows. He even helped me. But after he stole the money, he said he would go to the cops if I said anything. He kept the knife."

Angela lay in bed, covered herself with a blanket, and found more tears, which went straight to her dusty pillow.

———

Later that day, Rick told Angela he had to run an errand. He didn't tell her where or why. "I'll take care of it, as I promised."

For the first time in her life, she didn't believe him. The David she knew couldn't do those things. And Rick couldn't kill a man.

But could he lie? To me?

When Rick returned, he refused to tell her where he had been. After he fell asleep that night on the floor, she stepped over him, walking as quietly as she could. She used the keys he had left on the desk to open the door. The door squeaked, and she froze. She looked back at Rick. He didn't open his eyes.

Angela shut the door behind her and walked to his car. She had seen him park in the bushes, much closer than she had to park her car. They argued about that, but he convinced her they needed *his* car, which David didn't know. David knew her car, so it had to remain hidden.

She used the keys to enter his car. She had never seen this one, even older than the one he had replaced the Camaro with. He told her he had bought another used car after he returned from New York so David wouldn't recognize it. He paid cash for it without knowing whether it would run.

She searched the trunk, glove box, under the floor mats, everywhere. She found nothing.

As she started back toward the barn, she remembered a movie she'd seen where some bad guy stashed drugs under the floor of the trunk where the spare tire should be.

She took a minute to figure out how to get it to open. Even though she grew up without a father and lived alone for a few years, she found it embarrassing to admit she always needed a man to help her with vehicle stuff.

So much for being a feminist.

When she opened the tire cover, her mouth fell open and she almost yelled.

Instead of a spare tire, she saw cash. A lot of cash.

She closed the trunk and looked around. *No one around.* She ran back to the barn.

Where the hell did all that money come from?

As she opened the door, she tried to think where he could have gotten the money. No scenario made sense.

She entered the barn and screamed at Rick.

He rose fast, startled.

"Relax, would ya? And close the door." He gestured for her to sit down on the bed.

He rose and walked back and forth aimlessly, looking around the barn but not at her. His face turned red. Then he said something Angela had never expected to hear from him. "Don't you ever go behind my back again, you fucking bitch."

Angela's mouth opened slowly. *Did I hear him correctly? He's never spoken to me that way before. Ever.*

He raised his big hand and simply slapped her on the cheek. Hard. She didn't even raise a hand to defend herself. Her mouth opened wider, her eyes got wet, and her cheek hurt as if someone put it onto a burning stove.

Her eyes blinked a million times a second.

The man she had married, the man she loved, had hit her. "Stay here," he said and went out.

She sat on the bed, crying, her cheek red and hurting.

When he returned, she looked up at him, amazed and ashamed.

When Rick had gotten mad at her one time before, she had thought he might have it in him, but it was only that one time, and he had never actually hit her. He had promised he would never be like her father.

Then he spoke, hardly moving his lips. "I'm sorry, honey. I am."

Just like a typical abuser.

She didn't reply.

"I'm sorry I lied to you. I took the money. Not David. I didn't know how to tell you this, so I lied. And I'm sorry I hit you." He tried to touch her, but she pushed him away.

"We can run away to Mexico together or anywhere else.

We're rich now. No need to chase people to pay us anymore."

After about an hour, she said, "I can't do it. I can't. You can return the money. We can explain it was a mistake."

Rick gave her a bottle of water and told her she needed to relax. They would discuss it later. Angela felt exhausted. She lay on the bed and fell asleep for a long time. When she woke, Rick had disappeared.

Along with the items he had brought.

Angela burst outside but couldn't find his car.

THIRTY-SEVEN

Day 9

David opened the kitchen drawer and stared at the big knife he'd considered taking his life with a few days ago. He took it out even though his hand trembled. He walked back to the door, peered outside again, and put the knife behind his back.

For a second, he felt stupid. A knife? Against *her*?

After what they did, you never know.

Rick could be right behind her.

David stared at the knife. He felt like a pretty young woman in a cheap horror movie.

In this case, he was not the pretty young woman.

What the hell is she doing there? What does she want?

He opened the door slowly, only his head showing at first. He hated to admit it, but she looked almost as beautiful as before. She wasn't wearing any makeup. He thought he saw some traces of old makeup smudged badly underneath her eyes. Her cheeks were red. Her forehead had scabs on it. A few more cuts went through the rest of her perfect face.

She had been crying. She still was. Her hands trembled.

She looked like an amazing flower that hadn't been watered for a long time.

He wanted to hug her and slap her at the same time.

He would never slap a woman. He would never slap *her*.

Did she come to apologize?

She didn't apologize.

Did she come to attack me?

She didn't do that either.

Then he remembered the FBI or the police should be outside.

Why didn't they arrest her?

David stuck his head outside the apartment, causing her to move backward to get out of his way. He checked the parking lot. No FBI or unmarked police car. No Rick in sight either.

He drew back into his apartment, the knife still behind his back.

"Wait here," he said. "I'll call the Feds."

"*Wait*," she said and held his hand.

His heart raced as though she'd never betrayed him.

Or maybe because she had.

"Why? You stole from me. You two are wanted criminals. You both should be in jail. You two helped me up just to kick me down again into a much bigger pile of shit." He tried not to look at her face. "If I wasn't a gentleman, I'd kick your ass right now."

"Please. Let me explain first."

For the first time he looked at her from top to bottom. He had never let himself *check her out* while she stood in front of him. This time he looked at her differently. She wore a sweatshirt and jeans, but it felt too cold for that. Her shoes and clothes were dirty. The bottoms of her jeans were torn.

What the hell happened to her?

He considered giving her a chance. He wanted to be wrong. He wanted to be wrong about her. About them.

He heard a door slam somewhere.

He moved aside and let her in.

"You have ten minutes before I call the FBI," he said and fished his phone out of his pocket.

She nodded and walked in.

———

Being a gentleman, David gave Angela water, but nothing more. He had to put the knife back in the kitchen drawer anyway. He couldn't risk her coming in and literally stabbing him in the back with his own kitchen knife. He hoped she had not seen it.

He found Bob's number; his finger hovered over it, ready to dial it at a moment's notice.

She told him her story, everything that happened since the day she left. David listened carefully, hung onto her every word. At first, he found it hard to believe. *No way she wasn't involved. She knew nothing about this? Rick screwed her over as well?*

He wanted to believe her.

When Angela told him Rick had hit her, his heart pounded. He struggled between not believing her story and not believing Rick could hurt her. *Especially after what she's been through with her dad? I hope I get the chance to chase Rick with a kitchen knife and stab him. In the back.*

And then to twist the knife.

"After he hit me"—she had tears in her eyes—"I fell asleep for a long time. Probably over ten hours. I think he put something in my water to get me to sleep."

David wanted to stand and hug her but couldn't.

"When I got up"—she tried to wipe her tears—"he was gone. He didn't leave me money, a car, or even the phone I had. I left the barn and walked to the road. I couldn't go into the woods and search for my car again. I think I walked for over two or three hours. Five different men stopped and offered me help on the way. Thank God they didn't try to hurt or kidnap me. Eventually, an elderly lady stopped and offered to help me. She drove out of her way and brought me here. She was so nice, waited until I entered the building."

"Is she still here?"

"No, she left a long time ago." She looked down. "I think I waited almost an hour until I knocked on your door."

———

"You expect me to believe you didn't know what he planned?" David asked after a while.

"I don't expect you to believe anything I say, but you know me better than that. I made a mistake by *believing* in my husband. I didn't know his plans to steal from you. I don't even know what really happened. The only thing I knew was he had planned the start-up thing *before* he met you. When we moved here, he looked you up online and said you'd make a great partner. I saw nothing wrong with that. I thought he pushed you at times, and I told him that, but that's it. Nothing criminal. I swear."

So he did plan this all along.

Should I believe her?

"You can't go into your apartment. They locked it."

"I don't even have the keys."

That's why she came here.

"What really happened, David?" she asked.

He told her. She listened carefully, shaking her head at times, trying not to cry at others.

"You can shower here, if you want." He couldn't believe he said that. "I'll get you some clothes, and you can get some rest. And food, if you want. You can sleep here, on the couch."

He never thought he would talk to her that way.

"I'm not hungry."

"I have the number of the agent in charge. Do you want me to call him now? He'll need to talk to you."

"Would you mind if we called him first thing tomorrow morning?" Angela looked at him like a puppy begging its master not to toss him outside after pooping on the floor.

For the first time since they'd met, David felt on top.

Day 10

It took David a long time to fall asleep. He thought about what had happened and how misled he had been. He still couldn't trust her a hundred percent. He had considered keeping the knife close to him but decided it was ridiculous. She borrowed his phone for an hour, and he overheard her talking to her mother. She told her a different story than the one she told him.

Does she not want her to worry, or did she also lie to me?

The following morning, he found her asleep on the couch. He sat in the recliner next to her, trying to be quiet, and stared at her. She had put on his sweat pants and shirt after she had taken a long shower the previous night.

I'll never wash those clothes again.

She woke after a long time.

"I'm sorry if I woke you, but I have to call the agent."

She nodded.

He called Bob, who arrived after fifteen minutes. *Did he come with sirens blazing?*

"Before you arrest her—just listen to her story. Please."

Bob looked at him with his eyebrows to the ceiling. Then he lowered them and nodded. He came in, sat down, and examined Angela, her clothes, the apartment, and then David.

"When did she arrive?" Bob asked him.

"In the middle of night. When I was sleeping."

"And you didn't call me because...?" Bob tilted his head.

David looked at Angela, then back at Bob. "It was the middle of the night."

"So?" Bob clenched his fists.

"You were probably asleep."

"A key person in a federal investigation comes to your apartment in the middle of the night, and you don't want to *wake* me? I should put you in jail just for that!"

"I asked him not to. I felt disoriented and couldn't talk anymore. Please don't be mad at him."

Bob looked at Angela, at David, then back at Angela.

David knew what he thought.

"Listen, she's a *victim*. Like me. She went through hell. I couldn't put her through another interrogation before getting a shower and a good night's sleep."

Angela almost smiled at him.

David surprised himself. *Do I believe her?*

Bob struck the table with his index finger. "If she's

found guilty, I'll have to think of what I'm gonna do with you."

David exhaled and nodded.

Angela told her story. Bob listened carefully, nodded a lot, and took notes. David had a chance to look at Angela from the side and noticed he felt bad for her. Bob asked a few questions: Did Rick tell her where he went? What kind of car did Rick drive? And what did Rick wear?

In the middle of the interrogation, the other agent joined them. Bob seemed mad at him for being late but said nothing.

"Do you remember where he took you?"

She nodded. "I can find it."

"Are you up for a drive?"

The four of them went in the agent's car. Angela sat in the front seat. From behind, David could examine her better. Even after a shower and sleep, she still seemed a few years older.

But she still looks amazing.

He tried to shake the thought away.

They got out of town to a rural area. It took Angela over forty minutes to find the barn. Bob parked the car nearby, almost next to the road. Angela seemed to have a hard time looking at the barn.

"Wait in the car." Bob examined her.

Is he considering cuffing her?

Bob examined David.

The agent didn't trust him anymore.

Bob and Stuber went into the barn, guns drawn like in the movies. Agent Stuber remained at the door; Bob entered the unlocked barn. Angela probably didn't bother to lock it on her way out.

Stuber peeked inside and looked at them every few minutes, his gun still in his hands.

David examined the barn from the outside. It looked ancient and in bad condition. He found it hard to believe that Rick had forced her to stay there. Bob remained inside for less than five minutes. When he came out, his gun back in its holster, he searched for Angela first. He seemed relieved to find her still in the car.

Bob made a long phone call, and they returned to the car. "Nothing there. I'll have a team go through it more thoroughly soon."

The agents dropped them back at David's apartment. "Don't go anywhere," Bob barked. He returned after a few hours and told them they had investigated the barn, and all the signs seemed to corroborate Angela's story.

"Did you find any signs of where the asshole went?"

Angela turned her head to David.

"I can't tell you everything, but we may have a lead." Bob looked at her. "We also examined your phone. David helped us unlock it."

Angela glared at David as if he had betrayed her. He felt bad, but what could he have done?

"It helped clear you. We believe you planned your life without this interruption."

She nodded.

"It'll be a couple of days until we can let you get back into your apartment. We'll give you your phone back by then as well." Bob looked at David, then at Angela. "Do you have anywhere you can stay until then?"

Angela examined David. He nodded at her.

"I'll be fine," she told the agent.

After Bob left, David went to his bedroom and lay on his bed. He returned after an hour and found Angela lying on the couch, covered with a blanket up to her nose, staring at the ceiling.

She's alone and afraid. Like me.

"You can stay here, if you want. I'll get the guest room ready for you. I should have a folding bed somewhere. I'll set it up. It's a small room, and it can get cold in there sometimes, but it'll do for now." He sat down next to her. "You can stay as long as you need."

"You fixed the folding bed?" For the first time since she returned, she smiled.

She hugged him. At first, he did nothing. Then he hugged her back.

She cried on his shoulder and didn't let go of him for a few minutes.

———

"How was your nap?" David asked Angela from his recliner as she came out of the guest bedroom.

"Good." She almost smiled. "I'm still catching up on my sleep." She sat on the couch close to him.

"Are you hungry?"

"No. Thank you," she said.

That's why she stays so thin, he thought. *She doesn't eat.*

"Are you sure? Did he give you any food?"

"He brought bagels and some canned food. Not much, but enough to survive."

"I don't think you've eaten in the past twenty-four hours, have you?"

She thought about it. "Probably not. But I'm not hungry."

"That's funny," he said, "when I get upset, the only thing I want to do is eat. Like a normal person."

She smiled. He could see a fraction of her teeth again.

———

They watched a comedy on TV, then a late-night show.

Angela sat on the couch, legs folded underneath her, covered with a blanket. David wished she'd ask him to come next to her and snuggle.

Did he still feel angry at her? He tried not to let the anger go but found it hard. He believed her story. Even Bob believed it. But David had been so upset with her in the last few days, he had a hard time letting it go.

But she was a victim. Same as him.

And she was now single, wasn't she?

Kind of.

"Are you sure Rick won't come looking for us?" he asked out of nowhere.

Angela gazed at the TV. "I thought I knew him. I thought he'd never hurt anyone, especially not me." She looked at David. "But I don't know him anymore."

———

That night he dreamed she came into his bedroom after a shower, wearing nothing but a robe.

The guest room is too cold, she said. *Would you mind if I slept in your room?*

THIRTY-EIGHT

Day 11

"Were you cold in the guest room?" David asked Angela over breakfast.

"No, it was great. Thanks again for letting me stay."

He nodded. "Did you sleep well?"

She shook her head. "I keep waking up. I get these dreams..."

Like mine?

"What kind of dreams?"

"Nightmares."

Not like mine.

"What about?"

"About Rick and about my father." She seemed to force herself to eat. "They both chase me, sometimes together, sometimes just one of them, and try to hurt me. It happens in different places and different situations, but it's basically the same thing over and over. I guess it's my version of PTSD."

The mad look on his face turned to bewilderment.

"Posttraumatic stress disorder."

David nodded as if he understood. He would have to look it up online.

She cleaned the table as he put the dishes in the dishwasher.

"You want to go for a walk today? I need to get back in shape."

She shook her head. "I don't think so."

That's it. She wants to move out. I was too harsh with her when she came back.

"I'd rather go shopping. I need some clothes."

"You don't like my clothes?"

"I need something more my size. No offense. Would you like to join me?"

"Of course. Being your shopping friend and all."

They smiled.

"It's great to see you smile again," he said.

"Thanks. You too."

———

Angela borrowed money from David to buy clothes. After that, they had lunch and went to a movie.

When they sat in the theater together, he could almost imagine they were on a date. For an hour and a half, he didn't care if he ever got a job again, if the FBI found Rick, or how he would pay back his debts. Maybe he didn't need to be Steve Jobs anymore.

Even getting stabbed in the back by his former best friend—again—didn't seem to matter much anymore.

Rick may have stolen a million dollars from me, but he left something much more valuable.

Day 12

Bob returned the next morning with Angela's suitcase. He examined her lying down on the couch, watching TV, and turned to David with a question mark over his head and almost a smile, but he said nothing.

I don't care, David thought. *He can arrest us both, if he wants.*

"I came to ask if you knew where Angela was." Bob turned to Angela, who sat up as she noticed him looking at her.

She smiled, but her lips were flat.

He knew she was staying here. Is he testing us or just teasing?

Bob leaned the suitcase against the wall and sat down on the couch. "I have some good news." The agent opened his bag and took out her iPhone. When he handed it to her, her smile curved.

"I missed it." She unlocked it with her thumb and searched for messages.

She looked disappointed. *Was she looking for messages from Rick?*

She seemed totally immersed with it when Bob said, "You can go back to your apartment."

"What?" She looked up at him.

"We had to replace the lock we broke, so here's a new set of keys." Bob handed her the keys.

"You know you *could* have asked the complex management for a set of keys." David grinned, leaned back, and put his hands behind his head.

But then he saw Angela's face brighten as she looked at the keys.

His heart sank.

———

The three of them went to see the apartment. It looked as if thieves had broken in and didn't find what they were looking for. The FBI had left nothing unopened or intact.

Angela stared at the inside of the apartment with tears in her eyes.

For the first time since David had met Bob, the agent seemed uncomfortable. "I'm sorry for the mess."

Angela nodded.

"Do you want me to help you clean it?" David asked.

"I'm not sure I can stay here."

"You want to grab some clothes, personal stuff, and come back to my place?" David couldn't believe his own ears.

Bob stared at him.

Angela nodded, slowly. Her lips thanked him, but no sound came out.

Bob left them, promising to be in touch. David helped Angela clear a path and helped her pack. She found a big bag and put her belongings in it. He carried it down to his apartment as Angela walked silently behind him, carrying nylon bags filled with clothes.

He wondered how many clothes she needed. He hoped it meant she planned to stay for a while, but he also knew women liked to have too many clothes. Just to be safe. When they reached his apartment, he opened the door and let her in first. He put the bag in her room—*hmm, in the guest room*—and brought her suitcase from the living room. She stared at it, lips trembling.

"Do you want me to take it to your apartment or throw it away?"

"No. It's okay. You can leave it here. Thanks."

He could never tell her he was happy that she couldn't stay in the upstairs apartment. In *her* apartment.

He was having a good night's sleep, with a nice dream, when he woke abruptly to the sensation of huge, thick hands choking him.

THIRTY-NINE

Day 13

Angela?

It couldn't be—

The hands were too big. Too strong. The person attached to them, holding David down, was much too big to be Angela.

David squinted fast and tried to adjust his vision to the darkness.

He tried to breathe.

"Wh—"

He could hardly open his mouth.

Was it Rick?

Did Angela let him in?

He tried to grab the man's arms and push them away from him, away from his throat. The man's arms were thick —David couldn't close his fingers around them. He pulled on them as hard as he could. He tried to push them away from his throat. When it didn't work, he tried to push them in any direction he could.

The big arms reacted like the iron bars of a prison cell.

David tried to use his legs. He raised and pushed them toward the big man's head. He tried to kick the man's head.

Could it be Rick?

His legs wouldn't go there. He couldn't reach the big man.

The huge hands deprived his brain of oxygen for too long, and he went crazy. He tried to push every part of his body in every direction possible. It didn't help at all.

He knew he would die.

He *wanted* to die.

But then he remembered Angela in the other room.

If she had not let him in, and if this big man found her, he could...

Oh God!

He found new strength and tried to resist, but it was like an ant trying to push a bear.

He had no air.

"Where's the money?" the big man asked.

It's not Rick.

"W—"

The big man let David's poor throat go.

Air flew inside his lungs. He sat up, coughed hard, and gasped for more air.

When he came to his senses, he knew he had to go to Angela. He used all the force he had in him and shoved his arms at the big man.

Pushing a huge, thick tree would have been easier.

The thick tree in front of him wouldn't budge.

The Tree sent a huge fist into David's face, almost making a hole in it.

It hurt like hell.

He had never been punched in the face before.

He had never been choked either.

"If you move again without my permission," the Tree said in a thick voice, "I'll kill ya."

David noticed the Tree also had a gun.

He heard a scream from the other bedroom.

Angela.

She didn't let him in. Good.

But it also meant she was in danger.

He tried to stand, ignoring the Tree.

But the Tree hit him again in the face. Softer this time.

David felt dizzy and could only stare at the ceiling. Did he lose consciousness?

A few seconds or even minutes later, he started to get his bearings back. From somewhere far away he heard her squeaking, "I told you I don't know where he is!"

Angela.

He wanted to stand again, but the Tree still stood there.

Someone else is in the apartment.

He had to get to her but couldn't overpower the Tree.

He searched for his iPhone. It had been next to him, on the nightstand, where it was placed every night.

But it was not there.

Had the Tree taken it?

The Tree noticed his gaze, grabbed him by the arm, and dragged him out of his bed. The grip hurt, but after the first punch, nothing resembled that pain.

David fell off the bed, and, even though he had expected that, it startled him. He felt his body collapsing in on itself. He had enough time to put his arms down so they would absorb most of the hit, and the pain ran through them to the rest of his already aching body.

Thank God for the damn thick carpets in this apartment.

The Tree dragged him to the living room, as if David were a weightless blanket.

David saw Angela, who shrieked when she saw him on the floor. "Leave him alone!" she screamed.

She seemed unhurt.

She cares.

The second man, who seemed a little smaller than the Tree, sat on David's recliner with a gun in his hand.

"Shut the fuck up," the second man told her and raised the gun as if to hit her.

David wanted to scream but couldn't. He was still trying to get air into his lungs. If the second man hit Angela, he would rise and hit him. They could both shoot him for all he cared.

The Tree told David to get up and sit on the couch. He grabbed his arm to help him.

"I told you," Angela said, talking to the second man but looking sideways at David, "we don't know where the *money* is, and we don't know where *Rick* is. We've also been looking for him. He abducted me. He almost killed me. He stole the money from us. Please don't hurt David any more. *Please.*"

David could see tears in her eyes.

For him?

Her last words made his suffering hurt a little less.

He examined the men, who were looking at each other. He had seen them before. Their huge bodies. They were wearing gloves, but their faces were exposed.

In the movies, that would mean they had no plans to let them live.

———

The Tree searched behind David's TV, under the TV stand, and inside the drawers. He then returned to the back of the TV and seemed to unplug it.

You don't want us watching TV? David almost said out loud, but decided the joke was not worth another hit to the face.

The Tree searched under the coffee table, in its drawer, and under the couch. While searching, he kept looking at David. The big man entered his bedroom for a few minutes, opened, closed, and dropped things. Then he searched the kitchen and Angela's room.

David wondered if he should make a move. Try to attack. But he still hurt, and they were too strong. They also had guns.

Not a good time to try to resist. They would kill him.

They would kill *them.*

"You don't know anything either?" The second man glared at David from his beloved recliner, not moving the gun from Angela.

David shook his hurting head.

"Even if this guy hits you again? I think he almost killed you in there."

They laughed.

David nodded; his eyelids twitched.

"Even if he hurts *her*, like he did you?"

David clenched his teeth until they hurt.

After a minute, he nodded.

His head started to clear, and he remembered where he had seen them before. He should have recognized them earlier, but his head hurt too much, and it was too dark. They were the two muscle men who'd come looking for Angela when they hid in his apartment.

The muscle men her dead dad had supposedly sent.

David and Angela stared at each other. He could tell she had recognized them long ago.

They didn't seem to care about Angela. They only wanted Rick and the money. They had been there before Rick stole the money. Rick had said he paid them, but he was a liar.

Rick stole the money and didn't even pay them?

Everyone wants the money I don't have.

His head hurt. His nose hurt more.

Out of nowhere, the man from the recliner jumped. He looked down at David, then leaned toward Angela, held her jaw with his big hand, and squeezed it.

Angela screamed.

David tried to stand, mumbling, but the Tree pushed him back down onto the couch.

The second man turned to him, still holding her face, and said, "I won't hurt her. Don't try to play hero. We don't hurt women. Unless we have to."

Great. Goons with a code.

"We're keeping you both alive 'cause we may need you. If you hear from Rick, text this number immediately." The second man put a note on the table.

"Don't call the police *or* the FBI. We'll know if you do. They may promise to protect you, and maybe they'll be able to protect you for a few days, but we'll be back the day *after* they're gone. *Are we clear?*"

Angela nodded. So did David.

The muscle men left.

———

"Are you okay?" Angela sprang to David as soon as the door closed.

273

He wanted to play hero and tell her nothing hurt, but he shook his head.

Angela helped him lie down on the couch. She brought wet paper towels and cleaned his wounds gently.

"I think they broke my nose."

She examined his face and nodded. "You look terrible."

"Thanks."

She brought a blanket and tucked him in, the same way as when he had been sick. She sat next to him on the other couch and tried to stop the bleeding.

For a few seconds, it was worth the pain.

"What do we do?" Angela said. "We must call the FBI."

"I don't know; they seemed serious about not talking to them. They said they would know if we did."

"How will they know?"

"I don't know." He tried to shrug, but it hurt.

He recalled the Tree had searched around the TV area. Maybe the big man wasn't searching? Maybe he *left* them something?

David tried to stand. Angela told him not to, but when she saw his persistence she helped him up. He tried to remember what the Tree did.

The Tree unplugged something from behind the TV.

David looked there but saw nothing. He searched under the cable box and behind the TV stand. He almost gave up when he noticed a small black flash drive in the USB slot.

He never had one of those.

When Angela opened her mouth to say something, he shushed her with his index finger.

The USB drive didn't have a flashing light like in the movies. He pulled it out and checked it. It seemed like a regular, normal flash drive.

"This must be it." He showed her. "They left us with a bugging device."

"Shh!" She raised her finger to her mouth.

"Don't worry. It shouldn't work without a power source. It's disconnected."

They stared at it.

"I have an idea. I'll plug it back in. Just play along."

She nodded. He put the device back and sat on the couch.

"I think we should go somewhere and hide. Let's go to a hotel. Okay?"

"Good idea."

She didn't act well. She was a bad liar. He had known that all along.

I should have known she wouldn't cooperate with Rick on such a scam.

But she said yes to going to a hotel with him.

"Go pack. Let's go in fifteen minutes."

He glanced outside the window and saw no traces of the muscle men. They made some packing noises, and after a while he gestured for her to open and close the door. He went to the back of the TV and pulled out the bugging device, took it to the kitchen, found a hammer, and put the bugging device on the floor. Angela looked at him quietly.

After he broke it into a few pieces, he tossed it in the trash can.

"I thought you said it didn't work without power."

"Just wanted to make sure." He smiled. "I saw the Tree Man's face when I smashed it."

Angela laughed.

"Also Rick's face."

She stopped laughing.

Later she told him he needed to rest. She helped him to

the bed, picked up his iPhone and Apple Watch from the floor, and put them beside him on the bed.

She leaned in and kissed him—on the cheek, on the side that hurt less—but for a few seconds, his eyes sparkled.

"Thank you," she whispered.

"Don't mention it."

After she left, he fell asleep.

———

While they waited for Agent Bob, David told Angela he had seen them before.

"Same muscle men my father sent."

She doesn't know about her dad. She really doesn't know. Should I tell her?

"He told me he paid them. And it was before he stole the money."

"He did?" Her blue eyes almost melted him.

"Angela." He wanted to stroke her hair but didn't. "I think Rick lied to you about that too. To both of us. I don't think it had anything to do with your father. I think they were looking for Rick this whole time, not you."

Her eyebrows drew together.

"Angela," he said. "It had nothing to do with your dad."

"How do you know?"

"The FBI searched for him. They discovered your dad died ten years ago."

"*What?*" Her eyes dropped to the floor and filled with tears.

Did she cry over her dad? Or over Rick? She despised her dad, but hearing news like that couldn't be easy for anyone.

"Why did he lie about that as well?"

David wanted to hug her. "I don't know yet. He must've planned it all along. My theory is he owed them some money, but they wanted more when they discovered he stole a million dollars."

"But why did he let me get scared like that?"

David lowered his eyes and shook his head. "I don't know."

FORTY

Bob copied the muscle men's phone number and took the bugging device David had fished out of the trash.

"Too bad you smashed it," the agent said, almost to himself. "But good idea about the hotel thing. Maybe you should go to one, just to be safe." He looked at David. "If you don't, at least hide your car as best as you can, and try not to be noticed, especially if you leave the apartment."

David nodded.

Bob examined his face. "You should see a doctor. He roughed you up really bad. I think they broke your nose."

David nodded. He never liked doctors.

"Rick had another bank account, alone"—Bob looked at Angela—"which he took a few loans out of."

"It would explain a lot," David said.

"He even paid most of his debts on this account on time."

"Odd," David said.

"We're guessing he paid the legal loans with the money he stole or borrowed."

David nodded.

"I had no idea," Angela said.

"I'll send a technician to check for fingerprints," Bob said.

"They wore gloves," Angela said.

"I'll send them anyway, just to make sure. Maybe they can get DNA samples. And I also want to make sure they didn't leave any other bugs. Don't touch or move anything. If they installed more bugs, the hotel thing won't work, and I'll have a police car patrol the area all the time."

Bob left.

More bugs? I should have thought of that.

"Do you think we should really go to a hotel?" Angela asked.

"Do *you* want to go?"

She said nothing.

"Let's stay here. We can get a bar for the door. Maybe even an alarm. Okay?"

She nodded.

"I'll go move the car." He drove it to a different parking spot, farthest from his apartment, his only license plate facing a bush. Then he walked slowly back to Angela.

Day 15

"I'm feeling much better today."

"I don't believe you."

"Are you calling me a liar?"

"If you insist on not seeing a doctor, let's at least go for a jog." Angela smiled and reminded David of how Rick had nagged him to work out. He decided not to share the irony. They left from the back side of the building and ended up walking. He hated to admit it, but his head and body still hurt from the encounter with the Tree and his wing man.

"It's okay," she said, "I'm also not in shape. Rick didn't let me work out much. We only did some short walks. But let's commit to doing this every day from now on. What do you say?"

"We're supposed to be hiding, but okay."

They showered simultaneously. She used the guest bathroom while he used his private one.

"That shower was never used as much as it has been in the past couple of days. Come to think of it, I don't think anyone ever used it."

He didn't know why he said that.

"I'll go back to my apartment soon."

"That's not what I meant." He moved uncomfortably on the couch. "I'm happy you're here. I mean, under the circumstances...I mean—"

"It's okay." She put her hand on his arm. "I understand what you mean. I appreciate everything you've done for me."

"You don't have to go."

"I know."

"Do you want to watch TV?"

"You know what? I miss reading. Do you have a book I could borrow?"

"I don't have that many books, but the ones I do have are in my bedroom." He showed her the one shelf he had with a dozen books on it. "I *should* read more." He stared at the shelf.

Some of them were the self-help books Rick had given him. He should get rid of them. Most of the books he owned were about business. A few were about Steve Jobs, one about Elon Musk, and a few others on how to succeed in business.

"You really like Steve Jobs, huh?"

"Yeah, well." He shifted his weight from one foot to the other. "You know, almost every entrepreneur wants to be Steve Jobs. I've been following him for years, especially since he died when a lot of books about him came out. In the start-up community, most of us wish we could stand one day on a big stage in front of hundreds of people, maybe thousands, and announce the next iPhone."

She nodded with a sad smile.

"It's funny," he said, "I never told this to anyone, but I used to stand in front of the mirror and announce the new iPhone the same way he did." He raised his iPhone and spoke in a deep voice, which didn't resemble Jobs's. "'Tonight, Apple is going to reinvent the phone. And we are calling it—iPhone.'"

She smiled.

"When we started the new app thing, I had a daydream where Rick and I would announce it on stage, in front of the whole world. We were going to *revolutionize the coaching industry*."

She sat on his bed, her eyes never leaving his.

"Anyway," he said after a while, "I should give up on those dreams. I'll never be Steve Jobs."

"I don't think you should give up on your dreams. But there was only one Steve Jobs. Most people will not *be* Steve Jobs. I mean, it's great to have him as a role model, but most people need to be realistic. I never agreed with Rick about having to be the best all the time. I think even *his* mentors don't say that. I think this attitude pushed him over the edge. He always dreamed of being Tony Robbins."

"By now I think I trust *you* a little more than I trust *Rick*."

"I also believe coaching's not enough. In many cases, therapy with a licensed psychologist is essential for getting well."

"You mean in *my* case?"

She nodded slowly.

"Why didn't you say anything?"

"I think I did, but you weren't ready to listen, so I didn't push. The doctor at the hospital told you as well. I also didn't want to hurt Rick. He thought his way was better. We had a lot of arguments about that, but I didn't feel I could contradict him in front of others."

David nodded. *Maybe I should have seen a shrink, like they told me to. Maybe I'd be in a better place now.*

"No books for me here," she said.

They both looked back at the shelf and saw only one old novel there. "Stephen King?" He raised the book and showed her.

She shook her head. "His name alone gives me the creeps."

"It's a great escape. And he's a good writer."

"I've had enough scares in my life recently, thank you."

"Tell you what. Let's go to Barnes and Noble and get you some books. My treat."

Days 16–18

David suggested Angela return to the university. He thought she should do normal things. He wished he had normal things to do.

The FBI recovered her car, examined it, and returned it

to her. She parked it far from the apartment, close to David's car. Agent Bob still insisted on not sharing with them what they found in the barn, which David found odd but hopeful.

Could it be fingerprints? Maybe a map with a potential hiding place they put under surveillance. Maybe a phone with information.

Angela jumped every time her phone made a sound. She examined it immediately or rushed over to it if it was far from her. She didn't admit it, but David knew she hoped for news from Rick.

He was afraid to ask.

He could hear her cry sometimes in the shower or in the guest room.

He searched for work but not in his old profession. He couldn't handle it. He looked for jobs as a retail salesperson. He wanted to go work at an Apple store but figured it was too much hassle. He tried other technology retail stores and sent them his resume.

He wondered what they would think when they saw his MBA and worldwide experience.

David and Angela took walks every day, which felt good. They knew it was dangerous—but the benefits of exercise were great. They could see a police car driving by every now and then, and at a certain point, they started exchanging hellos with the police officers.

Angela talked to him about "shooting for number three," as she called it. He needed to be the best *he* could be, not better than others.

"You should find a job that will make you happy. I'm sure everywhere you go, they will recognize your talents and promote you."

He nodded. "You have a point."

"You need to get out of the apartment every day to get moving. Meet people. Make friends. Even *women*."

She smiled at him, but his heart stopped for a second. He tried to force a smile back.

He didn't want to hear that.

———

"There's something I need to tell you," David said over dinner. "It's been eating at me for a long time. I didn't want to tell you because I didn't want to hurt you, but I guess it doesn't matter much now." He played with his fork. "When we were in New York together, Rick...Rick went with another woman, with a waitress we met there."

Angela didn't blink. She didn't seem surprised.

"You *knew*?"

"I didn't *know*, but I'm not surprised," she said after a while. "Looking back, knowing Rick, it was obvious he was not the type to stay loyal." She sighed. "I once caught him kissing a woman in my car. *My* car. He said it was nothing, but I found some text messages that proved otherwise. I didn't confront him again because I knew he would lie—and charm—his way out of it."

"I'm sorry. I didn't know what to do. I didn't want to hurt you. I tried to stop him. I made him promise it wouldn't happen again. He promised me, and I believed him. It happened before I knew how big of a liar he was."

"That's okay. I don't know what I would have done either."

He wanted to hug her but didn't.

She excused herself and went to bed.

He heard her cry herself to sleep.

———

"Why didn't you bring her to *me*?" Boldy said.

"Because we knew what you'd do to her," Trever said.

"So you just beat the crap out of *him*? That's it?"

"Yeah."

"You should have brought her to me, man. She's so *tasty*. I'd eat her alive. I'd fu—"

"Enough with that!" The boss slammed his hand on the table. "It's time to end this shit. Get the money, or kill them all."

FORTY-ONE

Day 19

David helped Angela clean and arrange her apartment, and she felt ready to move back. She said she considered renting a new apartment, but if she broke the lease she would have to pay a fine. She couldn't afford it along with the additional expenses of moving. She also hated packing everything. Their complex was one of the cheapest-but-normal apartments they had found in Tulsa, and she knew her way around. The thought of starting over in a new place felt harder than dealing with the ghost Rick had left behind.

She also said I live nearby and that she needs me.

David noticed she cursed at times when she mentioned Rick's name. It stood out each time she did.

Or at least he noticed it more than she did.

After she packed, they took a walk and had dinner. The last one in his apartment.

"How are you doing?"

"I'm starting to doubt why I was with him in the first place. I mean, I loved him, but *why*? I always had a thing for bad boys, I guess. Probably an unresolved issue with my father. Next time I'll choose a nice guy."

"How do you explain what happened to him?"

"I am starting to think he has some personality disorder."

David nodded. "It would explain a lot."

"It would." She slipped her hands into her pockets. "To add insult to injury, I should have recognized it and maybe helped him."

"I'm not sure you could have. You were too much involved. You *loved* him."

She nodded. "I mean, we had our problems, but it seemed like any other normal couple. And as far as I knew, he did well at work." She gazed at an unidentified spot in the room. "That's what I thought until all this happened. It revealed a different side I didn't see—or *chose* not to see."

They cleared the dishes and cleaned the table for the last time. He stared at her packed bags.

His apartment seemed much smaller.

He didn't want her to leave.

He needed her to stay longer.

"Why don't you stay for some late night TV, and then I'll help you with your stuff?"

She agreed. He sat next to her on the couch. They watched *Pretty Woman*, which he had recorded earlier that day.

He took a blanket and covered both of them with it. She didn't mind. They were not touching, but he could feel her. He could smell her. She had an amazing smell. A combination of her own smell and a new perfume she had bought, which wrapped her body like a direct sunray on a freezing day. She had smelled good even after a thirty-minute run—

but tonight, after the shower and perfume, he wanted to sniff her, kiss her, and—

Her head dropped slowly to his shoulder. She got comfortable, and he loved it. He wanted to touch her. He had wanted to do it a million times in the past few days. Every evening, every hour of the day.

Is she hitting on me? Or is she just getting comfortable? Or is it unconscious?

He tried to see if she was awake, but from his angle he couldn't.

The third time she said she needed to go, he couldn't ask her to stay longer.

He had brushed his teeth and used mouthwash three times that evening. He had two pieces of gum.

He was ready.

"Wait."

She examined him.

He leaned in and kissed her.

She didn't resist.

Not at *first*.

After half a second of the best feeling in the world, she pushed him away gently.

She was stunned. *Did she not see it coming? Didn't she want me to do it?*

"I'm sorry. I don't know what came over me."

"It's okay. Maybe I misled you. I see you as a good friend. As my *best* friend." Then she said the worst thing a man in his situation could hear. "I see you as a brother."

He nodded. "I want us to stay friends. I'm sorry. I can't lose you."

"It's okay. You won't." And as if to stab him in the gut one more time, she added, "Please don't ever do it again."

———

David couldn't sleep. He kept hoping she would come back.

But she didn't.

He went to the fridge and got ice to put on his broken nose.

Had she misled him? Was he so naive to think he had a chance? Had she not misled him since the first time she came to his apartment when Rick was missing? Did she play with him?

Or had she been a kind and friendly person and he had misunderstood her all along?

Or had she felt sorry for him and wanted him to feel better?

After he had helped her move her stuff into her apartment, she didn't even hug him.

She remained alone for the first time since she returned from Rick's barn. In the middle of the night he texted her, *How are you feeling?*

She texted him right back: *Relatively well.*

Please don't ever do it again, she had said.

He apologized again. She replied that it was okay. *Let's meet for dinner tomorrow*, she suggested.

He agreed. He wanted to text her and tell her that he couldn't stand her being alone. He wanted to tell her he missed her already. He wanted her to come back. He wanted to tell her he would never do it again. He would never hurt her again.

He wanted to tell her he loved her.

———

Bob got off the phone and looked at Stuber. "Cash pressed charges against David and Rick for stealing his money."

"Is that good or bad?"

"It means the money was legal. It's not cartel money."

"That's good news for David."

"Yes, but it means we have much less interest in this investigation now. They'll pull us out soon."

FORTY-TWO

Day 20

After a long, sleepless night, David had dozed off in his recliner when his phone rang. Hoping it would be her, he jumped.

But it wasn't. She had a special ringtone on his phone.

It rang on his iPhone, and his Apple Watch vibrated on his arm. Waking up, it felt like an alarm going off all over the place.

Could it be Bob? Does he have any news?

He checked his iPhone. An unknown number.

He had Bob's number, and Bob always called from his cell phone. It couldn't have been Agent Bob.

David wanted to let it go to voicemail, but his gut told him he should answer.

When he heard the voice on the other side of the line, he stopped breathing.

"Long time no see, *buddy*," the familiar voice said. "How have you been?"

David's jaw dropped. He pulled the phone from his ear and stared at it.

"You still there?" the familiar voice asked.

"Where the hell are you?" David yelled at the phone. "What *the fuck* did you do? Why? How could you do this to me? To *Angela*?" He rose. "You crazy fuck! Come back with my money!"

For a few seconds, no sound came out of his phone.

His right hand clenched the phone, his left curled into a fist, turning his fingertips red.

"Relax, will ya? I didn't mean for you to take the fall."

"*What?* Of course you did! You—"

"I didn't *really* care. You were just the scapegoat. I needed the money. All that bullshit I told you about working hard? I lied. I don't believe that shit."

Rick didn't sound smug. Rick tried hard to sound confident.

Maybe he cared, just a little?

"I needed money fast. I didn't want to hurt Angela, but, as *you* know, I only held her as a trophy, not much more than that."

David felt his blood leaving his heart and going straight to his face, which felt as if it would explode soon. His mouth dried. His legs caved in, and he fell back into his recliner, almost tripping.

"What about that stunt you tried to pull with that email you sent me?" Rick asked. "It almost worked. Thank God I had help and let you waste your time. I was about to get rid of the phone anyway."

When David didn't reply, Rick continued. "Anyway, I didn't call to apologize. Well, maybe a little. I need your help."

"Wh—*what?*" David almost hoped the neighbors would call the police when they heard him.

"I need your help to withdraw the rest of the money in cash. I could only get part of it. Those fucking investors of yours tried to stop me from taking my money. I need your signature and ID. The bank won't give me the money without *you.*"

"You're kidding, right?" David said, his voice hoarse.

"I'll pay you for your trouble. I'll give you a *quarter* of the money."

"Go to hell."

"You sure? It's better than nothing. Think about it, will ya? This way you get some of your money back. You probably won't make that much money in your whole life."

David closed his eyes. *How mean can you be?* His hands still clenched, he said, "No way."

"Just think about it. I'll call you back in a day or two, and then I'll come by the hotel, okay?" Rick said. Then his voice became grave. "Oh, and one other thing—don't try to fuck my wife."

Rick hung up.

FORTY-THREE

David paced in his apartment, trying to lower his pulse, and considered his options. Go to the FBI and have them track Rick, or maybe go along and meet him? Try to hurt him? Maybe do what he said?

I could use the money.

He wanted to consult Angela.

Bob would know what to do. The right thing to do was to go to the FBI.

Or was it?

David climbed the stairs to Angela's apartment. It felt as if someone had installed more stairs since the last time he climbed them. He stared at the door. He raised his hand to knock but stopped. What would he say to her? That her abusive, cheating bastard of a husband called him and wanted to meet? How would she take it?

I have to tell her.

After a while, he summoned the courage to knock on her door.

"Is it dinner time already?" She invited him in.

"I need to talk to you." He almost pushed her in.

They sat in her living room. The apartment looked good. Clean and tidy. It seemed as if she had started to get her life back in order.

He was about to crush her life. *Again.*

"He called me," David said finally.

"Who?"

"*Rick.*"

Angela stared at him with blank eyes. Then her eyes twitched. A subtle twitch, but he noticed. A stream of tears came down her cheeks. She didn't speak for a few minutes. He wanted to wipe off her tears, but after the previous night, he couldn't touch her.

"What did he—" she said as her tears dried. "What did the son of a bitch say?"

Angela didn't wait for an answer. Without excusing herself, she walked to the bathroom. David could hear the water running. When she returned, it seemed as if she had washed her pale face and dried it. She looked as if she had seen a ghost.

"Are you okay?" he asked.

"I don't know." She sat down. He could see her hands were shaking. "What did he say?"

"He wants me to go to the bank with him to withdraw the rest of the money. He said he'd give me a quarter of it if I did. I didn't even ask if he meant a quarter of three hundred thousand dollars or—"

"*What?*"

He nodded.

"I don't even know why I'm still surprised by this man. Did he say why?"

"Just that they wouldn't let him withdraw it without me."

Angela's eyes examined the floor. After a few minutes, she gazed at him.

"Did he...did he mention me?"

I only held her as a trophy, Rick had said.

David shook his head. "I'm sorry, Angela."

Angela nodded. "What do you want to do?"

"I'm not sure. I think the right thing to do is to go to the FBI." He searched for confirmation, but her face said nothing. He lowered his eyes. "For a few minutes, I considered taking the money."

"No way!"

He nodded. "I thought if I paid them back part of the money, they might leave me alone and go after Rick."

"You know it's unlikely. And you would be a coconspirator."

"You have a point," he said. "Would you like to be with me when I talk to Bob?"

"Yes." She rose. "Let me change."

———

Agent Bob returned the car to the rental agency at Tulsa International Airport. He wondered if he should have updated David but decided he would do it while waiting for his flight. Agent Stuber had left the previous night. Their supervisor had had enough, especially after they discovered the money had no connections to the cartel.

It was not worth the FBI's time anymore. Time to go home.

He needed to go home.

"Rick called me," David blurted into his phone.

"*What?*" Bob glared at the gate agent. "I'll be there in

forty-five minutes." He disconnected the call and called Stuber.

"He took the bait. I need you back here."

———

David returned to his apartment. Angela arrived a few minutes later, dressed in her jeans and a white T-shirt—a casual but amazing outfit. Over her T-shirt was a half-open white sweatshirt. She wore little makeup and had color back in her face.

"He didn't seem surprised. He said it'll take him forty-five minutes to get here."

"Forty-five? He sure is taking his time."

David nodded.

"Did Rick say anything that can help us find him?" She looked ready for battle.

He shook his head. He reviewed the conversation with Rick in his mind.

Don't try to fuck my wife, Rick had said right before he hung up. David couldn't share that with Angela.

Then it hit him. He jumped out of his seat, hands in the air.

"What?"

"He said he'd meet us at the hotel!" he said.

"What hotel?"

"Exactly! Do you remember when we found the listening device the muscle men put in my apartment after they left?"

"He heard us say we were going to a hotel before you broke it! Oh my God, David!"

He nodded slowly.

"You think he works with them?"

"Sure looks that way."

"It doesn't make sense. They seemed to be genuinely looking for him and the money. He couldn't have been working with them."

"You have a point. But how else did he know?"

Angela seemed to consider. "Maybe they were pretending to threaten us so he would have leverage? He figured we'd be scared of them and want to cooperate."

"You could work for the FBI." David smiled. "The only issue with this theory is that they attacked him *before* he ran away with the money. Maybe he faked that as well. Maybe he had them come search for you when you hid in my apartment to disguise all of this?"

"Knowing Rick—the new Rick—anything's possible."

———

"When you called me, I was ready to get on a plane," Bob said after almost an hour.

"Where to?"

"Never mind that now. Tell me exactly what he said."

David updated him except for the parts he didn't want Angela to hear. He figured they didn't matter for the investigation. Then he shared their theories about Rick working with the muscle men. Bob took notes and nodded every now and then.

"The more I think about it, it makes sense he had help from the beginning. They also helped him fake the whole dad thing."

Angela crumpled onto the couch.

Bob updated Stuber over the phone. "That's amazing." Bob pressed the end key. "He must be stupid or desperate."

"I would say *desperate*," David said.

"I agree," Bob said. "I don't think he would have called you unless it was a last resort. Besides, to pull what he pulled—you can't be *that* stupid."

David and Angela nodded almost simultaneously.

"Good thing he didn't take all the money that day," Bob said.

David nodded. "I thought Mr. Cash froze that money."

Bob filled his lungs with air and smiled. "We unfroze it."

"Why?"

"Bait. We wanted Rick to think he had a chance to get the rest of the money. We asked the bank to flag the account and not let Rick take it out by himself."

"Nice," David said. "But he had three hundred thousand dollars. He could have run away with that."

"I had a feeling he needed more than three hundred thousand dollars," Bob said. "Besides, it was worth a shot."

"Why didn't you get an alert from the bank when Rick tried to withdraw the money?" Angela asked.

"My people are checking it now. Looks like the bank had some bug in their system."

"You mean if I went along with him, we could have taken the money and run?" David asked.

Bob nodded.

Do they trust me, or are they following me all the time? If they were following me, they should have come to our rescue when they heard we were in trouble.

Or did they hear it and not do anything?

Should I have taken the money with Rick and run away?

Bob looked at his phone and rose. "Excuse me for a minute." He didn't wait for an answer and left the apartment.

"Do they trust me, or are they following me?" David asked as Angela sprang to the door and peered outside.

"Can you hear anything?" he whispered.

She shook her head.

He put his ear to the door and tried to listen.

When Bob knocked on the door again, David jumped away, startled, and almost fell to the floor.

Angela tried to grab him, and they both burst out laughing.

When they opened the door, they stood next to each other, trying to look serious.

Bob examined them. "Were you able to hear anything?" He smiled and walked in. "We want you to do exactly what he says when he calls you back." He stared directly at David. "Can you do that?"

David looked back at Bob, then looked at Angela for an answer, but she only seemed scared.

"Can't you trace his call?" David asked.

Bob snorted. "We'll try, but it takes time, and we probably won't find him. He probably used a burner."

"A what?" Angela asked.

"A disposable prepaid phone you can buy cheaply anywhere. You don't have to identify yourself to buy it," Bob said. "It won't be traced to him easily."

"It's like the one he left you when he escaped," David said. "I guess he had a bunch of them when he got ready to run away with my money. *Our* money."

Bob nodded.

"Couldn't you find the serial number and then trace it to the store where he bought it and then look at surveillance camera footage?" David asked.

"You watch too much TV. It doesn't work that way in real life. It's difficult; he probably has more than one phone, and there are too many stores in Oklahoma he could have bought it from. He may have bought them a long time ago."

David cleared his throat after a minute and said, "I'm not sure I can do this. I'll want to hit him if I see him." He looked at Angela as if he didn't want her to hear this. "I'm afraid to meet his muscle men again." He touched his nose, which still hurt.

She raised her hand to touch his but then noticed Bob and dropped it.

"I know how dangerous they can be," she told Bob. "They almost killed him."

"We had less than three weeks for this, and it didn't go anywhere. We have other, more important cases to take care of. My bosses already called me to go back to the office. That's why I was at the airport when you called," Bob said. "The call I made outside? I tried to convince my boss we had a new good lead. The fact that we can connect Rick to those muscle men who attacked you makes it a much more serious crime. He's tried to kill you twice now. The only thing that can help us find him is if you meet him and we catch him then. I'm sorry, but we need you to do this."

They were all quiet for a few minutes. "We'll have your back all along. We'll know when and where you meet, and we'll grab him there. It's as simple as that."

David considered it. Knowing he would never have Angela, the thought of taking the money seemed more attractive. *But the FBI will know when and where we meet, which might be a problem.*

Day 21

301

Rick called again from an unknown number the next afternoon.

David answered it from his Apple Watch, just to spite him.

"I bet you didn't think you'd hear from me again."

"I *hoped* I wouldn't." Talking from the watch felt like Michael Knight talking to his car. Under different circumstances, it could have been cool.

"If you do this, you won't have to hear from me again."

In the movies, at that point, David would have a million FBI agents around him, asking him to keep the bad guy on the line for as long as he could. They would trace the call in a few minutes, storm out, and get the bad guy.

But his apartment was empty.

Rick had filled it with laughter, optimism, and good times. Now Rick's voice filled the apartment with darkness.

"Rick, how could you do this to me after all we've been through? And to Angela?" It was *worth another shot.*

"I'm sure you'll take good care of her, right?"

"She's n—"

"Anyway, how's that two hundred and fifty thousand dollars sound to you?"

So he meant a quarter of a million dollars. It would be a nice sum of money to have.

"You know I have no choice." *The FBI might be listening to this call.* "I have to do it just to pay back *some* of what you stole. Their lawyer wants to eat me alive. I trusted you—"

"It's better than nothing."

David sighed. "Okay."

"Great!" Rick said. "I'm in Oklahoma City. I need you to meet me here tomorrow morning at the bank. I'll text you the exact address when you get to downtown OKC. Eight a.m. sharp."

"We have banks here in Tulsa, you know."

"Too much FBI and police you have there in Tulsa. I'll talk to you tomorrow morning."

"Whatever."

"And David"—Rick paused—"*don't* pay the investor. They'll go after you for the rest. Just take the money and run. You can have a great life. Angela won't go with you, but you knew that all along, didn't you?"

———

"That's good news," Bob said over the phone. "We'll follow you there with a lot of backup. You don't have to worry about a thing. We'll try to grab him before you meet him. Sound good?"

David nodded but then realized he was on the phone. "That would be nice."

He texted Angela. It took her two minutes to knock on his door.

"I'm not happy about this," she said.

"Agent *Bob* was happy."

"I bet he was. You're doing *his* job. Are you sure you want to do this?"

"No." He avoided her eyes. "But I don't have much of a choice. I want to get this over with. I want them to catch him, put him in jail, and pay the money back. I want to get this over with."

He noticed she flinched when he mentioned jail. She still had feelings for Rick. Had he known that all along and tried to ignore it?

"Are you sure you don't want me to come with you?"

I don't need her to defend me. I need to be the one who protects her.

"No. I don't want you anywhere *near* him. I'll be fine. The FBI will be right behind me." He held her hand. "Also, I don't want to put you in harm's way. I'll be fine."

"Make sure he doesn't persuade you to run away with him and the money. He can be persuasive, as you know."

She hugged him at his doorstep, longer than usual, and then he watched her climb the stairs.

———

Rick sat in the dark, inside a car parked across from David's apartment, and watched them hug.

FORTY-FOUR

Day 9

After leaving Angela for the last time, Rick drove further out of the city. He stopped at a small gas station, went into a stinking restroom, and locked himself in. He dyed his hair blond in front of the cracked mirror and put on fake eyeglasses.

Nice look, he thought and smiled at himself.

He'd gone to the barn a few weeks earlier and pretended he wanted to buy it. The Realtor gave him the key. Rick expressed interest, paid a small down payment, and kept the key. He had promised to return and pay the rest of the money and even called the Realtor a few times and promised to pay him the following month.

By the time the Realtor realized the scam, Rick would be long gone.

At first, he felt bad and even considered sending the Realtor some cash in the future. But he forced himself to stop caring. He had to. No other way to deal with what he had done in the past few weeks.

He became a terrible man.

For years he trained himself to change the way he felt in an instant. He became a master at that.

He found driving without GPS hard but eventually located the small town he was searching for. He had never heard of it before, but the guy on Craigslist had promised him it existed.

Rick saw the cabin from the main road, drove into the woods, left the car, and walked for fifteen minutes back to the cabin. His ribs hurt with each step he took. He probably broke at least one from the beating he took from the muscle men, but he couldn't get medical care. He considered torching the car to eliminate evidence but figured it would draw attention if he burnt down the forest. He was tired of switching cars and figured Angela wouldn't be able to tell the police which car he drove—but she had surprised him when she found the hidden money, so he couldn't take the risk.

When Rick reached the house, an old guy opened the door.

"How the hell did ya get up here?" The old man searched behind Rick.

Rick put on his charming smile. "My wife dropped me down the road. I'm David. I'm here for the car."

"Oooh." The old man nodded and examined the dirt road driveway. "That's weird. I usually hear when cars arrive." The old man stared at Rick. "Never mind, then. Come on in. Would you like a drink?"

If the man had come out with a shotgun, I would have had to kill him. If it were an episode of Criminal Minds, *my character would have killed him anyway. But I'm not a killer. Not without a reason, anyway.*

Considering killing people started only a few weeks ago

when he'd had a run-in with the muscle men. He wanted to kill them.

Does it happen to everyone and they just don't act on it? Or am I finally going crazy?

"No, thanks. I'm in a hurry. Here's the cash. Where can I pick up the car?"

The old man backed up but quickly took the envelope. "Of course. Let's go."

The white rusty Saturn from the previous decade was parked in the back, behind the house.

"The keys are inside." The old man pointed at the car.

Rick found the keys in the ignition and figured he could have stolen the car. *Too late now.* After a few tries, the engine turned on.

"It just happens in the morning, as I told you on the phone. Don't worry about it. Take care, sir."

Rick wondered if the old man lied to him. He couldn't afford to get stuck in the middle of nowhere. He listened to the motor while the old man counted the cash.

I miss my Camaro.

———

Rick checked into the first motel he found along the main road, about ten minutes from the old man. He had read somewhere that those motels were best for hiding. The cheap motel disgusted him, but it was better than sleeping on the floor in the cold barn. He took a shower, put some ice he had bought on his broken ribs, and went to sleep.

Days 10–13

Rick switched motels every day as they had told him. After a few days laying low, he went to the bank and tried to withdraw the money.

"Hi." Rick gave the young female clerk one of his famous smiles. "I'm here to make a withdrawal." He gave her the account number.

"I would need to see your ID, sir."

He should have thought of that. The bank account was under his name, but he was in disguise. He didn't want someone watching the bank footage to identify him. He wondered if they would be able to identify him with his disguise, but he had no choice.

He gave her his real driver's license, and when she seemed unsure, he told her he'd just dyed his hair.

She believed him.

When he told her he needed seven hundred thousand dollars, her jaw dropped.

"The money isn't there?" he asked.

She read something from her screen. "It's here, but it says you need another signature. From a"—she looked back at the screen—"*David Pascal.*"

Who?

David's last name had slipped his mind. Rick had seen it when he looked him up and on some of the legal papers, but David had never used it. David was just David.

"Are you sure? It must be a mistake."

"Yes, I'm sure. I'm sorry, sir."

Cute, but not nearly as cute as he would have liked her to be.

"I'll have him fax me his signature. Would that work?"

"I'm sorry, sir." She returned his smile. "But he needs to come here in person, and he would need to bring a valid ID."

"Oh, okay then. No problem. I'll call him right now and ask him to come over. I'll come back tomorrow." He smiled at her with his large white teeth. "I have a *much* more important thing on my mind. When do *you* get off work today?"

They went to her place, which was much nicer than his cheap motel. He felt too embarrassed to take her there anyway. She made him dinner—a nice change from the fast food joints he had gotten accustomed to. After dinner they had sex, which was better than he had expected. He liked not having to impress her too much. He knew he was way out of her league.

The following morning, he took her to work. He told her David had betrayed him with *his* money, and it would be hard to bring him there. Was there any way she could help him?

"I'm sorry, sweetie, but I'd lose my job if I did that." She stroked his hair. "I'd probably go to *jail* if I did that. And they have cameras everywhere, so they would know I helped you without his signature."

She was *so* sorry.

If only I had a few more days to persuade her.

Rick promised he would pick her up again that evening, after work, but she never saw him again.

Days 14–18

Rick tried a few different branches, but none were willing to help him. He tried to avoid the cameras by wearing base-ball caps and fake mustaches. He decided he had to get David on board. He considered threatening him or apologizing and asking him for a favor. He should be able to sweet talk David into helping him. David was weak, and Rick could take advantage of it, as he had done in the past. But it may take a few days, and he didn't have that much time.

He even considered threatening Angela to get David to help.

The best way would be to bribe David. The fool needed money, and this would be an easy way for him to get it.

Why didn't I try to get him on board in the first place? We'd probably have been able to get more money together. Getting David to cooperate would have been nearly impossible. As charming as I can be, David was too honest. Almost as honest as Angela. Another problem with David was that he was proud. He believed in the start-up thing and prayed for it to work. He cared about his name too much.

Rick wondered if he could tell them David was the only thing standing between them and the money. They had ways to persuade people to do things. Like they did with him.

Maybe he should try to convince David? To start with, at least.

If he won't cooperate, I'll unleash the hounds.

Day 19

Returning to the old apartment complex felt better than Rick had expected. He parked at the farthest place with a view to David's apartment, but he couldn't find David's car anywhere.

Were they really in a hotel? For a full week? Together?

He thought Angela didn't find David attractive, even

though David had lost a lot of weight and looked better. Thanks to Rick.

I hope she didn't sleep with him. David wouldn't do that to me. Angela wouldn't either.

But they both hated him at this point.

Angela needed a shoulder to cry on after what he had done to her. And Virgin David would be perfect for that. She never truly believed him that David was the crook in all this.

Rick decided to wait for them to come back. Every time a car passed, he ducked. But none of them were David's old car. Rick giggled when he realized he had a much older car.

He had almost dozed off when David's door opened. *He was home after all? The son of a bitch.*

To make things worse, David and Angela exited David's apartment, both wearing sports clothes.

Are they going for a run? Without me? It didn't take them long to copy my routines and do them without me.

Rick forgot how hot Angela could be in those clothes.

David wore the clothes Rick had bought him, but it seemed as if David had gained some weight since he'd last seen him.

All their hard work. Gone down the drain. *What a waste.*

It was probably *his* fault.

He imagined David going back into depression as soon as Rick ran away with the money.

He thought he saw David wearing the watch he'd gotten him. That had been a waste of good money. Even though he needed David and bribing him helped.

He considered going into the apartment but feared they would return and catch him. He had no way of knowing when they would return. David didn't seem in shape, and it could be a short walk.

They returned after less than thirty minutes, which would have given Rick enough time, but he was glad he didn't risk it. At night, after David's lights were off, Rick walked up to David's apartment. David, stupidly enough, had let Rick borrow the key once, and he'd made a copy.

The idiot didn't even consider changing his lock.

Rick used a flashlight to walk around. He could hear David's snores. David was a sound sleeper, he remembered from when they shared a hotel room in New York. David's apartment looked the same.

He searched for the bug they had planted in David's apartment. As they had suspected, it was gone. He took out two listening devices he had bought with cash the previous day and planted them. He needed to know what they talked about in the living room.

Rick had seen the guest bedroom once before. He walked into the room, which had a single bed, a nightstand, and a small trash can. *Did David have a spare bed here before?*

Rick almost left the room when he noticed a strange item in the trash can.

Angela's empty perfume bottle.

She slept here.

At least they weren't sleeping together.

Rick would kill him if they did. He would kill them both.

FORTY-FIVE

Day 22
The Longest Day

Rick left to sleep at a nearby motel. He knew it was dangerous but probably safer than staying in the car. When he drove in and out of the complex, he saw David's and Angela's cars parked far from the apartment building. *Smart.*

When he returned to park in his new spot across from David's apartment, Rick could see the lights were off in the apartment.

He had heard most of the conversation with the FBI. They wanted to get a head start on him. But he was smarter.

He walked fast, almost ran, to David's apartment. He used his copied key to open the door and let himself in.

Rick held the gun they had given him. They had taught him how to use it. He had never fired a gun before.

He could hear David's snoring from the living room. He walked quietly into David's bedroom, grabbed his phone, used David's thumb to unlock it, and texted Angela that he needed her help, that he'd heard from Rick and needed to consult with her ASAP.

I'll be there in a minute, she responded in less than five seconds.

"Bitch," he said.

Three minutes later, she knocked on the door. Rick opened it in the dark and stood behind it. She walked in slowly as he grabbed her and pushed her to the couch.

She screamed.

Rick pointed the gun at his wife's head.

———

A scream woke David up. He stumbled when he jumped out of his bed.

What the hell happened? Did it come from inside the apartment?

He reached for his phone but couldn't find it. Only his Apple Watch was next to the bed. He used his fingers to search for the phone on the carpet, but it wasn't there. He grabbed the watch and tried to put it on but was too disoriented, so he stuck it in his sweatpants pocket and rushed to the living room.

He saw a man with a gun pointed at Angela. It took him two seconds to recognize Rick. He seemed skinnier, and his hair was blond.

"What the hell?" David yelled. *"You son of a bitch!"*

"Sit on the couch. Both of you." Rick kept his eyes on David and the gun on Angela when he walked backward and locked the door. Rick dragged the small living room table over to block the door.

"We were supposed to meet tomorrow morning."

"You think I'm *that* stupid? I know about the FBI. I know about *everything*. You two were going to screw with me. Turn me in."

David stared at Angela. She looked back at him. Both of their mouths were ajar.

"How did you know?" No point lying.

"The three of us are going on a little field trip together. Bring your wallet, and let's take your car, David. The one you tried to hide."

They all went out together to David's car, a few minutes from his apartment. Rick hid the gun in his pocket and let David and Angela walk in front of him. David thought he heard a noise from a neighbor, but no one came out to help them.

David contemplated making a scene, but Rick could get jumpy and shoot them.

David recalled the first time he saw Rick next to his car. Rick apologized for the scratch he'd made.

Did he plan this all along?

David and Angela sat in the front seats. Rick sat in the back, gun still pointed at Angela's back.

"Start driving," Rick said, his voice hoarse.

David obeyed after he figured Rick was serious. He checked the rearview mirror and noticed Rick didn't put his seat belt on. *Good.* David gestured for Angela to put hers on, and she complied. He had seen a movie once where the main character hit a tree and the bad guy without a seat belt was thrown out of the front windshield.

A nice trick, if push comes to shove.

Rick looked alternately at them, at street signs, and at a paper map and gave David directions. They followed the signs to Oklahoma City. Besides the directions, no one spoke for over half an hour.

David looked at both of them. *Barbie and Ken* seemed ninety years old, sick and beaten. David had been jealous of them. Under different circumstances, he might have been able to gloat.

He wished he had his iPhone to try to get a message to Bob. He succeeded in taking the watch out of his pocket and putting it onto his wrist without Rick noticing, but this model had no LTE, which meant it was useless without the iPhone nearby.

"Why are you doing this?" Angela asked.

Rick stared out the windshield.

"Why did you do this in the first place?" David yelled, looking at his face in the rearview mirror. "I thought we were *friends*. I *trusted* you." He looked at Angela. "We *both* trusted you. Angela loved you. Even *I*...did."

David could see Rick's face change a little. He stopped staring outside and looked around the car. Rick stuck his hand in between the back seats, under the front seats, then rose and leaned between them to the dashboard. Rick's free hand fumbled for something. He also searched under the visors, causing David and Angela to move out of his way.

David considered hitting Rick in the stomach, or the face, and saving Angela. He could pull over, take Rick's phone, and call the police or Bob.

Too dangerous. Rick was stronger, so it would be hard to overtake him. Rick still held the gun in his right hand. He could shoot them.

Should I hit a tree? A pole? He'd fly out of the car and die for sure.

But what if we get hurt?

"What the hell are you doing?"

Rick turned his head to him fast, as if to hit him. David drew his head to the side to avoid the hit. But then he noticed Rick didn't try to hit him—Rick put his index finger to his own mouth.

"Shut the fuck up and drive. I don't want to hear another word from either of you."

David slowed down and tried to get a better look at what Rick was searching for. *Did he hide another gun in my car?*

Rick pulled a small black item out of the cigarette lighter socket. It resembled what David had found in the back of his TV.

A listening device.

Who the fuck got in my car and put it here? David almost said out loud, but then he remembered Rick had shushed him.

Rick returned to the back seat, opened the side window, and threw the bug out.

"I'll tell you the truth."

Angela turned in his direction, and David watched him through the rearview mirror.

"That'll be nice for a change," Angela said.

David saw another change in Rick's face. It became softer, calmer. It reminded him of when he first met Rick. Almost nice and friendly. It reminded him of Rick in the hospital, worrying about him. It reminded him of when Rick bought him gifts and healthy food and took him out to exercise.

The Rick who he thought had loved him.

The Rick he had loved.

Rick started to cry. David and Angela stared at each other. David had never seen Rick cry.

"I think I can talk here now." Rick wiped his tears. "I

couldn't talk in your apartment. They had it bugged as well."

"In *my* apartment? No. I found it and threw it away."

"You did, but they put another bug there after they figured you threw it away. Actually, *I* put it there. I could hear everything you said for the past couple of days. They did too. They caught up to me a few days ago and made me do it. That's how I knew about the FBI."

Did he hear I tried to kiss her?

Would he even care?

"But you thought we were at the hotel, didn't you?" David said, but then it hit him.

"At first, yes. That's what *they* told me. But then they saw you around the apartment and made me put in another listening device."

What the hell's going on? Did they just blackmail him? Could this all be a lie? Could we ever be friends again?

Fuck no. I don't care what his excuses are. He abused Angela. He abused me.

"I've been bad to you both, and I don't deserve your understanding or your love again, but please hear me out. I'll start from the beginning. A few months before we moved here, I invested a lot of money into a seminar I tried to arrange for myself," Rick said. "Angela, it was the one you helped me with." Rick's crying became worse. He tried to wipe the tears off with his hand, then found a napkin in the car and blew his nose in it.

It doesn't sound like a good explanation so far, David wanted to say but decided to wait.

"I never told you this." Rick put his hand gently on Angela's shoulder. She didn't flinch. He continued, "I ended up owing the bank almost two hundred thousand dollars on my private bank account. I didn't want to worry you about it, so I borrowed some money on the black market, with enormous interest."

David wanted to remove Rick's hand from Angela's shoulder, but she didn't seem to mind.

"At first, I made enough money to pay them, but after a while I couldn't keep up with the payments. They threatened me and sent those muscle men to get me. That cost more money, so they charged me with it. With interest. I only paid them enough to keep them off my back a little, but then they said I owed them almost a million dollars. They threatened to kill you, Angela." He cried, wiped his face, then continued. "When they found me a few days ago, I told them I couldn't get the money without David. I told them you'd never cooperate. They were with me when I called you. If I didn't try to force you, they said they'd kill both of you."

David looked at Angela, then at Rick in the rearview mirror, and then at the road. Angela looked back at Rick. David saw a sparkle in her eyes. *Love? Or just sympathy?*

"You expect us to believe that?" David asked. "You almost killed Angela in that barn, you asshole."

Rick examined him, then Angela, and then he lowered his eyes.

"I'm sorry about that. I'm so sorry about *everything*." Rick continued to cry. "They had a *camera* inside the barn. You remember I told you not to get undressed in there? Only wash in the sink *with* your clothes on? They could see us the whole time. When you found the money and didn't want to run away, I decided the best thing would be to show them I didn't care about you. I had to make it believable. I'm so sorry. I tried to put your life ahead of mine. Ahead of our marriage."

Rick apologized a few more times before David interrupted. "You left her there!"

"I'm sorry for that too. I was afraid they were watching the cabin from the outside, and I didn't want them to follow me if I drove you somewhere. I did my best to lose them and come back before you woke up. I followed you from a distance and saw you get a ride with an old lady. I even followed you all the way to David's apartment. I made sure you were safe."

Can he eventually become the hero in this whole mess?
Oh God.

"And they *didn't* follow you?" David asked.

"I did my best to make sure they didn't."

After a while, David asked, "Did you plan on screwing me all along? Did you help me just to get me to get you the money?"

"It—" Rick said.

"Because I gave you *everything*, Rick. I gave you my *life*, and you threw it away."

Rick stared outside at the road, silent for a few minutes. "I'll tell you the truth, David. I did target you. I read about you online and knew your background. I needed your help. And I wanted to help you so you could help me. But I didn't set out to cheat you. Not at first. I was hoping to get a loan from you, that's it. When I figured out you didn't have money, I wanted the start-up thing to succeed. But when they started threatening me, hitting me, and especially when they started looking for Angela, I panicked. I saw a loophole with taking the million dollars I owed—and I took it."

Rick told him to enter Oklahoma City. The streetlamps disappeared, and it became dark.

"I didn't think you'd get the blame," Rick said. "I

thought that if I stole the money, they'd only be looking for me."

Rick looked at Angela. "Angela, I'm sorry. I really am. I love you. I didn't want them to hurt you."

Angela didn't reply. David tried to detect if she believed him or not.

"You tried to kill me with rat poison."

"I did a thorough research on how *not* to kill you. I gave you the exact amount to knock you out but never to kill you."

In some weird way, it almost made sense.

Rick took his hand off Angela's shoulder and sat back.

In the rearview mirror, David saw Rick with his head down in both of his hands. It meant he was not holding the gun. *On the seat next to him, maybe.* He considered making a sudden stop, to throw Rick forward and go for the gun.

But Rick could grab it and shoot either of them.

Was he telling the truth or lying again? He could be lying to get them to cooperate. It had been a long and crazy road for it to end as simply as Rick owing bad people some money. Was that it?

But they had threatened to kill Angela. I probably would have done the same thing.

Or maybe worse.

"Make a right here." Rick pointed at the upcoming intersection.

After a few more turns, they parked next to a closed Starbucks. "Park here somewhere, but not too close."

David parked the car at the farthest spot from the coffee shop he could find, but he could still see it in his rearview mirror. In front of them the woods were full of quiet, leafless trees.

"I lost it. I was too blinded by the chase after fame and fortune. I think I lost my mind at some point."

Angela nodded. *Did she accept Rick's apology, or does she agree Rick has lost his mind?*

"And then they wanted to kill *you*." Rick stopped looking at her and burst out crying again. It seemed real.

"Guys," Rick said after he caught his breath, "I'm sorry. I didn't mean for all of this to happen. I didn't know how to get out of it. I'm sorry I hurt the two of you so much. I'm *so* sorry."

"Why did you lie about Angela's dad? You scared her!" David said.

Angela turned to Rick for an answer.

"I know. I regret that. I got scared at one point, and that was the only explanation I could think of without telling you the truth. Then I just couldn't get out of this story. I'm sorry, honey."

Angela stared at her feet with tears in her eyes.

David stared at the woods in front of them. Looking in the rearview mirror, he could see Rick holding the gun again.

"You don't expect us to believe that with a gun in your hands, do you?"

Rick gazed at the gun, looked briefly at David, and then put the pistol on the back seat next to him.

"I don't expect you to believe anything I say. I understand that. But I didn't know what to do. I *still* don't."

"Why didn't you tell us that to begin with?" David hit the steering wheel hard. "We could have tried to help you."

"He's right," Angela said.

"I didn't want them to get to you." Rick looked at Angela. "They were threatening you, so I had to find a way out."

Rick grabbed the gun again and pushed the car door open.

"I'm sorry." He sprang out of the car.

Angela's eyes and mouth opened wide. It took them both three seconds to understand what was happening. They opened their car doors simultaneously and ran after Rick.

"*Rick!*" they both yelled. Rick ran into the woods. David and Angela chased him, moving around a few trees, and almost tripped on some fallen branches. After a few minutes, they caught up to Rick, who had stopped running.

Without looking back, Rick raised his hand and pointed the gun to his head.

"Rick!" Angela screamed. "*Don't!*"

"I can't take it anymore," Rick said without turning around.

David stopped a few feet behind him, but Angela continued running, her arms in front of her, aiming to grab Rick.

David grabbed her around her waist and stopped her short.

She fought him and tried to get away. She stuck her elbow in his ribs.

But he held her tight. Almost hurt her.

"Rick!" David yelled, still fighting Angela not to move. "They'll still come after Angela. Let's find a way to resolve this!"

Rick turned and stared at them blankly, the gun still to his temple.

David had never seen a man with a gun to his head in real life. He tried to erase the image from his mind of Rick shooting himself. The thought was horrifying.

"Rick!" Angela yelled. "Please don't do it. You're sick—

you probably need help. We'll get you help. We'll get through this. I *promise*."

After a minute, Rick lowered the gun.

David let go of Angela. She didn't move.

"Let's get back in the car," David said. "We don't want people to call the police on us."

Rick nodded. Angela rushed over to him and hugged him. He put the gun in his pocket and hugged her back for what felt—to David—like hours.

A million different feelings went through his mind. Through his heart.

The three of them walked slowly, side by side, back to David's car. Rick and Angela had their arms around each other. The distance they had run when they chased Rick seemed much longer now.

David sat in the driver's seat; Angela and Rick got into the back seat, together, and sat close to each other. David wanted her to sit next to *him*. Rick and Angela hugged each other again. For a long time.

She forgave him quite easily, he thought. *Too easily. Is it possible she was in on it to begin with?*

The sun rose as a few cars drove into the drive-through to get their morning shot of caffeine on their way to work.

David did his best not to look at the couple in the back seat. He stared blankly at the woods, which refused to let the light in.

He felt like a child watching someone steal the last piece of candy in the world, which for a few seconds he thought was his.

"Where were we headed?" David asked, looking at Rick in the rearview mirror.

Rick drew away from Angela. "To the bank. I needed you to sign a document to release the money. They'll wait for us outside the bank. It's a two-minute drive from here."

"And you think they'll let us go if we give them the money?"

Rick stared back at him in the mirror. "I didn't think that far ahead."

"I think we should call Agent Bob, explain everything, and have him and his friends figure it out. I trust him."

Angela nodded.

"I don't know about this," Rick said.

"You almost killed yourself back there. Please let us take the lead now," David said. "Give me your phone," David told Rick. "I couldn't find mine when you woke us up with a gun."

Rick looked guiltily at Angela, apologized to David, and gave him his old phone. He took it and tried to remember the agent's number.

"Damn it!" he said. "I can't remember a simple phone number even when *literally* my life depends on it."

"Call the police, then."

"Wait!" Rick said. "Try this." He handed David another phone. A familiar phone. "I believe that's yours."

For the first time that day, Rick smiled. David joined that smile.

"*Shit!*" Rick said.

"What?" David took his eyes off his iPhone and looked around.

"They're here."

"Who?" Angela said.

A big, brand new black Mercedes parked behind them and blocked their exit.

"How the hell did they find us?" Rick asked.

David checked his iPhone. "They must've tracked my

phone in your pocket. Or your phone. Or maybe they had a tracking device in the car."

The two huge men who had visited his apartment recently got out of the big car and walked over to the Honda.

Both carried guns.

FORTY-SIX

Agent Bob picked up Stuber from the small international airport in Tulsa before sunrise. "I talked to the Oklahoma City PD. They have a tactical team for us on standby."

"Why Oklahoma City?"

"I guess he was hiding there. It's about ninety minutes away. Big enough to have many banks and many places to hide. He could even hide there as a homeless person. Or maybe his partners had a base there."

Agent Stuber nodded.

"We were able to locate him on three different bank security cameras," Bob said, "but only after he contacted David. He tried to change his looks by dying his hair blond and putting on fake mustaches."

They reached the apartment complex and parked in front of David's apartment.

"Where's David's car?"

"I told them to park their cars farther away to make the assailants think they're in a hotel after they bugged his place."

"Wouldn't *David* like that?" They smiled. "Maybe we should look for it?"

Bob nodded. They drove around the parking lot but could only find Angela's car.

"That's odd."

"Yes," Stuber said. "I don't understand why you trusted him in the first place. I think he's guilty as hell. All three are."

Bob didn't reply.

He had known a young man in college who suffered from depression. No one helped him, they all thought he was lazy with school, and no one talked to him.

They found him dead before the end of freshman year. Suicide.

"Did you ever confront him about what we found on Rick's computer?" Stuber asked.

"You mean that he searched the internet on how *not* to kill someone with rat poison?"

Stuber nodded.

"I didn't. I wanted to save that piece of information."

They knocked on David's door, but no one replied. They tried to peek through the windows but could see nothing.

"Maybe he's at Angela's apartment?" Bob asked.

"You're kidding, right?"

Bob shook his head. "She stayed in *his* place for a while."

Stuber's eyebrows rose to the sky.

"I couldn't believe it either. It's all in my report, if you had bothered to read it."

"You know I hate reading those."

"*And* you hate writing them."

Stuber nodded. "That makes me even more suspicious.

In what universe does a guy like him have *any* chance with a woman like her?"

They climbed to Angela's apartment, but she didn't answer either. Neither one of them answered their phones.

"It doesn't look good," Stuber said as they walked back down to the front of David's apartment. The agent seemed mad at Bob.

Bob almost cared.

"What can we do?"

"We can break in."

"We don't have a warrant or probable cause."

"We can find one."

"You know I don't work that way," Bob said. "I'll have their phones traced, but it'll take a while."

An older man opened the door behind them. Both agents turned quickly, then nodded hello. They had questioned him at the beginning of the investigation.

"Are you looking for David and his friends?" Barton asked.

"Have you seen them?"

"The three of them left a couple of hours ago. I didn't see where they went, but they were walking."

"The *three* of them?" Bob almost yelled at Barton.

Barton nodded.

"With Rick? The tall guy?"

Barton nodded again.

Both agents stared at each other, shocked.

"They got a head start without us," Stuber said.

"Damn it!" Bob closed his right hand into a fist. "We should never have trusted them. Damn it!"

As Stuber opened his mouth to say something, Bob's phone rang.

FORTY-SEVEN

The muscle men opened the back doors from both sides and yanked Angela and Rick out of the car.

Rick pulled the gun from his pocket and tried to aim it at one of the muscle men, but the thug moved faster, bent Rick's hand behind his back, and forced him to drop the gun. Rick screamed with pain. The assailant hit him in the head, grabbed the gun, and put it in his pants.

The other muscle man, the Tree, who had enjoyed beating David in his apartment, held Angela by her arm, her face filled with pain.

"Let her go!" David yelled from inside the car.

"You just need the two of us," Rick yelled from the ground. "We are...we *were* going to the bank to get your money."

The big men looked at each other. A third man inside the car opened the window just a crack.

"Bring the men," the third man said and then glanced inside the car. "You stay with her. But you don't touch her unless I tell you. You hear?" Then he looked back outside and pointed at David, still in the driver's seat. "*You* leave the keys in the ignition and come out."

Another muscle man, whom David had never seen before, got out of the black Mercedes and went over to Angela. He grabbed her, pushed her back into the Honda, and entered the car behind her.

The muscle men worked like a well-oiled machine. Each thug knew exactly who needed to do what.

The Tree went to the driver's side door. David wanted to take out the key and throw it away, or hide it, but there was no point. They would find the key and beat the shit out of him again. The only thing he could think of was to push the key down as hard as he could while it was still in the ignition, bending the key. He played with it again, hoping to break it, but then a huge hand yanked him out of the car.

I hope that's enough to stop them from driving away before the FBI gets here.

If they arrive.

David never got the chance to call Agent Bob. Would he look for them? Probably, but it may be too late. He peeked at his Apple Watch—the FBI should be at his place by now, an hour and a half away. But they could get the local police to help. He had to think of a way to get a message to the agent.

But how would they find us?

If the muscle men could find them, the FBI should be able to as well.

David wished he had more time to share his location with the agent, but he had to think fast. Just before the Tree pulled him out of the car, he dropped his iPhone under the driver's seat.

It would be more helpful with Angela.

The Tree held David's left arm, which enabled his right hand to press the crown button on his Apple Watch.

"Call Agent Bob!" he yelled. "*Someone* call Agent Bob!"

He then scrolled down the crown button, hoping it would mute it, and lowered the watch behind his back.

"What the fuck you talking about?" the Tree said, then hit him hard in the head with an open hand.

David fell to the ground like a slice of ham tossed to a dog.

He saw it coming, but it still hurt like hell.

He thought he heard someone talking from his watch. *Or is it my imagination?*

The Tree helped him up, hurting his arm on the way.

David hoped Siri in his watch had heard him.

He waited a few seconds and yelled, "Don't hurt us! Please! Don't hurt us! You and your three goons with guns in the black—in my Honda! The FBI can trace my iPho—"

That got him another hit on the head. This time harder.

"If you yell again, I'll kill ya." The Tree threw him toward the Mercedes.

"If you hurt her—" Rick yelled as the other muscle man pushed him into the car.

That got Rick a hit on the head.

"Search them," said the man who had barked orders from inside the car, and his thugs happily obliged. He seemed smaller than the other three, almost normal. He had a black suit, white shirt, and no tie. The man looked like a boss.

One of the muscle men drove while the Tree sat in the front passenger seat, looking back and pointing the gun at them. The boss sat next to them in the back.

They drove away. Rick and David could see Angela, terrified, with a strange, crazed-looking man inside the car.

David didn't know if he would ever see her again. He figured Rick thought the same thing.

We don't hurt women, unless we have to, the second man had said in his apartment.

"Why don't you let her go?" David said. "We're coming with you willingly."

"She's collateral," the boss said. "If you give us any trouble, she'll die. *Slowly*. But if you cooperate, then maybe she'll live."

David and Rick stared at each other, eyes filled with terror.

What'll happen to her? He could hurt her in the car. In my car. There were many people there, not far from them. They might see or hear something and help her.

But he could also take her into the woods and—Oh God...

Is she scared? She must be scared. How will she handle herself?

Poor Angela.

David tried to look at his Apple Watch to see if the call went through, but the screen didn't respond. The iPhone was too far away, which meant they couldn't be paired by Bluetooth anymore.

Maybe the FBI would show up soon. If the call went through. They should be able to trace them. Actually, to trace *her*. The iPhone lay under the driver's seat in the car with Angela. They would come and rescue her.

If the bad guy doesn't find it and toss it away.

And if the call went through.

How long does it take the FBI to trace a phone? Do they use the carrier, or will Apple help? Apple probably won't help. I should search for it when I get home. If I get home.

What if the Feds are too late? What if he kills her as soon as the FBI arrives? What if he hurts her before they arrive?

What if he killed her as soon as we left in the black Mercedes? What if he rap—

He couldn't complete the sentence in his head.

Oh, dear God.

———

Agent Bob checked his phone. The screen read *David*. He studied his partner for a moment, then pressed the answer button. He put the phone to his ear to yell but could hear David scream, "*Someone* call Agent Bob!"

"Wh—" Bob started but heard an unfamiliar voice say from a distance, "What the fuck you talking about?"

Bob heard someone hit someone else. He heard David scream.

Bob put the call on speaker for his partner to hear and tried to pull him away from the nosy neighbor. Then David screamed again, "Don't hurt us! Please don't hurt us! You and your three goons with guns in the black—in my Honda! The FBI can trace my iPho—"

Another hit.

"If you yell again, I'll kill ya," the other man said.

Static noise filled the air for a few seconds, and then they heard another man say, "If you hurt her—"

Then the call disconnected.

———

David, Rick, the two huge muscle men, and the guy in the suit drove for a few minutes until they reached the bank.

They waited in the brand new black Mercedes until the bank opened.

"You know, even if you give me my money back," the boss told Rick, "I'll have to hurt you for making me leave New York."

David searched for a funny comeback, but his head hurt too much. He didn't want to get hit again.

"I don't usually get out to the field anymore," the boss continued, "especially not for peanuts. How much you owe us by now? A million? That's a couple of days' work for me." The boss crossed his legs, kicking Rick as if by mistake. "But you gave me such a hard time, and it took *them*"—he pointed with his thumb in the muscle men's direction—"so long to find you. *Too* long. My Oklahoma guys are not bright."

David expected them to hit the boss, but they didn't even look at him. *Well-trained dogs.*

"I decided I had to supervise this personally." He rubbed his forehead as if he was thinking. "You first fooled us into thinking you didn't care about that beautiful piece of ass we have back there. Well played. But we were on to you quickly. And—not sure if you know this or not—while *you* were running around the country, your friend here banged the shit out of her."

David and Rick looked at each other, stiff in their seats. David shook his head at Rick.

The boss took out an iPhone, similar to David's, read something on it, typed one word, and put it back in his pocket. "Getting me out of the office and all the mess you cost us *will* cost you. First, you give me my money back. Then, if I decide to let you live, you'll owe me for the rest of your life."

Rick stared at the boss, eyes blank. David tried to understand if Rick wasn't scared or if he just didn't care anymore.

"If you don't make it out of this alive"—the boss looked at Rick—"your two friends will owe me for the rest of their lives." He snorted. "*If* they live."

He pulled a knife out of nowhere. "To make sure you don't try anything stupid in there." He raised the knife and thrust it fast into Rick's leg.

Rick screamed.

FORTY-EIGHT

Bob made calls and barked orders into his phone while his partner drove the car, sirens wailing. He figured it would take him less than an hour to get to them but only if they could trace David's phone fast enough.

"Do you have any idea where we're driving?" Stuber asked, eyes still on the road as he passed other cars. Most cars moved out of the way as they heard the sirens, some even stopped on the side of the road, but driving that fast required a hundred percent concentration.

"No, but I hope they'll find him fast enough. We know they're in Oklahoma City. If they can't trace him, we'll have to start searching bank by bank, the old-fashioned way. The local PD are doing it as we speak."

———

The Tree told Rick to take his pants off, then took out a bandage from the glove compartment and put it around Rick's wounded leg.

It looked like they had done this before.

Many times.

"If you don't stop crying like a baby, I'll shoot you," the boss said.

"He needs to go to the hospital!" David yelled.

They all laughed, and the Tree surprised David with a slap to the face, which turned red again.

Rick limped into the bank with David's help, accompanied by the Tree. As directed by the boss, they walked to one of the small offices and said they needed to make a big withdrawal.

The Tree stayed next to the office door, eyes everywhere, looking like a bodyguard. The man they spoke to introduced himself as the manager and kept glancing at the Tree.

David could feel his heart pounding. Many thoughts ran through his head. Did he like Rick again? Did he still hate him? Did he feel sorry for him?

He tried not to think about Angela. Was she alive? Was she hurt?

He couldn't shake off the images in his head of the rapist-looking thug trying to take her clothes off.

He shivered.

She would fight; he knew it. But would that be a good or bad thing? Would it give them and Bob more time to find her, or would it make the goon angrier?

He wanted to cry.

What is a geek like me doing in a mess like this? I just wanted to make mobile apps.

He tried to get himself to think straight. No time for self-pity. Time to act. Time to be a *hero*.

Or to at least try.

He considered jumping on the "bodyguard." Rick would help him. Hopefully. The people in the bank would help them when they explained. *Hopefully*. They would call the police.

He examined Rick, trying to assess whether he would be on board.

Rick seemed numbed. He just held his wounded leg.

He looked as if he'd given up.

One of Rick's stupid mantras had been that if you *give up*, you *die*. He had hated Rick's mantras. Then loved them. Then hated them again.

It looks like both of us may die.

They explained they needed the money urgently. The manager checked the bank account and told them he needed an ID from each one of them. After he confirmed their identities, he asked why they needed the money, and maybe they wanted a loan instead or something.

David noticed the Tree moved uneasily.

"Can you tell me more about that loan?" David asked.

Rick looked at him with questioning eyes. Then the Tree moved forward and put his big hand on David's collarbone. "We're in a hurry," the Tree said and squeezed it a little. "Sir."

David's collarbone hurt. He nodded without looking at him. The manager stared at the Tree but said nothing.

"He's right. I'm sorry. Could we just get the cash and leave, please?"

"Is everything okay?" the manager asked, examining all three of them.

"Yes. We're in a hurry."

Please call the police, David wanted to say, even though he wasn't sure if that would even help.

The manager nodded. "Sure, but it'll take some time."

We don't have time.

David recalled when he started liking Rick. Was it

when Rick made him write the stupid list of things he liked in his life? Or even before that?

When Rick escaped with the money, David had wanted to kill him.

Rick still seemed frozen. *Will he help me if I try anything?*

If they attacked the Tree, the other muscle man might know and kill Angela.

If he hadn't already.

Anyway, he couldn't risk—

From the corner of his eye, he saw Rick jump out of his chair and land on the Tree.

What's going on?

What the hell is he doing?

He's risking Angela's life!

Damn!

David jumped in to help him.

They both struggled with the Tree. Rick punched him in the face; David tried to hold his huge arms.

"He's robbing us! Please! Call the police!"

The manager seemed shocked at first, then he pushed a panic button.

An alarm went off.

That can't be good.

"Turn it off! Turn it off!" David yelled, still struggling with the Tree. "Just call the police, but turn the damn siren off!"

The manager did nothing. He stared at the three men on the floor.

"They'll kill my...our...they'll kill his wife if they hear the siren! Turn it off *now*!"

"I...I can't turn it off. I'm sorry."

The Tree threw Rick to the other side of the room.

"Help us!" David yelled, but the manager did nothing.

Then the Tree pushed David to the other side of the room and rose.

David and Rick jumped on the Tree almost simultaneously, causing him to fall and hit his head on the glass door, which didn't break.

It didn't seem to hurt him much.

Two other bankers came into the office. They saw the men struggling with the Tree, who had pulled a gun by then but couldn't aim it at anyone because David held his hand down. When the Tree overpowered David, the gun simply waved aimlessly in the air. The two bankers froze and stared at them.

David remembered he had read somewhere that bankers were not supposed to intervene.

That can't be good.

But then one of them interfered. He helped David and Rick keep the Tree pinned down. The other banker jumped in as well, which enabled David to yank the gun out of the Tree's hand and throw it under the desk.

Rick and the banker were sitting on the Tree, Rick trying to hold the big man's arms down. The Tree seemed to give up as half a dozen other bankers and customers came to see what was happening. David reached into the Tree's pocket, grabbed his phone, and went outside the bank. He had wanted to take the gun but knew he probably wouldn't know how to use it. Or know where the hell it was.

As he ran out of the office, he decided he had a better chance *with* the gun in his hand.

He returned and searched for it. He searched under the frozen manager's desk, chair, and feet. He looked everywhere else but couldn't find it. He had wasted valuable time searching.

He got up and checked the desk. He remembered he had seen a letter opener behind the manager. He grabbed it, put it behind his back, and walked outside the bank toward the black Mercedes, which seemed sealed and calm. No one in there knew what had gone on inside the bank. He guessed the car was soundproof.

He felt bad leaving Rick alone, but Rick had help.

And Angela is more important.

The muscle man who had been driving the car got out, gun in hand, pointed at him.

"A *policeman* was in there. They flagged our account or something. I could get out, but Rick and your guy didn't. They're under arrest. Quick, we need to run before more cops show up."

David had no idea where that came from, but it almost made sense. The muscle man stared at him, trying to decide whether he believed him. He stared at the bank, hearing the alarm—probably for the first time—and then looked back at David, lowering the gun.

"Quick. We have to go to your other friend and Angela."

"I think our friend is busy with her." The muscle man laughed.

David's breath stopped. He decided to do something he had never done in his life. He took the letter opener out of his back pocket and, as he got closer, he stuck it as hard as he could in the muscle man's right arm.

He had wanted to go for the belly, or the chest, but couldn't. For a second, he considered whether it would be self-defense. The man held a gun, after all, but it wasn't pointed at him.

He tried to tell himself he didn't care.

The muscle man's eyes opened wide as the letter

opener went through his shirt and into his big, muscular arm.

It went in much smoother than David had expected.

But the muscle man didn't scream. He barely made a sound.

The gun dropped to the ground, the letter opener still stuck in the man's arm.

David hoped they had not alerted the third guy—the one who held Angela.

———

The boss closed his eyes in the back seat of his huge, beloved Mercedes and listened to classical music on the amazing speakers. He knew his bodyguards hated it, but he couldn't care less. Soon he would have some more money in his pocket, and he could get rid of the three clowns. He hated them. He hated Rick especially. The two others were collateral damage.

He knew what Boldy might do to the beautiful model. Boldy texted him saying he couldn't wait. It may have been a mistake leaving him with her.

Did it matter? She was going to die anyway. Why not let him have some fun first?

He heard his stupid driver exit the car. Probably had too much Wagner, his favorite composer. Or maybe he needed a smoke. His trained dogs knew they couldn't smoke in his car.

He should get rid of them. He'd used them only once before, in another matter in Oklahoma City. They performed better then, but this time they blew it.

When he opened his eyes, he saw someone fighting

with his stupid driver. That someone was Rick's geeky friend.

"What the fuck?" The boss cracked the tinted window open and yelled from inside the car. He then reached for a gun and aimed it at David.

———

David grabbed the muscle man and tried to push him toward the boss as a shield, but the goon weighed a million pounds.

He didn't want to die, but he had to keep them busy until the police arrived.

Hopefully, the police would get to Angela first. He tried to think if he could explain where she was. He had a hard time keeping track of where they had been driving.

The boss got out of the car, pushed the goon out of the way, which caused him to fall, and aimed his gun at David's face.

"You're all dead," the boss said and moved his index finger.

Like in a predictable low-budget movie, the sound of a gunshot rang out from the opposite direction. A bullet exploded from behind David and into the boss's chest.

The boss fell down.

Did the goon shoot him?

Why?

David turned around, mouth open wide.

Rick stood a few feet behind him, a gun in his hand.

David wanted to say something, but the muscle man, shockingly, pulled the letter opener out of his own arm, raised it in the air, and lowered it fast toward David's face.

———

"We got an alert from one of the banks that they were trying to take out the money," Stuber said as Bob drove fast into Oklahoma City.

"About time those notifications started working. Do you have an address?"

"Not yet, but the police got an alarm in the same bank. Seems like a robbery attempt."

"Why would they—" Bob started but then figured it out. "Shit. That means something went wrong."

Bob's phone rang. He glanced at it and saw it was his daughter. He had not spoken to her in a long time.

His heart sank when he declined the call.

———

David raised his arm in time to defend his face. The letter opener scratched his arm. The muscle man pressed down the letter opener, lowering it slowly toward David's face.

David knew he couldn't defend himself for long.

He hoped Rick would shoot the goon. But Rick didn't.

He tried to look back at Rick but couldn't find him.

Did he bail on me?

As the letter opener came within an inch of David's right eye, the muscle man was hit from behind and fell to the ground.

The muscle man tried to grab David on his way down, which caused him to fall as well.

David looked up and saw Rick, who must have hit the muscle man.

"You sure took your time," David said.

"Next time I'll shoot right through you," Rick said and almost smiled.

But the muscle man was not done. He pulled a gun out of nowhere and aimed it at Rick.

Rick pointed the gun at the goon's chest and, without flinching, shot him.

—————

Rick extended his hand to help David up, but they both almost stumbled.

"You could have hit me," David said.

"Better me than him."

Joking around like old times again?

"Thanks, man." David took his hand and rose. "Where did you learn to do that?"

"Ironically, they taught me how to shoot."

"How's your leg?"

Rick leaned on the side of the car. "Hurts like hell."

"What about the Tree in there?" David pointed at the bank.

"He does look like a tree." Rick smiled. "A bunch of people in there are holding him down."

David nodded. "How do we get to Angela?"

"Let's see if we can call the guy who's holding her and pretend to be the boss."

As Rick bent over to search the boss's pockets, the Tree —who somehow had gotten away from the bank employees —came out of the bank with a gun in his hand.

It was a smaller gun he must have kept hidden on his body somewhere.

Rick saw him first, pushed David to the ground, and stood between them.

David heard a gunshot.

The Tree fired the small gun.

Rick fell on top of David. Not thrown away, like in the movies. He simply fell.

The Tree walked closer, gun still aimed at them. David could only stare at the Tree from underneath Rick and do nothing.

He decided he wouldn't go down without a fight. He searched for a gun. He knew he could shoot the Tree—or at least die trying.

Another gunshot hurt his ears. This time it was followed by a sharp pain in his leg.

The Tree had shot him.

It hurt like hell.

Again, like in the movies, police sirens cut through the air and forced the Tree to turn and aim his gun at the police.

David couldn't find the gun Rick had used, but he wanted to take advantage of the situation and maybe jump on the Tree. But that could risk Rick's life. Or his. He thought he felt Rick breathing.

Let the police do their job.

They're probably better shooters than me anyway.

He could see two police cars stopping; four police officers stepped out of the cars and hid behind their doors, pointing their guns at the Tree.

They yelled at the Tree to drop his weapon. He lowered the gun but then raised it and fired at the police.

A big mistake.

David closed his eyes and could hear at least a dozen bullets coming from the police officers into the Tree.

He tried to pull himself and Rick to safety but could hardly move Rick.

The Tree fell like a log in a forest. There were no other

trees next to it to cushion the fall. His bloody face hit the ground a few feet away. Even though David had seen many deaths in the last few minutes, this one was the most gruesome, and David had the front-row seat.

———

David sat up. He heard the police officers yell in his direction but didn't care. He posed no threat to them, so he should be fine.

He held Rick in his lap, even though his leg hurt as if a car had run over it. Twice. Rick was covered with a lot of blood, took shallow breaths, and stared at him blankly.

"Get an ambulance!" David screamed toward the police officers. "*I need an ambulance.*"

He thought he heard someone say they were on the way.

"I'm sorry, David," Rick mumbled. "Please tell her I'm sorry."

Her.

For a few seconds, David had forgotten about her.

He looked around him. He would tell the police officers to find her.

"You're not going anywhere," he told Rick. "You still have time to make it up to her. And to me. You saved my life here, man. *Twice.* You're a hero. We're even now." He examined the area, then looked back at Rick. "You remember you promised to take me to a Tony Robbins seminar? I need you to keep that promise."

He could hear more sirens coming closer. He looked around again. "Here's the ambulance," he said but saw nothing.

FORTY-NINE

Angela stared at the big, black, shiny car as it drove away with Rick and David inside. After they were gone, she glared at the man who stayed with her. He stared at her breasts and then down at the rest of her body. To make things worse, he stared at her and grinned with crooked, stained teeth.

Then he laughed.

She wanted to puke.

She tried to hide her trembling hands. She had seen disgusting men check her out in the past, but not this way. Not this close. Never alone in a car in the middle of nowhere.

Never from a killer.

He reminded her, for a few seconds, of her father.

Her lips trembled. She worried about Rick and David. She knew they would do anything to rescue her, but she didn't know if the bad guys would keep their end of the bargain. Would they hurt them after they got the money? Would they tell this disgusting creature to kill her?

Or worse?

She considered springing out of the car and running as fast as she could into the Starbucks, where there may be people, or into the woods, but the guy had a gun. And a phone. He could shoot her if she ran. He could call the other bad men and tell them she ran. They would hurt Rick and David.

She promised herself, after what had happened with her father, that she'd rather be killed than be raped. Fortunately, she had not had the chance to test this promise.

Until now.

If he tries to rape me, I'll kick, scream, and run. No matter what.

She looked outside. Cars drove by the coffee shop. He couldn't hurt her. She could scream. People will hear and come to her aid. Or call the police.

But then he took out something that seemed like a long, white, bendable plastic pencil. He grabbed her arms. She resisted at first, but he was much stronger. He put the plastic thing around her wrists and pulled it up hard, making a zipper sound. It hurt.

She was handcuffed.

The backs of his hands brushed against her breasts. On purpose. She tried to move back but had little room in the car.

At first, she couldn't be sure if he meant to do it or not, but then she saw his disgusting grin.

His breath stunk.

He tightened the zip tie on her wrists. He grinned again as she screamed.

He likes to hurt people. He likes to hurt women. Maybe fighting him off wouldn't be a good idea?

But she had no choice.

Then the disgusting man bent down to cuff her ankles.

She considered trying to kick, but he was much stronger. "You're so pretty," he said, looking up at her. "They told me to kill you, but that would be such a waste." She considered hitting his back with her cuffed hands but figured he would hardly feel it. He stared at her.

She noticed the zip tie on her ankles was looser than the one on her wrists.

"First, me and you are gonna have some fun."

He put his hand on her left thigh.

She lifted her legs up and down, trying to kick his hand off. She threw her legs everywhere. She also screamed as loud as she could, which made him jump.

He quickly looked out the window, then slapped her cheek. Hard.

The slap threw her backward across the back seat of David's car. The amount of pain in her face felt overwhelming. She had been slapped on the face twice in the past few weeks, but Rick's slap had been gentle compared to this.

However, the insult of the first slap had been much greater. She loved the man.

She'd recently learned Rick had been trying to save her. *Was he?*

She felt her lips bleed and started to cry. Her head shook, and she felt as though she might faint.

She did her best not to. Only God knew what he would do to her if she fainted.

He stared at her. She raised her hands, ready to defend herself again. Hopefully, this time she would hurt him more. But the man exited the car from his side. She wanted to scream as the door opened, but there were no cars around.

The disgusting muscle man did something to the side of the door that made a clicking sound and then closed it. He went over to her side, opened her door, pushed her hard to the other side of the car, did the same thing to that door, and threw the door closed.

She thought the door almost broke.

He got behind the wheel and locked the car doors.

He cursed and pushed the driver's seat all the way back, hitting her on the way.

He tried to turn the key in the ignition.

He planned to drive away.

She used her cuffed hands to try to open the door but couldn't. He had locked the door so she couldn't open it from the inside.

It would be much easier for him to hurt her if they went somewhere else, with her locked and cuffed in the back seat.

"Fuck," he said as he tried to turn the key in the ignition again.

But the car wouldn't start.

Angela moved to the other side of the back seat and tried to open the other door.

The disgusting man had locked this door from the outside as well.

The man cursed again, hit the dashboard, and tried to turn on the ignition a few more times.

She tried to get herself out of the zip tie. It hurt her wrists even more, but she didn't care.

The disgusting muscle man took the key out, cursed again, and tried to bend it.

When his eyes were on the key, she used her teeth to try to cut the zip tie open.

No luck.

After less than a minute, he stuck the key back into the ignition and started the car.

Shit!

He grinned and watched her in the rearview mirror. He drove the car slowly, probably not to draw attention. On the way out of the parking lot, she could see another car going into the drive-through.

She decided to take her chances.

She screamed at the other car, hitting the side door window with her cuffed hands. She thought the man in the other car could see her, but he didn't seem to care.

As they drove by, she thought she saw him use his phone.

Maybe he called the police? Or maybe he didn't care? Or maybe he didn't see me because he was too busy with his damn mind-controlling phone?

The muscle man drove the car aimlessly. She tried to decide if it was a good or bad thing. It could buy her more time. It could be enough for Rick and David—or the police —to try to save her.

Even if they got away, they wouldn't know where he took her.

Her heart sank.

The muscle man only drove for a few minutes. He found an opening to drive straight into the woods. He took an unpaved path, which made the car bump and hit the ground. Her body jolted back, and she fell to the floor of the car.

She hurt the side of her rib cage.

She couldn't get back up, so she decided to stay down.

She hoped he would never stop driving, but he did. He turned the ignition off and twisted around to face her. When he couldn't see her on the back seat, his eyes opened wide, but he quickly found her on the floor and grinned.

He stared down at her. She thought she could see him drool.

"You gettin' ready for me?" He laughed hard.

He looked around, probably to make sure they were alone. He checked his phone and texted someone. He seemed to wait for an answer and then texted again.

Angela didn't know how much time had passed. The muscle man unlocked the doors, took the key out, and exited the car. He walked slowly to the back door.

Those few steps felt like an hour.

She stopped breathing.

———

David had to let Rick go. He had to find Angela.

He picked the boss's pockets, found an iPhone, but couldn't unlock it. He tried the dead man's thumb.

It worked.

He searched for the third muscle man's phone number, and when he thought he found it, he texted him not to hurt Angela. To let her go.

Go to hell, the third muscle man replied.

I'm giving you an order! We don't need her anymore. Let her go!

A few seconds passed. Felt like an hour.

Fuck you. I waited a long time for her. Bye.

He had to find them.

But how?

Then it hit him like a brick falling from the sky.

My iPhone!

He launched the Find My iPhone app, put in his own username and password, and tracked his iPhone—which he'd left with Angela in his car.

They were close.

He knew he couldn't change the phone's passcode,

but he needed it to stay unlocked, so he changed the iPhone's Auto-Lock to Never.

That should work.

He looked around and saw the police were still hiding behind their cars. He heard more sirens. He considered going to them, but they would probably arrest him. They might want to shoot him. It would take too long to explain.

He made his move.

He entered the black Mercedes and searched for the ignition key. There was none, only a start button, which did nothing when he pressed it. He needed the key to drive away.

He opened the door, and the police officers yelled at him to stop moving.

Shit!

The keys should be in the driver's pocket. He searched for it. The police officers screamed.

They wouldn't shoot him. He didn't pose a threat.

But they did.

———

The disgusting muscle man opened the back door, and as soon as his body was exposed, Angela kicked him as hard as she could in the groin with her cuffed feet.

He was thrown back to the dirt, hitting a tree on the way down. He yelled, then cursed.

Still on the floor, she pulled her legs up and down as fast as she could, aiming to release the zip tie. She took off her shoes and forced her left foot upward. The zip tie loosened, and miraculously, she could pull her foot out, then the other one.

She tried to get the zip tie off her wrists. She pushed her

hands back and forth, up and down, but unlike the ankle zip tie, it was too tight. It wouldn't budge. She broke two nails trying to get it loose.

She needed her feet more anyway.

She pushed the door open with her cuffed hands. She noticed the thug had started moving, so she sprang out of the car. He saw her and tried to stand, one hand still on his groin. She considered kicking him again while he was down but decided it would be too risky. Having no shoes on would hurt him less, and he'd probably be able to grab her. She'd had the element of surprise before. He wouldn't let it happen again.

Time to run.

She ran in the direction of where she thought the Starbucks was. Her bare feet hurt from the stones on the ground, but she didn't care. She could hear him yell and struggle to run after her.

She didn't look back.

———

David couldn't believe the police had shot in his direction. Should he raise his hands? He never ran away from the police.

He found the keys and got back into the car.

But then they shot at him again.

Many more bullets this time.

The side windows cracked. Then the windshield cracked.

He raised his hands to defend himself. Not that it would help.

He heard many bullets flying, but, for some reason, none of them hit him.

None of them entered the car.

Are they such bad shooters?

Then it hit him. The huge new black Mercedes was bulletproof.

Thank God.

No time to think about it. He had to drive away and find Angela.

———

After a few minutes of running, the disgusting man caught up to Angela and jumped on her.

She fell to the ground, and her head hit the dirt.

The disgusting muscle man sat on top of her and grinned.

———

David looked down at the blood coming out of his leg. A lot of blood. He had to stop it. He looked in the glove compartment and found another bandage.

Those guys are sure ready for anything.

He needed to get to Angela but wasn't sure he would make it. He patched his leg wound like the Tree did with Rick.

He heard the bullets and sirens behind him as he escaped the police, navigating through the cracks in the windshield. He drove over something, probably a body, which made him shiver. He hoped it wasn't Rick. If more cars showed up, they would stop him. Would he try to drive through them?

How many more bullets could this car take?

As he got closer to where his iPhone was located, the sirens got stronger.

When I find her, having the police behind me would be a great help.

If they don't kill me first.

A black SUV with sirens pulled in front of him and forced him to stop.

Shit!

Two men wearing suits came out, guns drawn and aimed at him.

I could drive through them.

One man screamed at him to get out of the car. The windows were so damaged he couldn't see their faces.

What do I do?

The rearview mirror filled with police cars.

He looked at the boss's iPhone, which signaled David's iPhone was close.

Angela is close.

One man forced David's door open, gun aimed at his head.

He considered giving up.

They will shoot me. They—

Then he noticed a familiar face.

Bob.

Thank God.

David raised his hands. "It's me! David! I'm alone. One of them took Angela. Please help me. I'm trying to find him. Follow me. Fast. Please!"

David didn't wait for their reply. He closed the door and continued driving toward Angela. They could try to stop him, chase him, or even shoot him.

I don't care.

But they didn't stop him. They stayed behind, flashed

their badges at the police officers, talked to them, then followed him as he chased his iPhone down a dirty, bumpy road between many large trees.

He bounced against the sides of the car, his whole body aching, but he didn't care.

He screeched to a halt at the sight of his old Honda, threw his door open, and limped as fast as he could.

The car's two left doors were open, but Angela and the muscle man were gone.

He looked behind him and saw the agents were close. He looked around as he heard her scream.

———

Angela tried to resist with her entire body. She pushed, she kicked, and she spat.

But the disgusting muscle man was too strong. He held her down with one hand, and with the other he ripped her blouse open.

She screamed.

———

David half ran, half limped in the direction of the scream. His leg hurt but he ignored it. A minute later, he saw the third muscle man sitting on top of Angela.

He wished he had a gun.

"Leave her alone!" He screamed like he had never screamed before.

The third muscle man's mouth opened when he saw David. The muscle man searched around for a gun, still holding Angela down.

He found one and aimed it at David. Then he grinned and aimed it at Angela.

David found a huge rock, picked it up, then ran and launched himself at the thug. He smashed the rock as hard as he could into the muscle man's head.

The goon fell on top of Angela, blood gushing from his head. David pushed him away and discovered Angela's shirt and bra ripped open.

She cried. She didn't cover herself.

David wrapped what remained of her shirt around her and helped her sit up. He hugged her as the sirens grew louder.

"FBI! Put your hands up!" Bob aimed his gun at the muscle man.

"Where's Rick?"

"I'm sorry, Angela." David looked into her eyes. "I'm so sorry."

FIFTY

Day 30

The FBI traced most of the million dollars Rick had stolen. They cleared the seven hundred thousand dollars in the bank account under David's and Rick's names and returned it to the investor. Rick had deposited the stolen money in a bank account he had opened with a fake ID. Twenty thousand dollars was still missing. The investor insisted David pay the rest of the amount. He promised he would. They gave him a few months to pay it and promised they wouldn't pursue prosecution if he did.

Angela insisted she would pay half of what he owed.

———

"You mean Cash had nothing to do with the stolen money?" Stuber asked Bob in his office.

Bob shook his head. "It appears that the money he gave them was his own legit money. Nothing laundered. He was really being mobbed."

"I can't believe Cash didn't kill all three of them," Stuber said.

"I know," Bob said. "Rick probably didn't know Cash was bad, and Cash probably didn't want to attract attention by making them disappear. We'll get him another way."

———

David stayed a few days at the hospital, but luckily his gunshot wound was not serious. He left the hospital to attend the funeral.

A few people arrived at Rick's funeral, and they were greeted by rain. It poured on them during the short service at a local cemetery. Bob and Barton were there as well as a few people whom Rick had coached. They told Angela he had helped them a lot and they would miss him. David still limped, even though the doctor at the hospital said nothing major had been hit and that he should be fine in no time. He noticed a few more people at the cemetery whom he had never met before. They probably worked at the funeral home.

Rick had wanted to touch millions of people, but eventually he had touched only a few.

———

David and Angela stayed in their own apartments. He considered asking her to room with him, to save money, but decided against it.

With her encouragement, he became a salesperson in a local, privately owned computer store. He sold well and helped them with strategy and marketing. For maybe the first time in his life, he felt calm.

He and Angela would meet for dinner whenever he didn't work late and talk about their day. Slowly they went back to jogging; when he worked late, they jogged in the mornings.

He dreamed about Rick from time to time. In one of his dreams, he went to a self-improvement seminar led by Rick, with thousands of people watching, learning, and cheering.

"In the dream," David said, "I go backstage afterward. He hugs me. I tell him he helped me a lot."

"He did," Angela said.

"Yes."

"If it hadn't ended up the way it did, I'm sure the two of you would have gone on to rule the world."

David sighed. "I thought you said I didn't have to rule the world."

"Before what happened—I mean, before Rick disappeared—I truly believed that you two, together, could have made it. Not everyone can. Actually, most people can't. But now, after all that's happened, I think you're doing well. You'll rule the world in your own unique way."

"Thank you." He blushed.

"I don't dream of him at all, you know?" she said. "I want to, but I don't. It's too complicated. I wish it had ended differently." She stared at the floor. "I wish it didn't end."

"Me too. We hated him so much just before he died. We never had the chance to try to forgive him."

"I'm not sure I have. I'm not sure I'll ever be able to fully forgive him."

———

A few months afterward, Angela had taken extra courses and completed her studies. David had made a special dinner to celebrate it—with candles. They smiled a lot. They had red wine. Rick had said it was good for the heart.

David had planned to use that special night to talk to her. He had planned it for a long time. He was going to suggest they move in together.

He even considered trying to kiss her again but decided against it.

They spent a lot of time together, almost like a couple. The only thing missing was sex.

"So you're now a psychologist, eh?"

"I guess." She smiled with her perfect teeth.

"Congratulations!" he said and raised his glass. She thanked him, and they clinked glasses.

"I wanted to tell you something," she said, looking beautiful in the candlelight.

"Anything."

"I've decided to leave Tulsa and go back to my mother in Chicago. I'll probably look for my own place there."

David almost dropped his glass.

"What?" he whispered and lowered his eyes.

"Will you be okay?" she asked after a while.

Even though the air was still, the candle blew out.

"Um...yeah. Sure." He tried to relight the candle. His hands were shaking. He wondered if he wanted her to notice it. She didn't say anything or try to help him.

"Are you sure about this?"

"Yes. I feel it's time. I can't stay here any longer."

He let go of the candle and did his best not to cry.

"I'm sorry," she said.

Not as much as I am.

EPILOGUE

Five years after his best friend died, David Pascal went to Chicago on a business trip. After a good meeting, he sat down at a local Starbucks, drank coffee, and almost allowed himself to have a piece of cake but decided it wouldn't be worth it.

He sat facing the front door and examined the people coming and leaving. Some were couples, some were alone. After almost an hour, a beautiful blonde woman entered the coffee shop. He recognized her immediately. She had a couple more wrinkles and had even added one or two pounds, which looked great on her.

She's still the most beautiful woman in the world.

He wanted to reach out to her but froze. She didn't see him at first, but when she stood in the long line to get coffee, her gaze wandered and fell on his face.

Three seconds later, her eyes lit up and a perfect smile ignited her face. Her teeth remained as white as he had remembered them. She left the line and walked over. He rose, and they hugged.

A few moments later, they moved apart, and she sat

down at the table in front of him while the strong smell of coffee surrounded them.

"I missed you," she said.

"I missed you too."

Angela held his hands in both of hers, their arms over the dirty table. She held them as she had never held them before.

"What are you doing in Chicago? Do you still live in Tulsa? What are you doing these days?"

He opened his mouth to talk, but she cut him off with another question. "Did you ever get married?"

He shook his head. "I had a couple of girlfriends I met online, but they couldn't live up to—"

Had enough time passed to tell her the truth?

"They could never live up to my expectations."

She nodded slowly.

"Did *you?*"

She shook her head. "I only dated one man a year ago. It took me a long time to even think about dating."

He couldn't help but feel jealous.

"But, as luck would have it, he was a bit too slick for me, so I gave up on him. I think I gave up on men in general."

"They *are* pigs."

She laughed. "Not all of them."

After a long silence, she said, "I'm sorry I never called you. I wanted to, but I couldn't. I'm sorry, David."

He loved the way she said his name. It stayed the same.

In his dreams, they were married, had two children, one boy and one girl, and lived happily ever after. But dreams, for him, never came true.

"It's okay," he said. "I didn't call you either."

"Yes, but..."

After a few more minutes of silence, he said, "As for

your other questions, here goes. Do you remember the store I started working in before you left?"

She nodded.

"I helped the owner grow, and he made me a small partner. We opened a chain of five stores in Oklahoma; most of them did pretty well. Actually, I'm here in Chicago to negotiate with someone who wants to open a store here with our name. A franchisee. It'll be our first one. He'll pay us a lot of money for the name and for our tactics."

"That's amazing." She smiled. "I'm happy for you."

"Thanks. I got this part of my life taken care of, I guess. Maybe I needed to adapt to my abilities. I'll probably not be a part of the next iPhone, but maybe a small Best Buy would be enough."

He noticed she didn't have a drink, and when he offered to get her coffee, she shook her head, smiled, and took a sip from his.

"Believe it or not," he said, "I'm even going to a therapist."

"*What?*" She drew back. "That's great. I'm proud of you!"

He smiled.

"What about friends?" She asked.

"I got back in touch with my brother," he said, and she clapped her hands. "And I kept in touch with Bob. Agent Bob. Remember him?"

"Of course. That's great."

He nodded. "I stuck with a few things Rick taught me. I work out, eat well, think positively, and some other bullshit he talked about."

They laughed.

She examined his body. "I can see you eat well and work out." She smiled.

"I miss him, from time to time."

"Me too."

They looked at each other for a few minutes.

"You know, I think you two had a lot in common."

He raised his eyebrows.

"You both chased unachievable dreams."

He considered what she said. After a while, he nodded.

They watched a couple who entered the coffee shop, arms around each other, laughing.

"What have you been doing besides dating only one man? Are you the world's most famous shrink yet?"

Probably the prettiest one.

She giggled. "Nah. But I do pretty well. I completed my PhD here in Chicago, I have my own practice, and I'm full most of the time. I work a lot of nights, so I probably wouldn't have much time for family anyway."

"How's your mother doing?"

Angela lowered her eyes. "She passed away a few months ago."

"I'm sorry."

She nodded.

"Do you still jog?"

"Yes, from time to time."

"I'm staying in a hotel not far from here," he said. When she didn't react, he added, "I have a morning flight, but is there any chance you'd want to join me for an early jog before I leave? Like the old days."

Or stay the night with me? he wished he could say.

"That would be great. You still have my number?"

He smiled. He took out his phone and showed it to her, her name first on his favorites list.

"It took me a long time to erase Rick's number," he said.

"I used to call him, after he died. Just to listen to his voice on voicemail."

"I think I did that once, accidentally."

They stayed in the coffee shop, talking, until an employee told them they were closing.

"I thought Starbucks stayed open all night in Chicago."

"No. Not this one, anyway."

"How do you like the big city?"

"I love it. I've always loved it. Besides the weather."

"You know what they say about Chicago's weather?" He had looked it up before his flight from Tulsa. "If you don't like it, don't worry; it'll change in five minutes."

They laughed and walked outside, and then they stood in the cold, dark street.

After a while, she said, "Do you want to see my place? It's not far."

It had been a long time since a beautiful woman had asked him such a question. With Angela, even though they had not met in over four years, it seemed natural and innocent.

"I'd love to."

They walked for a few minutes and entered a nice apartment building with a lobby and a doorman. She smiled at the doorman as he greeted her. The doorman seemed surprised to see David. As they entered the elevator, he looked back and saw the doorman checking her out.

He felt a little jealous.

They took the elevator up to her apartment, which she had decorated nicely. It had an amazing view of a nearby park.

"You did well for yourself," he said. "It's a long way from our apartment complex in Tulsa."

She smiled but blushed. "I've been working hard. I'm probably *married* to my job."

She made them coffee, and they sat on her fancy couch. Angela took her shoes off and folded her legs underneath her.

He loved it when she did that.

They talked for a few hours, then he realized the sun had risen.

"Wow, we talked all night."

"Yes. We had a lot to catch up on." She rose. "I want to show you the view. You'll appreciate it."

They went out to the balcony, both taking in the air.

When they were close, he wished he could kiss her.

"There's some traffic here that I hate," Angela said.

"Yes, but you have to look at the glass half-full," he tried to imitate Rick, "and focus on the amazing view of the park you have here."

They laughed.

He checked his watch. "I have to go now. I need to catch my flight."

"Oh. Yeah. Sure."

She walked him to the door and opened it for him, and they stood there.

"I hope we can do this more often. I would hate to wait another almost five years to see you again," he said.

"Me too."

They hugged and said good-bye. She shut the door after he pressed the elevator button.

After a few seconds, Angela's door opened again. "David?"

He turned, startled.

"Is there any chance you could postpone your flight?" she asked. "I can cancel my patients for today. I haven't taken a day off in years. I need to get some new clothes. Maybe we could go shopping. You were a good partner for that, if I remember correctly."

He walked over to Angela, who still held the door open.

Her feet were bare, so their eyes met at the same level. They stared at each other, examining the other one's face, less than an inch away.

Rick will have to forgive me, he thought. *Maybe he was right. Maybe I* should *dare to dream.*

Neither of them had brushed their teeth since the previous evening.

He didn't care.

She walked him in and asked him to wait in the living room.

He fished his phone out of his pocket and sat down on the couch.

Thank you, he texted Agent Bob.

PLEASE LEAVE A REVIEW

If you've enjoyed this book, it would be great if you could leave a review.

Reviews help me bring my books to the attention of other readers who may enjoy them as well.

Thank you!

AUTHOR'S NOTE

If you haven't read *Never Reply All*—the prequel novella to *Don't Dare to Dream*—and want to learn more about Agent Bob and another case he worked on, you can get it here:

Amazon.com/dp/B07ZRJ4CXN

Stay in touch

Please subscribe to my mailing list on my website to stay in touch:

www.danfriedmanauthor.com

ACKNOWLEDGMENTS

Many people helped me with this book, and I hope I'm not forgetting anyone.

People who read and suffered through old drafts of the book and helped me improve it immensely: my teacher and mentor William Berndhardt, my wife Avital Friedman, my brother Sharon Friedman, Ken Darrow, and my editors Kate Schomaker, Bryon Quertermous, and Teresa Frith.

Even though the book is more FBI than the police, the people who helped me with this part were my dear cousin, Sergeant Dekel Levy, and my friend and a fellow author Sergeant Brandon Watkins. I'd also like to thank Chief Derek Pacifico, whose course on police interrogation helped me a lot. All the mistakes and inaccuracies are mine. Stay safe guys.

Others I wish to thank are Michael Omer, Ido Manor, Liron Fine, Lara Berndhardt, Nikki Hanna, Ruth Penn, and, of course, the Internet.

I'd also like to thank the people of Tulsa, Oklahoma, who welcomed me and my family for two great years. As David says—I met some of the nicest people in the world there.

ABOUT THE AUTHOR

Award-winning author Dan Friedman likes to write thrillers where regular people deal with extraordinary situations.

He is also an entrepreneur, has an MBA, and in the past was a technology journalist and a programmer. Dan lives with his wife, two children, and their dog. He lived for two years in Tulsa, Oklahoma—where Don't Dare to Dream was born.

His debut novel Don't Dare to Dream won the 2019 Reader's Favorite Gold Medal Mystery Book Award and was a finalist thriller in the National Indie Excellence Award!

For more information:
www.danfriedmanauthor.com
dan@danfriedmanauthor.com

facebook.com/danfriedmanauthor
bookbub.com/authors/dan-friedman
amazon.com/Dan-Friedman/e/B07KDWZ95G
instagram.com/danfriedmanauthor
twitter.com/danfr

ALSO BY DAN FRIEDMAN

Never Reply All (a prequel novella to Don't Dare to Dream)